THE
VULCAN HUNTER

E. G. GARDNER

written between
May 1998 and October 1999

BALBOA
PRESS
A DIVISION OF HAY HOUSE

Balboa Press books may be ordered through booksellers or by contacting:

Balboa Press
A Division of Hay House
1663 Liberty Drive
Bloomington, IN 47403
www.balboapress.com.au
1-(877) 407-4847

ISBN: 978-1-4525-1047-7 (sc)
ISBN: 978-1-4525-1048-4 (e)

Printed in the United States of America

Balboa Press rev. date: 07/24/2013

CONTENTS

PREFACE

What if you had the key to the beginning and the end of the world as you knew it, what would you do with it? Open a door to know the truth? Or pray you never understood it so you wouldn't know what was coming!

When Dr. Peter Cashman was sent a book purported to be a chronicle of just such a happening he almost passed it up as a good story, albeit a very old and partly illegible story, but nothing more until his Seismologist father read it and started Peter on a quest. The quest would involve as few as possible to save as many as possible. The hardest part was first to convince himself the book was written as truth, the next hardest part, once he was convinced, was to convince other scientists to work with him without reason and without knowing what the end of all their study may be.

A series of cataclysms around the Earth lent speed to the search for the elusive writer of the tale. Cataclysms so horrendous the world changed shape forever and whole land masses would be no more.

Peter his father and their trusted few colleagues would work frantically to prove or disprove the theory of total devastation in hopes that all would not be lost.

Surely someone could survive, someone or some part of the world must have or the story would not have been written.

They needed to find those places that survived to have any hope of saving the human race. The clock is ticking.

PART 1

CHAPTER 1

Lord Vulcan growled in anger. He could no longer find his love, his goddess: Idoli. He roared his fury to the black sky, throwing down a challenge to all who would hear him. They had taken her away, and from this day, he would roam the earth seeking her. He would kill all who stood in his way: god, man, or beast. "Idoli!" he screamed *"Idoliiiiiiiiiiiii!"*

Peter Cashman replaced the book on his side table. It was now 4 a.m., and as tired as he was, he was unable to sleep. The book had been sent to him anonymously. It was very old and many of the pages were almost illegible, but it was compelling. The cover note said it was prophetic, an encoded tale of Lord Vulcan. Tomorrow he would go through the book again, download the information, and see what he could find—if there was anything to find.

The day dawned bright and sunny, a great start to Easter. The roads were packed with holidaymakers heading away from the city and into the mountains, down to the beaches, and anywhere else that would take them far from the great rat race. By some sort of unwritten understanding, the opposite side of the highway was jammed with country people heading into the city to share in the delights of theatres, restaurants, and shopping in the big stores.

Jennifer Bannon, her sister Erin, and her cousin Michael were packed into Jennifer's little car heading for the mountains. Their destination was Lake Marnie high on the plateau of Boulder Mountain. The three had spent months collecting camping gear and saving money for this long weekend.

"Want to stop for coffee about eleven?" Jennifer asked.

"Let's just keep going. We've waited long enough. We can make coffee when we get there," Erin answered.

Michael nodded in agreement. "Yep. The sooner, the better."

They sang along to the radio while Michael checked his video camera for the umpteenth time.

"This is going to be so much fun," Erin said. "Just the three of us. No parents, nothing for the whole of Easter!"

Jennifer grinned. "Yeah, just think about it."

At one thirty that afternoon, the road-weary travellers reached Boulder Mountain. True to its name, the mountain was covered in huge boulders all the way down to the valley floor on one side. The road had been built through this area, as thick rainforest covered the other side of the mountain.

The little car climbed steadily until finally reaching Lake Marnie camping ground. They piled out of the car and began the search for a suitable campsite.

The lake was beautiful. Most of it was surrounded by thick rainforest, except where the road came in. This area was covered in groves of conifers. Jennifer and Erin chose their site a little way up the slope on the west side of the lake, about ten metres from the water's edge. They positioned between two large trees to take in the view across the water. The two girls set up in one room, and Michael went in the other with the packs.

Outside under the fly, they set up their barbecue, tables, and chairs.

It took most of the afternoon to complete their camp, haul water, and locate toilets and washing facilities. By early evening, they had stretched out in comfortable chairs and were grilling steaks on the barbecue as they watched more tourists pour into the park.

Michael sighed and said, "This is so good. Just smell that air! It makes me wonder why I even live in the city."

"Money, by any chance?" Erin offered.

They all laughed.

Over the next three hours, many young people came to their tent to talk, have a drink, or just pass the time. Most came to introduce themselves and find out where the three were from.

They were very tired young people when they finally rolled into bed at midnight.

Peter Cashman sat crouched over his laptop. The book had been loaded into his computer and he was now working on a variety of codes to try to find out if any existed within its pages. He was coming up empty at home, so with his laptop and camping gear loaded into his four-wheel drive, he set off for his father's cabin high on the east side of Boulder Mountain.

"I may as well enjoy the weekend if I have to work," he muttered to himself.

The cabin was about sixty metres from the lake via a narrow path. Near the cabin, a spring bubbled out of the rocks, one of the reasons his father had built there. The land wasn't owned, but his father had taken a fifty-year lease as part of his job as a seismologist.

It had been very convenient for the family. It meant that while his father was officially working, the rest of his family could enjoy holidays at one of the most beautiful spots on the map. When Peter had grown up and followed his father's footsteps, the cabin just naturally became part of it. Just as it would when he married and had a family.

Without bothering to stow his gear, Peter threw a meal together and unrolled his sleeping bag on one of the bunks. He was dead tired from lack of sleep and the long drive, but he needed to get this part of the work finished before he could determine if the book was a prophecy or just a good story.

As he worked, he slowly came to the decision that in fact the book was just a good story. There was no hard evidence to suggest that anything in it could be construed as a real-life happening. Even looking into the past gave him no clues.

He shook his head, exasperated at the work he had done and the fact that there were no answers. The field was so narrow. People spent their whole lives predicting earthquakes, cyclones, and wars, yet no one had come up with any real information on volcanoes. He, like others in his field, could locate fumaroles and steam vents, make predictions on the presence of quakes and tremors, or even on the past performances of the mountain, but there was no real prophetic evidence of what may be.

He plugged the small seismograph into the computer. He walked outside and within a thirty-metre radius of the cabin placed five small echographs. He set up a sonar in the pit his father had dug for just such a purpose. Thermographs would allow for changes in the soil and air temperatures to be recorded. He had only one paper to write this year, and allowing for lack of practical evidence, he figured he would still be able to present it with some authority.

The moon was bright silver, the night was warm with barely a breeze, and the sound of happy people floated up to him from the camping ground near the lake. He dragged in a deep breath and then returned to the cabin where, within seconds of falling onto his bunk, he was asleep.

CHAPTER 2

The sun streaming through the window woke Peter early. He sat up while scrubbing at his short, curly hair. His first job was to put on the coffee pot—"real coffee" his father called it. His second was to get water for his shower.

Outside, the world seemed to stand still. Sun poured through the trees, but there remained patches of fog and mist—soft, white, ethereal. The trees were still. Some were dark and mysterious in their depths while others were adorned with colour as autumn took over from summer.

Even the birds were quiet, as though not wanting to disturb the absolute peace of the forest.

Peter stretched and yawned; it sounded unnaturally loud.

He filled the hot-water tank for the shower then piled it up with chips from the woodpile. Soon steam was hissing and spitting from the old heater. Peter went inside and threw himself under the shower.

He soaped up quickly, as they had done when children, and then he was able to stand under the water until it was gone. He knew from experience that the fire would also be out, but cold water had to be added to the tank so that it didn't buckle with the heat.

He wrapped a towel around his body and headed out the door. As he opened it, he lurched. The door swung away from him then came back and hit him hard. "Jesus!" he yelped, and then he was on the floor.

He got to his feet, dragging the towel around him. The computer and printer began chattering and ticking, demanding his attention. The *ping ping* of his seismograph told him something was happening.

He crossed quickly to the table and checked the readings. Almost as soon as he got there, silence reigned. The readouts showed a small bump, and the seismograph detected only an echo, a minuscule 2.2. That was odd, he thought, given that he had hit the floor.

He shrugged. If it was close to the surface, it could be enough to knock a person over, especially one who had just woken up.

He mentally shook himself then returned to the mundane tasks at hand.

Outside, he drew another bucket of water and poured it through the shower heater. He drew more water for the coffee pot and breakfast dishes.

With breakfast over, he decided to check the collectors. He was surprised to see all of them showing a reading. This meant that the tremor had been very much localised. He checked through his files and read through as much as he could find on Boulder Mountain. There was no evidence.

The mountain had been formed some two hundred thousand years ago and was considered cold and stable. The lake was not at the top of the mountain but on one side where the old explosion had blown out the side. He decided to take some readings on the lake and the surrounding areas throughout the day. Satisfied with that, he headed down the path for a walk.

The camping ground was alive with chatter and the smell of breakfast. Jennifer, Erin and Michael had showered and were sitting outside the tent in the sun eating.

"How did you sleep Michael?" Jennifer asked him.

"Like a top thanks" he answered "and you?"

"Great I haven't felt so good in years, well, a long time" she sighed.

"What about you Erin?" he asked her "did you sleep well?"

"Well sort of it was bit hard getting to sleep I guess it was too quiet" she said.

They finished breakfast and were washing the dishes when the tremor rolled through the camping ground.

The plates rattled and jumped across the table Erin grabbing them before they hit the ground. Michael, who had been going into the tent, fell over.

"Hell what was that?" he sounded nervous.

Jennifer grabbed the tent pole and hung on

"It feels like a tremor, I guess some mountains do have them" but she didn't sound confident not even to herself.

A woman nearby yelped, and a toddler who had fallen over started to cry. Dishes and equipment rattled throughout the camping ground. Then it was gone.

"Phew that was interesting" Jennifer laughed nervously.

"Scary is more to the point" Erin added.

"Yeah both." Michael said.

"Do you think it will come again?" Erin sounded nervous "I hate things I don't understand".

"Hey lighten up it was only a little one, let's enjoy this okay?" Michael grinned at them "who's turn is it to make the coffee?"

Peter strolled under the thick green canopy, it was cool silent and dark. There was no sound no breeze to play hide and seek through the branches just floating mist and occasionally soft fingers of sun pushing down through the forest seeking to touch the ground and warm it.

He felt alone, he seemed alone, 'the last person on earth' he mused.

As he strolled the narrow twisting path to the lake he thought of the years he had spent here how he, his brother and sister, mother and father had played pretend. They were the last survivors how would they eat how would they live! They had planted vegetables and fruit trees. Invariably the vegetables had died over the winter but the trees survived and here and there the odd apple and lemon tree were still to be found bearing fruit.

The nearer he got to the lake the less alone he felt. Sound began to drift toward him. The smell of food cooking, children calling, laughing yellingparents calling their children and the almost obscene throbbing roar of a boat starting up on the lake. Soon it would be dragging skiers around behind it and by mid morning it and several others would be fighting for space to show off their prowess with their skiers, and high speed manoeuvres. The quiet fisherman in his little 'tinny' with an outboard or oars would have to watch his back or get run over. Children playing in the shallows would be hit by waves from the wash big enough to knock them over. Peter shook his head 'whatever happened to quiet family holidays, when a small sailing boat or a rubber inner tubes were about the limit.' Progress his father had said and sadly he had to agree. More money to buy more toys meant more noise yet still those people would tell you it was a 'quiet' holiday.

He came out into the clearing at the top of the camping ground. There weren't any campers in this area they had concentrated closer to the lake on the sunny side, the north and north west, where the tree canopy was at its thinnest. He surveyed the camping ground with his binoculars there were a lot of people here this Easter probably due to a long hot and dry summer in the city. The need to get away to the coolness of the country and in this case preferably the mountains, and memories of past camping trips probably drove them here. He strolled down to the water's edge and felt the water it was cool and clean he scooped some up to taste it had a satisfying mineral taste that comes from all natural springs. He continued along the edge of the lake heading east away from the main camping area.

He headed for a small headland of rocks which jutted out over the water. He and his sister, older by two years, had dared each other to jump from the top of these rocks into the deep cold darkness. The lake was at its deepest at this end, the assumption was that the spring that fed it had it's inlet in this area hence the coldness. He climbed the rocks easily now his long legs stepping over the spots where small rocks and stones had rattled away under bare feet and small steps all those years ago. The sun was already touching the camping ground and many people were simply lying about soaking it up. Peter raised his binoculars and watched as a beautiful blue and white craft glided around the northern edge of the lake heading in his direction. It wasn't moving very fast but it was sending twin curling creamy waves up in its wake. The nose was lifted slightly out of the water and it carried no skiers the driver was simply enjoying the buzz of still water riding. He stood up straight behind the wheel without a hat or dark glasses the wind streaming through his hair; he was smiling. Peter smiled, he understood the man's feeling of pure pleasure.

He climbed down from his rocky perch and headed around to the northern side of the lake. As he walked around the rocky outcrop he lost sight of the boat, when he got to the other side it was no-where to be seen. He kept walking.

Two hours later he headed back to the camping ground, he had exhausted all the places he and his family had visited, played in and generally made their own before the advent of the public camping ground. As he strolled the edge of the lake to where the main body of campers were set up he again noticed the blue and white boat. It was listing badly and appeared to be damaged. He walked over for a closer look. The left side of the boat was scraped and dented as though it had been hit by another boat. Just below the water line he could make out what appeared to be a hole. The inside of the boat had about six inches of water in it. He heard someone behind him,

"This your boat?" he asked conversationally.

The man nodded "yeah it's mine."

"What happened? I saw you coming around the north side of the lake she was just gliding along."

The man shook his head,

"I don't know what happened, one minute I was cruising the next I was doing flips. I guess I must have hit something in the water a log or something."

Peter shook his head, "no sir, you hit something more than that, that is the sort of damage you getting from something big hitting you."

"There wasn't anything in the water that I saw" he looked out across the lake "I am careful, I have to be you know, I take the kids out with me."

Peter nodded sympathetically "good luck then."

He walked off heading back to the cabin. He was quietly desperate for a good cup of coffee and to do some reading and catch up on his paper.

The gloom of the path was now lightened by the sun which had finally managed to push it's way through the canopy. Patches of sunlight where the trees were thinner, glowed through the forest floor. Areas where groups of trees had nurtured many young and then not fallen and had become densely grouped together, allowed no sunlight to penetrate. These groups were dark not just dark green but black within their groves. They remained damp and dripping throughout most of the day even hot summers did not change them. In winter when the snow came they were cold pockets of thick snow all day ideal for children who wished to build an igloo or a variety of snowmen in different guises. Peter continued toward the cabin remembering the fun they'd had scaring his mother who had come searching for her wayward children calling them for a meal. They would dress up in masks and hide in shadow deep trees only to leap out screaming when she neared them. They would hide behind grotesque snowmen and whine and whimper. Their mother took it all in her stride but he knew there were many times when they did scare her.

As he neared the cabin he heard a sighing through the forest as though a fresh wind had begun to blow, but there was no wind. Peter stopped and looked around, all was still.

Not even the birds called.

It was as though the world were waiting for something to happen there was an air of expectancy. He looked up to the highest reaches of the canopy. Sun dappling the branches sparkled off the droplets of moisture still clinging stubbornly to leaves. He realised he wasn't breathing it didn't seem right to even disturb this serenity by taking a breath.

He checked his sonar station but found nothing out of the ordinary. The collectors were back to normal, the computer and printer idle. He scrolled through the readouts of the tremor but there was nothing out of the ordinary. Peter knew from experience that localised tremors often felt bigger than they actually were, many parts of the country experienced these small quakes often up to dozens per day. People became so used to them that they never noticed them any more. Perth was well understood to have many 'bumps' daily so to Adelaide and the various mountain rangesparticularly the Blue Mountains of New South Wales and the Darling ranges of Western Australia.

He made coffee and took it out into the sun. The weather was beautiful he couldn't have asked for better he was glad he decided to come here his friends would not have let him work over the Easter if he had stayed in the city. The paper work took up most of the afternoon, he was quickly becoming bored with it but stuck it out until he had completed the outline. There was no easy way of getting it done it was pre-requisite that all papers be in the person's own handwriting, which meant no computers. Peter did cheat though he set up on his computer did all the hard work, printed it out then wrote it out by hand once it was edited.

The far off droning sound of the boats on the lake was the only disturbance in this otherwise peaceful place. Occasionally laughter and calling would float up to him and now and again people strolling through the forest would be startled when confronted by a little cabin in a small clearing. They called out to him or waved; he in turn would smile and wave back. He did not encourage conversation he preferred to be alone.

C H A P T E R 3

By early evening Peter had put away his work, collected samples of water from the lake and tested them taken the readouts from his sonar and collectors and transferred all the information on the tremor to his computer at home. He decided to drive down the mountain to Bayley a small town at the foot of Boulder Mountain, population 1500 souls, which boasted a great steak house.

He headed out before the sun set. He had left the generator running so he could keep the computer and printer powered. He didn't think there would be anything else to record but because the equipment was sensitive to the smallest changes in the surrounding area, he didn't want to miss out on anything. He had had a reasonably hard year and virtually no practical experience. Three weeks in the Philippines at Mt. Pinatubo had been just about all of it; no-where near enough.

He knew that next year, his final year after a long seven year slog, he would have to do more, travel more, experience more. He couldn't write a final paper without the practicals. The only thing that had saved him this year was the diversity of his study and the fact that Australia had experienced many small Temblors and some not so small up to 5.4 on the Richter. He had been able to get to those sites easily and was lucky enough to be able to record the thousands of aftershocks that manifested. Unfortunately Australia did not have any active volcanoes. In fact the only volcano in Australian territory was in the Antarctic and it did nothing. The only measurements he was able to take were heat and movement, not enough to write a paper on.

He pushed the Toyota to get down the mountain before dark, there was a fair amount of traffic behind him and he didn't want to be the object of someone trying to pass him on the steep and narrow bends. Halfway down the mountain was the Devil's Elbow, an extraordinarily tight U bend the only section where a rail was in place. As he began to turn into it he noticed the safety rail was no longer there. He completed the bend then pulled over into a parking bay. Jumping out of the Toyo he walked back to the bend and looked over the side. It was just a bit too dark to see anything very much but he was sure that the railing was down there below him. He looked up at the towering boulders above him scanning for loose rocks and dirt. Crossing to the other side of the road he ran his hands over the rocks they were covered in a fine layer of dirt. He walked about thirty feet along the dirt shoulder and around the curve of the bend, he looked up. Right above him a huge boulder appeared to be balancing. He was certain he would have noticed it if it had always been there but he really couldn't recall having seen it before. He scrambled up the rocks scattering stones and dirt which rattled and bounced off the road below. It was getting quite dark when he reached the rock he tried pushing it, it's sheer size prevented him from moving it, yet smaller rocks and stones rolled away from under it to fall in a shower below. He climbed above the rock and almost fell into a small cave like crevasse unseen in the now almost complete darkness. The wind had started and was becoming quite strong he could only conclude that the rock had been dislodged by the tremor, but didn't seem to pose a great risk to the road. Never—the—less he would report it tomorrow; it may have to be brought down. He clambered down gingerly almost getting run over as another vehicle took the bend too wide. The driver hit the horn startling him; he heard the abuse as they sped past him. He climbed back into the Toyota and continued down to the township.

The wind was quite strong and cold when he pulled up at the Bayley steak house, his thin cotton shirt was no protection. He hurried inside, the fire was lit and the smell of food cooking was overwhelming. He hadn't realized how hungry he was until his order of a large porterhouse with chips and vegetableswere placed in front of him. He followed this up with an equally large helping of sticky toffee pudding and cream. A bottle of Shiraz Cabernet and a roaring open fire stoked his feelings of well being. He sipped the wine taking his time to savour each mouthful.

No-one hurried him and when desert was finished he found a comfortable leather chair near the fire and there he stayed sipping his wine, pondering the events of the day, mentally cataloguing them in order to add to his paper. At 10 pm. with a noisy party going on nearby he called it a night. Outside the wind had grown colder, the sky black and littered with a billion wind blown stars, was a huge arch overhead. The minor street lights did nothing to detract from the magnificence of the night even the tiny sliver of moon seemed to pale into insignificance.

The trip home was uneventful; he didn't feel the need to spoil his mood or his dinner by working. The fire stoked in the pot belly stove, he helped himself to a glass of scotch settling down with the book on Lord Vulcan. Sometime during the night he woke stiff and cold having fallen asleep in his father's old leather chair. The wind soughed through the forest it was mournful like the cry of a wandering lonely soul, seeking, searching. He stood and stretched his aching neck his left shoulder felt stiff and sore. He walked to the window it was black outside not a glimmer of light anywhere he opened the door and stepped out into the wind; autumn was beginning to bite. The blackness under the canopy was complete even the branches had melded into one huge darkness. Only at ground level and then up close, was anything other than total darkness discernible. He stood waiting for eyes to adjust but there was no adjustment. Returning to the cottage he lit the carbon lamp, he wanted coffee but there would be no coffee for him the generator must have stopped a long time ago, he hadn't realized he could no longer hear it. He had also run out of water. With a shrug he dragged off his clothes pulled on an old track suit rolled himself up in his sleeping bag and fell into a long and dreamless sleep.

CHAPTER 4

By 6 am the camping ground was beginning to stir. It was Easter Sunday the sun was already touching all it could reach the wind had dropped in the early hours and that wonderful autumn stillness heralded the promise of another warm and beautiful day.

Jennifer rolled out her sleeping bag still half asleep; she could hear someone calling. She stumbled out of the tent rubbing her eyes frowning at the brightness of the day. The most amazing sight greeted her, she rubbed her eyes again, and she simply could not believe what she was seeing. The lake had disappeared! Gone! Nothing, just a big patch of mud. Boats lay on their side's tree roots showed stark like old skeletons, fish flopped around, and bits of flotsam and jetsam lay scattered around. A woman walked up and down the camping ground calling, Jennifer could hear the note of panic in her voice. She dragged her jacket on and went to see what the problem was. The woman was in tears.

"Are you okay?" Jennifer asked her.

"It's my husband" the woman sobbed "he went fishing last night and hasn't come back I can't find him anywhere"

Jennifer put her arm around the woman's shoulder

"I'm sure he's alright he's probably off cleaning his catch"

"No I don't think so and see the lake has gone" she sobbed harder.

"I'll go and round up some people and we'll look for him. There must be a perfectly rational explanation why the lake has disappeared, so I don't think he is in any danger."

Jennifer went back to her tent woke the others then dressed quickly.

"Come on guys we've got to help this lady find her husband"

Michael stepped outside into the bright day his eyes widened in shock at the sight of the huge mud flat where once was a beautiful lake.

"What do you think happened?" he asked his voice sounding small.

"I don't know Michael but it's probably quite a natural phenomenon" Jennifer answered.

Erin didn't speak she just stared.

The woman had gone and Jennifer could no longer hear her calling.

"She must have found him I can't see her anywhere" she said.

Michael picked up his video camera,

"This I have to get and when it comes back I'll have film I can show to the TV studios they might even use it in their news service."

"If it comes back" Erin muttered. She couldn't take her eyes off the giant mud pool.

Michael loaded the video camera and headed up the hill toward higher ground.

Peter woke. He rolled out of bed threw open the door and dragged in a lungful of fresh clean morning air. He grabbed the bucket off the hook and headed over to the spring. His head ached a little probably a combination of wine, scotch and bad sleeping habits, nothing that a stroll around the lake wouldn't fix. The musical bubbling of the water bursting out of the rocks did not greet him, there was no water. He stepped into the knee deep pool at the base of the rocks and peered through the crack, nothing, no sound of running water either. 'How strange' he thought this spring has never dried up in all the years he had been coming here. He drew a bucket of water from the pool where it hadn't been stirred up and headed back to the cabin. People calling out to each other from the camping ground surprised him, it was unusually loud and when he listened closely seemed close to panic. He checked his watch it was only 6.40 am perhaps they were on an Easter egg hunt. He had just started his first cup of coffee when there was a knock at his door. He didn't answer it straight away; he didn't know anyone here anyway.

The knocking became more urgent and a male voice called out,

"Anyone home? Hello?"

Peter opened the door,

"I am home is there something I can do for you?"

"Look I'm sorry to disturb you but seeing as you seem to be permanent here I thought you might be able to tell us what happened to the lake."

The man looked self conscious scrubbing fingers through his crew cut.

Peter was bewildered.

"The lake? what happened to the lake?" he asked.

"er . . . we don't know that's what I'm asking you, it's disappeared".

Peter stared at him a feeling of fear began to prickle his spine and scalp.

"Disappeared? You mean it's just not there anymore?"

The man nodded "gone!"

Peter grabbed a portable thermo scan and raced off down the path with the messenger hot on his heels.

When he came in sight of the lake he knew instantly what had happened to the spring.

People were milling around in groups discussing the disappearance. Peter walked to the edge of the mud where the lake began and pushed the probe of the thermo into the soft ooze. The reading jumped alarmingly from a cool average of 15c the lake mud was showing a reading of 32c.

"Jesus" he muttered "these people have to get out of here, something is going to give".

He stood up and turned around dozens of pairs of eyes were on him waiting for a reason an explanation anything to make them feel better, anything so they would stop feeling afraid.

"You have to leave here," he said "I don't know why this is happening but I think we have a geothermal problem here. I can't really explain it to you I only know that this whole situation could develop out of control and someone may get hurt. I think the tremor has set off a chain off events that has lead to a crack in the rock under the lake the result is the lake has drained away under ground. In itself that would not be a problem in due time it would probably return, but, and here is a problem, the temperature of the mud is rising and has reached 32centigrade. The crack that has allowed the water to drain must also be allowing heat to seep up into the mud and that makes it dangerous. I don't think there is any reason to panic, but I do think you should pack up and leave here as quickly as possible." Dozens of pairs of eyes stared at him; some people paled quickly and began fidgeting nervously nobody moved. He watched them watching him no-one spoke. Then a voice at the back came to him

"We've got to get out of here we've got to get down the mountain."

Peter watched in growing horror as the panic set in.

"NO, NO" he yelled "keep calm please".

They bolted then like a pack of startled ponies; they turned as one racing off in different directions. Children were knocked over and elderly man pushed against a tree, tents knocked down tent ropes torn out of the ground as people in their blind panic dragged them with them. People began screaming and crying.

Peter looked back out across the lake, a small puff of steam showed white in the cool morning air, nearer to the shore he noticed a small bubble appear on the surface of the mud rise up then break, 'oh god' he whispered 'no no please'.

He raced back to the cabin, halfway between the cabin and the lake, a new tremor, spreading out from the lake like a ripple in a pond when a stone is thrown in, caught up with him. As the ground rose and fell underneath him he was flipped up and over. The very gravity that he had so deftly defied an instant later brought him crashing winded to the earth. He lay there listening to the creaking moan of a tortured earth; the sound of a beast trying to break free. In the distance he could here the crash and clatter of rocks as the long fingers of the tremor reached out and pushed them out of the way.

The trees tossed and clattered their disapproval. He could hear the cries of people in distress and panic. Cars revved as those who had forsaken their belongings roared off toward the mountain road. Peter knew that some of those people would not survive the drive down the mountain. The mountain! They probably wouldn't even get through; if what he heard was rocks rolling then it was a good chance that the road was already blocked. He staggered to his feet completing the last stretch to the cabin like a drunken sailor. Inside his cabin was a mess papers all over the floor, his treasured coffee pot shattered the computer and printer had slid across the table and jammed against the wall but were still chattering like maniacs demanding his attention.

He crossed to the computer dragged it across the table and checked the readings. On the seismograph the reading had reached 3.4 still not that large by standards but if it was close to the surface or there were other factors involved it would make the quake appear stronger.

He tapped in a new graph and requested on going comparisons, the answers he was getting were not good. There was a build up of heat in the ground and all readings were fluctuating wildly. The sonar showed nothing of importance it sat in its pit pinging away recording every tiny fault crack or breach of density, which to date very little was showing. Peter was puzzled there had to something to show him what was going on. Two tremors in two days a missing lake, boiling mud and steam yet no breaches no sudden sliding of the strata, no sudden declivity's appearing, just the basic hall marks of a basin crack. Not that unusual.

At the camping ground chaos reigned. People sobbed in their panic, several had crashed into each other in their cars in their attempts to be first down the mountain. Children cried. Some though stood still, frozen in their fear, staring at the lake waiting for the next happening to galvanize them into action. Jennifer and Erin went quickly to their tent. Two of their tent ropes had been pulled out the chairs and table knocked over. Erin started to pick things up and return them to their rightful places. Jennifer watched her.

"Erin? We have to go now! Go and get you bag and clothes quickly and throw them into the car. Where is Michael?" she looked toward the lake someone was down on the shore taking a video film "Michael?" she called; the man did not turn.

"Erin put all this stuff in the car I am going to get Michael"

She turned and ran toward the lake.

As she neared the lake she called again "Michael?"

The man turned around but it wasn't Michael.

Up on a ledge way above the camping ground Michael Bannon filmed the chaos below. He had filmed the lake and now centred on the people he couldn't understand why they were running around in obvious panic but he figured it had to have something to do with the lake. He wanted to finish filming the general chaos before returning to the tent to find out what the problem was. He panned the video cam around the camping ground coming to rest on his cousin Jennifer who appeared to be talking to someone near the edge of the lake; As he zoomed in on her the world seemed to explode.

From the middle of the lake came a huge geyser of superheated steam and water it shot fifty or sixty feet into the air. Those standing on or near the edge of the lake died instantly scalded to death in one dreadful second. Michael still had the camera running and though stunned by the blast he could see his cousin crawling along the ground. Another blast ripped through the mountain as a second water spout tore out of the lake centre this time carrying burning rocks. It was twice as big, the rocks were flung hundreds of feet, and the camping ground began to burn.

Peter heard the explosion and felt the ground slide away from underneath him simultaneously. He started running toward the lake; he was only a few metres from the cabin when the second explosion ripped through the still air. Huge burning rocks and mud started to fall all around him. He raced back to the cabin grabbed his computer and bag and threw them into the Toyota. As he jumped in a large rock fell on one side of the cabin it began burning fiercely. He knew he would not get down the mountain on the road there was only one other way. He gunned the motor and tore through the thick forest at the back of the cabin. The ground sloped away steeply but somewhere nearby was an old fire trail; his father had used it many times during winter to get wood. He hadn't been on it for years and it was probably overgrown. He stormed through the forest driving as fast as he dared. There was no point he knew in taking too many risks he would not get down if he wrecked his vehicle. The ground moaned and rolled, the words of Lord Vulcan came to him as he 'roared his challenge to the black sky,' nothing would stop him, not god, man or beast, 'just a story Peter' he told himself.

The Toyota rocketed over a low unseen ledge the drop was a bit further than he had hoped but he landed on all four wheels safely, ahead of him was the old fire trail now he just had to keep it in sight.

Michael Bannon watched in horror as boiling mud burning rocks and super heated steam spewed out of the lake bed. Boats burned, tents burned; the pine trees looked like giant torches. The noise was dreadful. There was nothing he could do but watch as people died screaming their clothes burnt off them. He had zoomed in on the tent he shared but could not see Erin. The tent and car were burning, Jennifer he knew, was dead. He looked back to the edge of the lake where he had last seen her there was nothing there. He sobbed turned and ran; straight up. The camera bounced around on his chest but he could not leave it, it was his only chance to show anyone what had happened—if he survived. Rocks and burning lumps crashed around him, he crawled climbed and ran getting as high as he could. Then he could not go any higher he was faced with a huge wall of rock straight up. He couldn't climb it he wasn't that athletic, he couldn't go back and there was no way around. He turned around leaning against the huge rock wall and watched the carnage far below him. The screaming echoed through his soul the terrible sight of people running burning, was etched into his brain. Still the ground trembled, steam and mud poured skyward. Michael turned back to the wall squeezing his eyes shut to stop the tears. On his left he noticed a long narrow crack in the rocks. He eased his way across on a narrow ledge reaching over to slip his hand inside the crack. It was much wider than he first thought and appeared to be a small narrow cave. He took off his camera and jacket and threw them in. Turning sideways he forced his fortunately slim body through the opening. It was a struggle made even more difficult by the rocks and mud that were rebounding off the rocks all around him. Twice he was hit and screamed as he burned. Finally with one last effort he forced himself inside the cave.

There was very little room. He slid behind the big rock, wrapping his jacket over his head and arms he crouched as far from the entrance as he could get. The noise of rocks hitting the rock face outside the soft plop of burning molten lumps combined with the noise from below and the fierce crackle of burning trees was deafening; Michael was terrified. Then he remembered the camera. He grabbed the video positioning it far back to protect it from damage but far enough forward to capture some of the horror he set the lens to zoom and let it run. He crawled back into his corner and sobbed huge body wracking sobs of sheer terror.

CHAPTER 5

One hundred and fifty kilometres from Boulder Mountain on the west side where the hills met the wide open plains, where sheep grazed peacefully in a serene setting; was Fairhaven sheep station. Breeders of fine wool used specifically for carpet and rug making.

Fairhaven had been established in 1840 and had continued in the same family since then. It was the oldest family concern in the state and one of the oldest sheep breeding properties in Australia. On this beautiful early Autumnal morning a small sink hole appeared in the middle of the Ram paddock. Within minutes a geyser of super heated steam forced its way skyward out of the hole and twenty six pure bred rams died instantly, cooked to the bone.

In the homestead the lady of the house heard a distant 'whump' but thought nothing of it perhaps her husband was blowing a tree stump.

A further forty kilometres away the Bayley River (if it could be called a river) suddenly disappeared. Downstream and cutting close in to the town of Bayley where the river met another stream turned east then continued to the catchment area finally running into the Plains Dam, a bridge collapsed. The road running right up to the dam wall collapsed into a huge hole, small cracks like the pencil drawings and stick figures of a small child, began to appear across the dam wall. It wasn't a huge dam; walling off a valley to stop the heavy winter rains from running into the sea. It was also down on previous years because of the long hot summer, instead of the water being to the top of the wall it was at least fifty feet below. The usually placid surface of the dam was restless sending small waves rolling across the surface to slop against the wall with a wet smack. There was no-one to see it though as yet no-one knew.

Above, on Boulder Mountain, at the peak directly above the tiny cave sheltering Michael Bannon from the dreadful inferno, an ominous rumbling began. At first just a few small rocks and stones slid down the mountain, followed by a rain of shale broken trees and dirt. Within minutes huge boulders were rolling like marbles in a giant's game, rolling toward what was left of the Lake Marnie camping ground.

Michael heard the noise felt the ground shaking and screamed his terror as huge boulders rained down from the top of the mountain.

His tiny cave filled with dust and smoke he tried to bury himself further into the corner he didn't want to die like Jenny and Erin 'oh god please don't let me die' he sobbed over and over.

The noise seemed to go on forever.

"In the chaos and darkness Lord Vulcan rent the air with his tortured screams of defiance".

Michael was still screaming when he realized the only noise he could hear was his own. He sobbed his chest hitching as he tried to stop. Outside all was eerily silent the few pieces of burning matter that had gotten into the cave had been dowsed by the dust. Michael wiped his sleeve across his eyes and nose nursing his burnt arm he crawled toward the crack that was the opening. He couldn't see anything the dust hung thick in the air like a curtain. It was shockingly hot, the air almost unbreathable. Michael tied his handkerchief over his mouth and nose and attempted to squeeze through the opening to see the outside world. There was nothing to see the rocks were unbearably hot to touch he cried out in pain as his burnt arm and shoulder came in contact with the rock. He fell back into the cave unable to control the hysterical sobbing.

On the road down the mountain three cars, a Ford pickup, trailer still hitched and a 4wd had gotten as far as the Devil's Elbow before their world came to a crashing end.

The huge boulder that Peter had so carefully checked had rolled onto the road bringing down a multitude of smaller rocks. The first car into the bend had swerved to miss the heap and gone straight over the side. The Ford pickup had gotten around the rocks on the shoulder but his trailer had jack knifed slamming into the rocks spinning him around. He hit the wall with a resounding thud which brought down another shower of rocks on top of him. The second and third cars had slammed into the whole mess the old Nissan 4wd had stopped in time.

The driver jumped out and helped the people out of the mangled cars;, there was nothing he could do for the people in the Ford pickup the roof was crushed to the seats. He looked over the side but the car far below him was burning. He went back to his vehicle and tried to call out on his radio the people from the other vehicles crowded around him.

"Are we all there is?" a woman asked him

He shook his head "I just don't know I'm sorry"

He couldn't get through on the radio there was nothing but static.

He walked a little way up the road to the next bend and stood listening he could still hear noise coming from a way off but there were no more cars. The ground swelled and rolled away from under him. The people waiting by his vehicle screamed. He moved quickly to flatten against the rock face as more boulders roared down from above crashing around them. He felt the splinters of rock and shale scraping and grazing his arms and face as he crouched trying to protect himself.

When it settled down again there was one less person than before.

One man was sobbing quietly as he nursed his wife. The blood poured from the back of her head, he knew she was dead.

"We have to get off this road" he said "as long as we are going to get tremors we are going to get rocks. In fact they will probably just come down anyway even without any more movement they've all been loosened now. We have to find a safe place away from this area but we are going to have to walk none of these cars are going anywhere" he looked at his own vehicle which was now dented and battered with a sprung door after the last rock fall "we can't go back because there is nothing there anymore."

"How the hell do you know" asked a man "were you last out what did you see?"

"I only saw what was behind me, a car was burning, trees were burning and people were screaming. How many people did you push out of the way to get down here so fast?"

The man stepped toward him aggressively

"What are you saying—mate" he demanded.

He shook his head wearily "I am not saying anything. Look we can't afford to argue we have to stick together if we are going to find a way down the mountain—agreed?" he stepped forward to the aggressor and extended his hand. The man looked away hands on hips.

With his hand still extended he said.

"Don, Don Holman, retired geologist, farmer and amateur painter" he grinned.

The younger man stared at him for a while then shook his hand

"Geoff Tyrrel, not retired, not working, not anything."

There was no humour in the younger man's voice as they stood in the middle of a destroyed mountain road with four other people solemnly shaking hands.

Don Holman turned to the others all occupants of the second car. He addressed himself to the man nursing his wife.

"She's dead sir you're gonna have to leave her if you want to get out of this alive."

"I can't leave her" he looked up tears streaked through the dust on the old man's face "I just can't she is all I've got we've been together forever."

He took the old man's arm "Please we have to go now" he said gently.

The younger man Tyrrel stepped forward to help the old man to his feet. The others clustered around him "we'll take care of him" said a woman.

The mountain rolled the people screamed as Don Holman dragged them close to the rock face. Huge boulders crashed and bounced off the road and down into the gully. Pieces of razor sharp shale sent down in a thick shower cut into their arms hands and faces. When the movement stopped a huge pall of dust hung in the air. Don Holman realized he could no longer hear anything coming from the lake; the mountain was eerily silent.

CHAPTER 6

When the first explosion of superheated steam and mud had roared out of what was left of Lake Marnie, Erin Bannon was inside the tent getting her bag. She had put on her shoes and jacket and was retrieving everything she could carry to load into the car. The terrible noise and the ensuing screams brought her outside, for a heartbeat she stood transfixed as the great geyser roared skyward then showered the watchers, she saw her sister die. Jennifer had tried to run but had been caught and Erin saw in that instant a blackened form trying to crawl away from the lake. Then she was running. She ran upward away from the lake as she ran she dragged the hood of her jacket over her head. Hot mud and rocks began raining down around her twice she dodged being hit. Several burning rocks thumped into the trees which exploded in a shower sparks and flame. Still she ran.

She raced over the top of the hill behind her she could hear the screaming and a much louder, bigger explosion. The ground rolled under her she fell and rolled she got up and ran and fell again. She cleared the top of the hill and tore down the other side. The hill was steep the grass damp she could barely keep her feet. She plunged headlong into the damp darkness of the forest.

Erin didn't know how long she ran she fell often once she fell forward then slid all the way to the bottom of the hill sailing out over a fairly steep drop. She landed winded on her back against a tree. Still the mountain rolled and roared huge lumps of burning molten rock and mud fell all around her several times she felt the tingling as it burnt through her jacket; once her hair started to burn. Still she ran, legs pumping her lungs bursting. She jumped a small stream then to her right she saw a small overhang she waded back through the stream and crawled into the opening. At the back of the overhang it curved slightly into a small cave water seeped down the wall and a pile of animal bones lay in it. She crawled as far back as she could rolling herself into as tight a ball as possible. Suddenly the whole mountain seemed to be on the move with a great roar huge boulders tumbled down the mountain rebounding off the overhang bouncing off into the blackness of the forest. Fires burned but not for long the dampness held them at bay. Erin screamed as the front of the overhang shattered, rocks piled up in front of her small shelter the dust was thick and choking it was uncomfortably hot. Another tremor rippled across the mountain then it was gone, deathly silence reigned.

The wait seemed interminable but when no more noise came Erin sat up cautiously.

The air was thick with dust, choking and bitter she ripped her hood off and tied it around her mouth and nose. The silence was palpable. The rocks had piled up in front of her leaving only a gap of about 10 centimetres; she couldn't see anything. Inside the cave it was dark there was no room to stand or move around she started to cry.

Peter gunned the motor of the Toyota, this was the second time he had almost come to grief. In low range he was trying to manoeuver over a pile of rocks but they were sliding around under him and the vehicle kept crashing down hard. He backed off and went looking for another way around. He was driving along a stony ridge which had brought him out of the thick forest into the open. He had lost the old fire trail and couldn't pick it up again. Behind the racket continued the tremors rolled through the mountain, huge boulders were on the move he had to find a way out. He lifted the handset on the radio in another attempt to call the park rangers office. At last he heard a scratchy reply to his desperate call.

". . . . say again"

"Lake Marnie gone tremors increasing do you read over?"

". . . . Tremors?"

"This is Peter Cashman I am on the rock ridge halfway up Boulder Mountain overlooking the valley on the east side. I can't find a way down can you guide me? I'll explain soon."

There was a lot of static then a puzzled voice, clear but distant, came back to him.

"This is Boulder Mountain Ranger Station we hear you, we felt the tremors. We've got you on the map. You need to go back about I kilometre to where the ridge begins go down the hill, it's steep but there is no other way. The creek is on your right follow it down to where it turns right you'll find the old fire trail bearing left, it's pretty rough over".

Peter double clicked his handset to let them know he had received and backed up as quickly as he could. The 1 kilometre felt like forever, rocks were raining down on him large boulders were bouncing as they came fortunately missing him. He reached the end of the rocky ridge and stared straight down a steep hill.

"Oh Jesus here we go" he muttered "it's now or never".

He slipped the Toyota into low range for traction then took off. The vehicle didn't go straight it slid sideways, bucking and thumping occasionally straightening up. Rocks rained down on the roof and bonnet. Peter hung on grimly the steering wheel often being ripped out of his hands when he hit a rock or log. Twice the vehicle ground to a halt spun and nearly went down the hill backwards. He jammed on the brakes and gunned the motor to bring it back on track. He followed the creek, which had become non existent, all the way to nearly the bottom then it swung right. Peter veered left but couldn't find the track. He stopped the Toyota and leaned out; a tremor rolled through the mountain. Where the creek turned away to the right a large hole opened belching steam and mud. He quickly returned to his vehicle gunned the motor and took off through the bush. As he came out the other side of a grove of trees the old fire trail opened up in front of him. He floored the accelerator the Toyota jumped forward slipping and sliding as it followed the old track along the lower side of the mountain.

As suddenly as it all started it all stopped; Peter realized the only sound he was hearing was the roar of the engine as he pushed it to its limit. The tremors had stopped silence descended like an eerie curtain. When he reached the bottom he negotiated a rough patch of old creek bed warily half expecting it to blow up in his face. Once safely past it he stopped the vehicle and climbed out. Looking up at the mountain Peter was amazed at the sight. The top peak was gone, fell he supposed, the whole mountain was slowly becoming covered in a thick choking haze of dust and whatever else the mountain had thrown up. He could taste sulphurous bitterness in the air. Had the mountain been building up to blow? no that could not be his equipment would have told him. Had that first small and quite naturally occurring tremor set off some strange reaction within the mountain? Possibly. The bed of the lake may have been faulty for a long time the cold water draining away in to the chamber of the mountain below would have been like a kettle boiling, the lid would have to lift sooner or later. Or was there something more sinister about the whole thing. He watched as the mountain disappeared under its thick haze, any poor bastards that had not got out could not survive that; any who had survived the initial explosions that is. He didn't think there would be too many of those.

He jumped back into the Toyota and headed across country to the Ranger station. He would have to call his father no doubt he would know his equipment would have picked up the seismic disturbance, also the mountain was visible for a long way someone would be sure to advise authorities something was amiss.

CHAPTER 7

Half way up the mountain on a shattered road six injured bedraggled people argued the best way to go. Don Holman was trying to reason with two women who thought it best to stay where they were until rescued. The younger man Tyrrel was off scouting after giving up on the argument the two other males, by now, were saying nothing. As the silence became absolute across the mountain the thick dust descended over them, they began coughing and choking.

"Find a scarf or handkerchief quickly" Holman yelled "get it over you nose and mouth the thicker the better you have to be able to filter out this stuff."

They rummaged through the cars until everyone was provided with some sort of protection.

"Now we have to get going. It seems as though it's over but we still have loose rocks to contend with. The only way out that I can see is straight down there" he pointed down the gully where the other car plunged into a fiery death.

"Its good thick forest and there isn't much fire down there we can easily get around it, but it isn't going to be easy. Tyrrel and I will help any of you that need it but you have to help yourselves as well."

Tyrrel had returned from his scout and was nodding in agreement.

"There is no other way I've looked in every direction. Lower down the road has gone completely sheered off the side of the mountain the gully is the only way out."

One of the women crossed over and tried to peer into the gully

"It's so steep I am not very good at climbing . . . ." she sobbed "but I'll try."

Holman smiled at her "you'll be right love".

The dust thickened around them turning day into almost night. The group huddled together as Tyrrel slipped over the side of the gully looking for foot holds. Around his waist Holman had tied a nylon tow rope they had found in the Ford pickup. He climbed down about 20 meters before he called for the others to come down.

"I've found a ledge it's a fairly easy climb, come down one at a time."

Holman helped the two women over first. They climbed down gingerly slipping and sliding as the treacherous shale rattled away from under their feet. Small trees broken branches and part of the road railing helped them with their foot holds. Tyrrel leaning out on his anchored rope, helping each of them onto the ledge. It wasn't wide but it was enough to support them while he went on to find another spot further down.

All the while Holman prayed the tremors were finished, another one while they were climbing down and they would all go to their deaths.

The dust had become so thick it was near impossible to see beyond a meter or two. Their eyes were stung and watering their noses and throats itched, many times during the climb down they had to stop as one of the group had a coughing fit.

When they reached the ledge, they held hands more for comfort than any safety it afforded. These total strangers bound to a goal of survival.

The old man who had lost his wife proved to be an agile climber. On the next leg he accompanied Tyrrel down while Holman stayed at the rear supporting anyone who got into trouble.

It was long slow and laborious; they stopped often, breathing hard, their lungs burning with the exertion of climbing in the appalling conditions. Then disaster struck.

Tyrrel was slipping and sliding through a particularly heavily treed area. He stepped onto a fallen tree trunk anchored to a tree then bounced it to make sure it would hold the weight; it didn't. The trunk took off down the mountain side like some giant toboggan. Tyrrel lost his balance, sliding the length of the rope, the anchor held. Before the rope pulled taut it slipped up from around his waist to over one shoulder. He was hanging on desperately. It slipped over his shoulder then pulled tight on his arm. The others couldn't see him but they heard him scream as the force of his body coming to a halt at the end of the rope broke his arm. He was swinging, dangling at the end of a thin tow rope which creaked and rubbed against the trees. Try as he might he couldn't find a foot hold he couldn't see but he knew there was nothing underneath him. Far below him he heard the tree crashing to the bottom.

CHAPTER 8

High on the side of Boulder Mountain in a tiny cave the size of a stone coffin, Erin lay. The air was so thick she found it hard to breathe even through the makeshift mask. Her eyes watered and every ragged breath she took was painful. Twice she had soaked the mask in the dripping water on the wall of the cave. It wasn't much but it did help. She had tried to wet her mouth the same way but the water was slimy and bitter and made her retch.

"I survived" she told herself "am I all that's left? There must be someone else. But how are they going to find me and I can't even get out!"

Erin worked her way around so that she could feel the rocks against her feet then she pushed with all her might. Nothing moved. She hammered at the rock pile that had both saved her and had now become her tomb.

"I will not die here" she screamed at no one "I survived I must get out!"

She pounded her feet against the rocks screaming defiance until she was sobbing and exhausted. Her chest hurt her ears were ringing her eyes streamed and her nose itched.

"God please help me" she sobbed "please help me I don't want to die."

Further up the mountain above the wreckage of the once beautiful Lake Marnie camping ground in a small cave, a desperately ill young man lay curled in foetal position. Michael was no longer conscious. His breathing was ragged as he lay in the dark his jacket over his head. The burns on his arm and shoulder were weeping; he was in shock. Nothing existed beyond this flimsy shelter. All was silent except for the hoarse gasp that was the breathing of Michael Bannon. Just back from the entrance of the cave a small video camera continued to record the events as they happened in front of the cave and beyond; events which by now were totally obscured by the thick choking dust.

Peter drove the very battered Toyota into the car park of the Ranger station. He stumbled inside noting the long cracks through the walls and cracked windows.

Jim Milburn helped him in the door.

"You've suffered abit damage" Peter said.

The older man nodded.

"Yeah just a bit not too much though and we still have all our services—oh except water. I can't figure that one out" he scratched his head.

"Well I can tell you why. Have you looked at the mountain do you see what has happened up there?" Peter asked.

"All we can see is that strange cloud hanging over it. It came down very fast just after the last tremor we have no idea what is going on." Jim told him.

"Lake Marnie camping ground has gone" Peter said his voice flat.

Jim Milburn looked at him steadily

"You mean gone as in disappeared?" he asked

Peter nodded wearily "yes all gone nothing left, the Lake blew up."

Jim stared off toward the mountain through the cracked window of the office

"All gone" he said quietly speaking to no-one in particular "why?"

The question was simple and directed at Peter

"I don't know" he said "we had one small tremor on Saturday morning that sort of started it all. I could go into a whole lot of scientific jargon why this happens but it won't make any sense to you or any one else. Overnight the lake disappeared, simply drained away, the lake bed may have been cracked or it may have just been a natural phenomenon, whatever, it disappeared. This morning after another more violent tremor the lake exploded back into life when it sent up a geyser of superheated steam and boiling mud. The second explosion was more violent and twice as big. Those people up there never had a chance if it hadn't been for the old fire trail I wouldn't have made it out myself. The place just burned it was raining magma and burning rocks. The tremors kept coming, at one stage I thought the whole mountain was going to implode on itself. Then the peak must have come down because it started raining rocks and boulders the size of houses. When I first got down the dust hadn't started to settle I could still see the top of the mountain the peak was gone the whole lot must have collapsed. That cloud you can see is pyroclastic it is deadly and is made up of dust, sulphur and a dozen different gasses that have been thrown up. If there are still people alive up there I can't see them surviving long that stuff will eat their lungs."

Jim Milburn handed him a cup of coffee, he smiled

"We always keep a couple of buckets filled with water for the dogs but it's been boiled so it's okay."

Peter took the coffee gratefully,

"I don't care whether it has nor hasn't I need this coffee, dogs and all."

The phones at the Ranger station started ringing. Jim Milburn and another officer were answering the queries as best they could.

"This is hard" he said to Peter "what do I tell these people who want to know what happened to the mountain".

"Tell them the truth. Tell them there have been some problems and that the proper authorities have been informed and are investigating it. Don't tell them about the Lake Marnie camping ground the last thing we need is people trying to get up there to find relatives."

Jim nodded "okay".

When the phone rang again it was Peter's father.

Jim Milburn was nodding "yes sir, yes sir,. but . . . He's here sir" he handed the phone to Peter "it's your Dad."

Peter took the phone "hi" he said a bit to brightly even to himself it sounded false.

His father was concerned with the seismic activity that he had been picking up since Friday. He said that he was getting a lot of reports from all over Australia particularly the southern states, and New Zealand. When he couldn't reach Peter at home he figured he had gone to Boulder Mountain for the Easter. Then when he picked up several big tremors emanating from the area below the mountain he started calling him, by radio, by mobile and finally when he couldn't get him, he called the ranger station to see if they had heard anything from him.

Peter gave him a brief outline of what happened and how he had used the old fire trail to get off the mountain.

"I'm on my way Peter" his father said "is there somewhere we can stay?"

Peter thought for a minute,

"There is a pub at Bayley I could drive over there and find out if there is any space."

"Good enough, I'll be there in about four hours" he hung up.

"Do you think the pub will have any room?" he asked the Ranger.

Jim nodded, "it will if it's still standing. I'll come over with you I want to check it out for myself the lad can look after things here" he said indicating the younger officer.

They climbed into separate vehicles Peter following the ranger down the road to Bayley. All the way the mountain cloud was becoming denser and now had a distinctive yellow tinge.

Could anyone have survived? Peter doubted it very much but no-one could ever underestimate the human spirit and the will to survive.

CHAPTER 9

In a cave three quarters of the way down the mountain six people huddled together. Their coughing had eased and they could breathe more easily now but they were cold and it was very dark in the cave.

At first they had climbed below the cloud then Tyrrell had nearly taken a dive off the mountain held to a small tree by a length of nylon rope. Holman had scrambled down the slope dug himself in among the rocks and physically dragged the younger man to safety. He had screamed as the broken arm was released from the rope. Holman had held him like a baby as he cried in pain.

When the sobs stopped Holman helped him take off his shirt creating a makeshift sling to support the arm. The elbow was crooked from the break but the rest seemed intact. If he hadn't been reasonably physically strong his arm may have been torn out of the socket. He made the younger man comfortable then with the rope around his waist he went back to help the others down the slope.

"I'll be back for you Tyrrell" he said "I have to find somewhere for these people to stand first—okay?"

Tyrrell gave a weak smile "It's okay go ahead I'll be right here for a while."

Holman nodded patted his shoulder and returned to the others.

It was another long agonising hour's descent before he found the ideal spot, a cave which appeared small but would hold them all.

He shepherded the others in then went back for Tyrrell. By the time he reached him the cloud had caught up and it was almost dark except for the eerie yellow tinge to it.

The taste was awful and it was becoming difficult to breathe. At times during the climb down with Tyrrell, Don Holman thought he would never take another breath there just wasn't any real air. When they reached the cave the other four were still huddled together where Holman had left them.

"We didn't move" one of them said "we were too afraid."

Don nodded "It's okay, help me with him will you"

The four of them supported the younger man into the cave laying him on the floor. One of the men rolled up a jacket for a pillow and placed it under his head. By now it was pitch black Don Holman couldn't see beyond a metre in front of him.

"I need a match or lighter" he said

A box of matches was produced out of the jacket Tyrrell laid on.

Holman struck two matches at once walking forward into the gloom as he did so. Ahead of him there appeared to be a wall of rock but when he reached it he found that there was a split large enough to allow a person through. He struck two more matches and held them inside the next section. He could still see floor so he forced his way through.

The cave beyond was cold and water dripped constantly down one wall but it was huge. As he stepped cautiously forward he realized the cave spread out into a much larger room than he could see. He struck two more matches and there in front of him was a small stream of water; the cave went on beyond it. There was no foul smell or cloud from the mountain in here he figured they could probably block up most of the opening with smaller rocks lying around.

To save the matches he followed the wall back to the opening and squeezed through.

In the gloom he could just make out the group now sitting closely around Tyrrell on the floor.

"Come on" he said "I've found something bigger and better".

The two men helped Tyrrell to his feet stumbling in the gloom. Holman lit two matches to show them the opening then helped them squeeze through one by one.

On the other side he showed them the water

"I don't know if we can drink it so I'm going to taste it first"

He knelt down and scooped up a handful holding it to his nose first.

"Smells alright" he scooped up another handful and gingerly tasted it he nodded "tastes okay but it's a bit bitter probably something from the mountain in it so I wouldn't drink it just wet your mouth and lips and spit it out."

"Will we ever get out of here" one of the ladies asked him, Holman could hear the tremor in her voice.

"I don't know but we seem to be safe for the time being. If this cave has managed to survive whatever has happened here I guess we will be okay for quite some time."

"We don't have any food though" said one of the men.

"No we don't" Holman answered "but we are alive and there is water and we will stay here until either all that is going on outside is over or someone finds us, agreed?"

There was silence for a while then agreement.

Outside on the shattered mountain the cloud continued to thicken and roll down the mountain. Up on the peak thunder began to roll, in a small stone tomb a young woman sobbed herself into unconsciousness further up the mountain amid the deadly gasses still pouring out from the ruined lake a young man also lay unconscious. His breathing was slow and halting and rasped and rattled in his chest. Of Lake Marnie camping ground there was nothing to be seen.

A small video camera whirred the film tape long finished.

CHAPTER 10

The Ranger fairly flew across the dirt roads leaving a dust haze thick enough to cut behind him. Peter Cashman followed as closely as he dared. They rounded a bend which brought them onto the bitumen road. Picking up speed they raced toward the town of Bayley.

As they approached the town limits the devastation became obvious. At first Peter thought the rubbish dump was on the edge of town before realizing he was looking at the town.

Nothing was standing. Most of the houses and stores had been shattered by rocks and debris from the mountain. Only the rear of the Hotel looked anything like intact and that was leaning drunkenly to one side. The Steak House was a charred mess the owner sitting on the ground outside staring at it. Peter jumped out of his Toyota and walked over to him.

"You okay mate" he asked quietly.

The man looked up shaking his head tears streaming down his face

"My wife and baby are in there somewhere" he sobbed.

Peter stared at the burnt out restaurant "I'm sorry mate" he said.

He walked toward the hotel where the Ranger was talking to the publican.

"He said he thought the whole bloody mountain had come down on them. There was an almighty roar then rocks started crashing down around them." Jim Milburn told him.

Peter only nodded what could he say? He stared up at the mountain; way in the distance he could hear thunder beginning to roll perhaps it would rain and clear away the cloud it usually did in cases like this.

Not far up the mountain in a large damp cold cave six people heard the roar and shivered in fear. Holman told them it was thunder but it didn't make them feel better; they huddled together for warmth and security.

Two others further up heard nothing, instead they moaned and sobbed in delirious semi deranged unconsciousness.

"Lord Vulcan heard the voice of his Idoli on the wind and he followed it to the edge of the great northern continent where, on soft warm sand, at the edge of a wine dark sea, he saw her fleetingly in the sky. He roared in pain as he watched her leave him a point of light across a velvet black sky. His pain soon turned to rage and he screamed her name "Idoliiiii". The seas rose up to caress him but he would not be calmed. Soon the great ocean had turned to a roiling, spitting fury as he unleashed his anger upon it and the world shook as the great Lord Vulcan unleashed the terror and fire at his command. Idoli neither heard nor saw any of this as the spirit of the air and wind carried her to a safe place of light and beauty. In the midst of this maelstrom unheard by Lord Vulcan deafened by the sheer destruction of his own temper, came another sound to the world. The Lord of Earth began to rage at the destruction shaking his fist at Lord Vulcan. The ground split, the very bed of the oceans split, huge mountains of water rolled over the burning land putting out the great fires. The Lord of the Oceans joined with the Lord of the Earth and together they created new land and lakes and streams.

The Lord of the Wind and Air made clouds which became heavy with the water drawn from the earth. And soon it rained and the earth was washed clean and all manner of things began to grow. And so a new cycle began."

CHAPTER 11

The cruise Liner "Dolphin" left Sydney Quay and headed into the vast blue of the Pacific. Passengers toasted their departure with magnums of Champagne as the beautiful ship slid effortlessly through calm brilliant water.

For three days the water remained calm the weather fine the sky clear. On the fourth day as evening approached the skipper announced the small volcano of Teti was stirring and as night drew on; would be visible. People crammed the railings straining for the first sight of the belching volcano.

Soon a roar, similar to an oncoming locomotive, cut through the stillness; Teti was making its' presence known. The ship had slowed speed as the people watched one of the greatest displays of nature on earth. Their oohs and aahs could barely be heard above the echoing roar. The navigator noted that Teti appeared much larger than usual and mentioned it to the captain.

"All the better" said the Captain "it will give them something to watch and tell everyone else about".

As the ship continued to slip through the now wine dark waters of the southern Pacific, past the erupting volcano heading toward its first port of call at Vanuatu, the engineer was adjusting the air conditioners to balance out the rise in air temperature and humidity. Not unusual in this part of the world but slightly higher than normally expected.

The dinner chimes sounded and sighing with the wonderment of it all the passengers filed into the restaurant for the first dinner sitting. Few people felt or even noticed the rise and fall of the ship on the sea and if they did they would only have put it down to a natural action of the waves.

But not the engineer nor the navigator.

The first readings that alarmed the engineer were the rises showing in the surrounding water temperature levels. The other problem he encountered was the ocean did not appear to be as deep as it should be. He checked the instruments fine tuning everything but it made no difference. He called the skipper but was advised it was probably a system fault. He could not find one.

The navigator was also having his fair share of troubles.

Beneath him should be flat sandy ocean bed with only a few small rises which became more pronounced as they neared Vanuatu. From Vanuatu to Fiji navigation became an art as the ship was steered between the maze of small cones underwater ridges, reefs and coral. But not here, this should have been plain sailing. Twice he changed course in an effort to find the deep flat sections that made sailing these waters so easy. For an hour he strained to keep the ship in safe water, the skipper standing puzzled by his side.

"I simply don't understand this" said the Captain "the engineer is reporting problems all over the place, if it isn't the ship, and these readings indicate it isn't; what the hell is it?"

The navigator shook his head "some sort of disturbance I think".

"Disturbance? You mean under sea disturbance?"

The navigator nodded "uhhuh, well that's what it looks like."

The skipper stared at him "you did say Teti looked bigger didn't you?"

The navigator returned his stare "yeah I did, oh god I hope it hasn't gotten too big."

The words were no sooner out of his mouth than a huge wave crashed over the bow of the ship. It came out of no-where taking the deck strollers by surprises. Some were knocked down and pushed along the deck by the force of the water some managed to hang onto the railing as the water poured over them. A few unlucky ones were washed into the sea.

"All stop" screamed the skipper "oh jesus what's happening?"

The crew ran down the deck trying to see the people in the water. The search lights came on life buoys hit the water as they frantically tried to help those now rapidly dissolving into the wake of the ship. As the ship slid to a halt the engineer called the bridge,

"The water temperature's rising it's up to 34 degrees Celsius we have to keep moving."

"We can't" replied the skipper "we have people in the water chief, I repeat people in the water."

Four people found the buoys and were holding on while the crew threw ropes to them. Two men were crawling up the side of the ship when the ship lurched; they both lost their grip and fell back into the sea. On the starboard side a huge bubble like movement appeared on the surface of the sea from it burst forth a stream of lava, looking for all the world like a delicate burning veil. The sea hissed and roiled the Dolphin was tossed about like a cork huge globs of magma falling onto her decks burning through layer after layer. With a monstrous roar the sea became a cauldron, those still swimming for the ship died quickly those on the decks were burnt to death. The Dolphin did a death roll slid beneath the boiling sea and was gone.

When the sea finally subsided there was no evidence the Dolphin or her passengers and crew had ever existed.

The huge tsunami that followed the under sea eruption hit Vanuatu with such force a large portion of the population went with it. Parts of the islands were wiped clean leaving nothing behind. The shallow broken waters of the Pacific between Vanuatu and Fiji broke up the tsunami and it became nothing more than a surge tide when it arrived at Fiji.

Japan experienced a massive earthquake which took a large part between Kobe and Tokyo off the world map. Fujiyama blew its stack its pristine beauty forever desecrated by long rivers of lava which flowed endlessly to the sea taking most of the remains of Tokyo with it.

New Guinea's volcanoes erupted one after the other in a series of huge bangs that reverberated around the earth. Son of Krakatoa a small smoking cone close to the site of the old Krakatoa, burst into life sending huge streams of magma pouring into the atmosphere.

Off the coast of California the San Andreas Fault groaned and moaned as the southern end of the extrusions slipped even further apart. California shook settled and shook even harder; again. Under sea vents shot huge geysers of superheated steam and water hundreds of feet into the air falling on the whole of the west coast like warm rain. Slowly the edge of California from the tip of the most northern curve all the way to Mexico began to subside. The land did not sink though it simply pulled away from the main mass and stayed there, somewhat lower at sea level but intact.

Further north at the edge of the Bering Sea, the Aleutian Trench collapsed. The huge extrusions forced up by the constant movement suddenly flattened. From the centre of the trench an eruption roared into life, showering the Aleutian Islands with boiling water and mud. Across the Pole Siberia shuddered and shook as an earthquake at the top end of the Richter scale rolled across the frozen waste.

In Australia the sleeping giant slowly came awake.

Chapter 12

"Lord Vulcan wept, his Idoli had gone the Lord of the Earth and the Lord of the Wind and air had joined forces against him. He had reached the vast southern land where though he tried to put his heart into his rage, he was defeated. There he lay down and slept"

The shattered remnants of the once pretty tourist town greeted Alan Cashman as his Nissan negotiated the last bend before Bayley.

"Oh god it looks like a rubbish dump" he said to no-one.

His son and a Ranger were sitting on chairs having a drink when he pulled up.

"Nothing better to do?" he inquired sarcastically.

Peter stood rubbing his dirty hands down the side of his jeans.

"Hello Dad" he shook hands with the older man "this is the Ranger Jim Milburn"

The two men shook hands.

Alan Cashman surveyed the damage "can you tell me what happened?"

"No not really" said Peter "we had a series of tremors then the mountain lake disappeared. Some hours later the lake bed exploded throwing up steam, mud and then rock and magma. The camping ground was full but I doubt anyone has survived I only got out myself because of the old fire trail, then it was touch and go for a while."

"Well I have some rather bad news for you, the Pacific fault line is on the blink. I don't know exactly what is going on yet but just listening to some reports as I was driving up here indicates that New Guinea's volcanoes are on the rampage and there have been reports of tremors in the Pacific regions but nothing concrete yet. I guess we'll find out in good time." Alan told them.

All three stared up at the mountain watching the play of lightning around what was left of the peak hearing the thunder as it rolled over the devastation. As they watched light rain began to fall. The survivors of the town had thrown up temporary shelters of tents and tarpaulins they hurried into these now as the rain poured down on them. High up on the mountain drenching rain ran down rocks and into a stone tomb where a young woman lay unconscious. The cold rain slowly washed the deadly cloud away from around her. She would wake up, in time, but she would be shivering with cold and soaked to the skin. Even higher up the same thing was happening in a tiny cell like cave. Further down six people huddled together in a large cold black cave didn't hear the rain only the thunder they did not know the cloud was dispersing.

Slowly the Lord of Wind and Air was winning the battle against Lord Vulcan, putting out the fire washing clean the earth.

Elsewhere in the world the tortured earth groaned its dismay at the disturbances caused by Lord Vulcan slowly coming awake.

Within the hours it had taken Alan Cashman to drive to Bayley the seismic centre in Canberra was reporting and receiving reports of volcanic and seismic disturbances from all over the world. Vanuatu reported the huge tsunami and the loss of life. New Guinea was trying to evacuate many of its people in areas and on islands affected by the volcanic eruptions. There was a great loss of life and no-one had any idea how many villages had disappeared. A shipping company in Sydney was requesting help from the airlines and the Air Force to help it track one of their cruise ships which had not answered a call after reports of undersea disturbances in the south Pacific. The information came in slowly at first, an earthquake in Siberia, smoke from long dormant volcanoes some were only minor, but, some of the bigger mountains were showing signs of unrest. Then the collapse of California's coast! Amazingly many people on the subsided section had survived and had made contact with the rest of California, there was a rescue operation under way. The great lakes area in Michigan was also having problems with a series of quakes measuring around 3.4. The embankment around two of the smaller lakes had collapsed and water was pouring into the surrounding country side. Avalanches and rock slides roared down the sides of the Andes and the Himalayas. The Russian Urals were hit by a quake—probably from Siberia—which brought down tons of ice on surrounding villages and towns. Sections of coastline in New Zealand began sliding or subsiding into the sea after a series of tremors. The world was going crazy; yet it had not really begun.

For two hours Alan Cashman his son Peter and the Ranger Jim Milburn had been sitting in the Ranger's office listening to the reports pouring in from around the world on the radio Alan had set up.

"It doesn't make sense" Peter said "what do you think is going on" he asked the older man.

Alan shook his head "I don't know Peter. Certainly the earth has periods of extreme volcanic and seismic disturbance and being the volatile nature of the beast we must expect it, but this is something totally unexpected; there have been no warnings. That in itself is highly unusual."

"Is there anything anyone can do?" Jim asked quietly.

"No I'm afraid not we are totally at the mercy of nature" answered Alan

"The nature of the beast" Peter muttered "Dad there is something I want to show you." He crossed to his bag and retrieved the old book, the story of Lord Vulcan. He rummaged around and came up with a series of computer print outs he handed all these to his father.

"This book was given to me or rather sent to me I don't know who by but it was suggested that it is in fact prophetic and encoded" he shrugged "have a look at it. I've run it through the computer and tried to tie it to some sort of code but found nothing. I have printed out what little I could find that made any sense but still it doesn't jell maybe you can make something out of it." He handed the book and the printed material to his father.

For the next three hours the older man pored over the information given him by his son. Peter and the Ranger made a meal for the three of them, the younger Ranger having been sent home to help his family. Outside the night was black and cold and the rain continued to pour without abatement. The pyroclastic cloud that had so dominated the mountain was gone washed away unseen by anyone. The fires on the mountain were out, smouldering trees and a changed shape to the mountain the only indication of what had gone before.

In a small cell like cave above the remnants of Lake Marnie camping ground a young man stirred. Although he opened his eyes he could see nothing, he tried to cry out but the only sound was a ragged croak. He struggled for a while to sit up but pain tore through his chest forcing him to lie down again. He was cold, shivering; the rain was pouring through the small opening and running in rivulets across the floor. He dragged himself to the opening and opened his mouth the rain was bitter, acrid, he began coughing and gagging. In his effort to crawl back into his corner he knocked something. He drew back his hand thinking it was an animal but it was only the video camera he left in place to capture the scenes below. He crawled away from it dragging his pain racked body away from the opening. He sobbed and once again tried to call out; mercifully he lost consciousness.

Further down the mountain Erin Bannon woke, she was freezing cold and soaked through. There was no room to move but she wriggled around until her head was near the opening. There was nothing to see, she had no idea if she was blind or it was just as black outside the cave as it was in. The rain came in on her face, sharp needles which stung, she opened her mouth but it tasted terrible; she spat it out. The pain in her chest was awful breathing was difficult she tried to say something but nothing came out. The water seeping down the wall of the cave had become a stream she was forced to sit in; there was nowhere else. She began hallucinating and in her mind she could see the replay of the terrible carnage at the camping ground. Squeezing her eyes tightly she tried to block out the screams and the burning figures but she could not. Jenny! Jenny! She tried to call, she sobbed dry racking sobs no tears came to wash the burning from her eyes. Again she laid down her body heaving with sobs she could not control. It would be a long night for her.

In a large cavern six people remained huddled in a tight group. They were damp and cold they had neither wood to light a fire nor torch to bring light so they sat in the darkness not speaking each lost in his or her own thoughts.

The younger man Tyrrell had managed to get himself in to sitting position as the awful pain in his arm steadied down to an almost acceptable level.

"Do you think someone should check outside?" he asked hopefully "you never know maybe it's all gone now. If that was thunder before then perhaps the storm has blown it all away."

Don Holman was weary, wearier than he had ever been in his life. He had been retired a while now and was not used to climbing. His bones and muscles ached so badly he wanted to cry but he knew he would not.

"I guess I'll go" he said "someone has to".

He hauled himself painfully off the floor his buttocks were damp and numb and his back ached abominably.

"Perhaps the walk will help get the kinks out of my back. I really think we should be doing exercise anyway instead of just sitting here. There isn't much chance of sleeping."

He staggered to the rock face and painfully squeezed himself through the opening into the outer cave. It was pitch black he couldn't see where the entrance was. To avoid walking straight out and falling off the mountain he struck two matches. The light glinted off the rain he slipped and slid across to the entrance. Cautiously he leaned out, ice cold rain poured over his head, he tasted it, it was bitter like the water in the other cave. He shook himself drying his face with the sleeve of his shirt. The thunder had gone but he had no idea if the cloud had also gone, he knew nothing about eruptions in any form he only knew rocks. There was no point trying to leave the rain would only make the final descent slippery and dangerous they had to sit it out until morning and hope someone would come looking. If it did clear outside once the rain stopped he could probably get them the rest of the way down the mountain. He went back into the other cave feeling his way along the wall not wanting to use any more matches. The others heard him coming and all spoke at once,

"What's it like out there?"

"I don't really know" he answered "it's pitch black it's pouring rain, and it's undrinkable, but I can't see anything so I don't know if the cloud has washed away or it's raining through it."

"Can we climb down"? Asked one of the women.

"'fraid not we'll have to wait until morning. If the rain stops then we'll try if we can't do it we'll just have to wait until someone finds us".

"How do you know anyone will even be looking?" asked Tyrrell "after all anyone who comes to find out what happened probably won't be looking for survivors."

"How do you know they won't" said Don Holman "we survived and there are probably more out there, we don't even know what happened we only know what we heard and saw."

Tyrrell gave a non committal grunt "yeah well . . . . whatever."

CHAPTER 13

Down in the Ranger's office two calls came in, one from the army and one from the SES, in reply to messages left by Jim Milburn. Both calls brought the same response from the Ranger.

"Look we don't know exactly what has happened up there but we do have a vulcanologist and a seismic specialist here . . . . we can't get up there it's pouring rain, tomorrow morning will be the soonest we can find out just what there is to know . . . . I can't tell you any more than that but I would appreciate if you could send everything you've got including ambulances and medical staff we can only hope there are survivors."

He caught sight of Peter's face

"although we are not holding out a lot of hope for that."

Putting the phone down he said to Peter

"No-one Peter?"

Peter looked tired and drawn "I just don't know Jim I don't know just how far it all went, but no I would not hold out any real hope."

Alan put down the sheet he was reading.

"Peter do you know what this book is?"

Peter shook his head "a good story?"

His father looked disgusted "it's a chronicle".

"A chronicle? Yes it could be I never thought of it like that, if it's true that is."

I believe it is true" the older man said "I believe it was written not as a story of the beginning of the world, though that is what it pertains to, but as a warning for the future."

"I'm sorry I don't see . . ." Peter left the sentence unfinished

"It is, I believe, a forecast of the end of the world" his father said quietly.

"You mean to die by earthquake and volcano? no, no, dad that's old hat the scientists from the beginning of time have been touting that very argument and here we are thousands of years later getting better and better and the earth is getting cooler and cooler. No sorry I can't wear that."

Peter walked back to the kitchen and helped himself to coffee.

"Is this possible?" Jim Milburn asked him.

"Yes I think so, but not as Peter sees it. I don't believe it means we die by earthquake and volcano simply because the earth has them I think there is a catalyst for these 'quakes and eruptions; . . . . Something external." He added.

"Like a comet or asteroid chunk?" asked Peter returning from the kitchen. He placed steaming mugs of coffee in front of his father and Jim Milburn.

"By the way we're out of water Jim."

"Not to worry there should be some in the fire fighting tank of the truck I'll siphon some out."

"Something like that" Peter's father continued "amongst the Aborigines of this country and I believe there is a similar story amongst the American natives, in dreamtime stories they talk of the rivers of fire but there were no volcanoes in this country in the time that the Aborigines have lived here assuming that these stories were created over the last sixty thousand years. There is no evidence to suggest that the Aborigines lived in this country any longer than that yet it seems implausible that there were no people living here. Those stories could only have come from first hand experience so we can assume rightly or wrongly, that the stories have been handed down by an earlier race. This being the case the rivers of fire had to have occurred over one hundred and fifty thousand years ago prior to the last ice age. There is no evidence to suggest that anything has occurred since then; seismic, yes, but not volcanic. We do know that the Flinders Ranges in South Australia have warm spots also the Blue Mountains of New South Wales but they have shown no indication of smoking. We do know the Flinders Ranges were created by volcanic activity in the first place but that was eons ago long before the last ice age. Australia's mountains and gorges are between two hundred and fifty million and seven hundred and fifty million years old, does it make sense?"

Peter stared at his father saying nothing the words slipping through the filing cabinet of his brain. He was recalling information and cataloguing it making comparisons to the information he was receiving from his father. Jim Milburn just looked puzzled it was almost beyond him though it did make sense.

"What are you saying dad" Peter asked.

"I am trying to say that this is not a natural occurrence;natural perhaps in the universe, but not natural to Earth. There has to be an outside influence something of tremendous force possibly with a huge magnetic field."

Peter shook his head "if that were so why haven't the scientists found it why haven't we heard anything about it? There is nothing in our universe that is big enough to do that without us knowing about it."

"Don't be naïve Peter, we have very little knowledge of the universe and what is in it. Our little section of the galaxy barely rates as a speck of dust. Our world is so small and insignificant we barely rate a mention. There are planets and stars, asteroids and comets out there that could destroy our galaxy. Huge wandering worlds of destruction we could not even imagine. If by chance one of those monsters were to arrive in our particular area, if it were large enough it could exert huge forces on this tiny planet without even becoming visible. We are on the outer edge of the spiral with little protection."

"So you are saying that something this big could be surrounded by a magnetic force field this in turn could exert tremendous pull on the Earth causing upheavals on a scale we have never seen before. I suppose the high iron content of the Earth's core would be the great attraction. This would force magma up through every crack or breach in the Earth's crust . . . . yes it's possible" there was an excitement in Peter's voice that had not been there before.

His father watched the animation grow and marvelled as his son's superb analytical mind began collating information drawing on previous experiences and computing them with the data he had received.

"I have to get this down I have to be able to get home Dad I need to use your Lab. This is too big for one person I need a team I can trust. If you are right we have to break this book down into tiny pieces and find out what will happen next and how, and how long will it last. We must survive this. We don't know what happened last time but obviously someone did survive otherwise the Aborigines would not have these stories." Peter began packing up his bag and laptop.

"That's if I am right Peter" his father told him "this is how I see the book."

Peter was nodding "it's a start it's more than I had let's work on that principle."

"Alan can I ask a question?" Jim Milburn inquired.

"Go for it any input no matter how small is useful."

"If there is something out there and it is exerting enough force on this planet to cause these upheavals, could the force become great enough to actually force the planet into leaving its' orbit or perhaps tip it over?" Jim Milburn's face was creased into a worried frown.

Alan and Peter exchanged a glance, there was dead silence in the room.

They suddenly spoke together

"The ice age . . . ."

Nodding Peter grabbed the laptop and began typing furiously.

Alan thought for a minute then "it's a common belief Jim that the ice age's were caused by a comet or an asteroid slamming into the earth. It has also been blamed for the death of the Dinosaurs and the very fast evolution of a lot of other species including man. However apart from the devastated areas in Siberia, no other site large enough has been found to be able to say 'this is what has happened'. No-one has ever given thought to an outside influence because comet and asteroid hits are common throughout the galaxy and therefore not considered an outside influence. Rather they are just part of the make up of the universe and we are uncommonly lucky that this doesn't happen more often. However if the book shows that turmoil on earth in the form of volcanic eruptions, earthquakes, tsunamis etc. preceded the ice age, and I am hoping this is what we will find, then a major outside influence may have been behind it all. It could be a large wandering star that perhaps only comes back every million years or so and stays around for a while. Perhaps it is moving very slowly and takes a million years to leave. This is one scenario we can hope and pray is wrong."

"If what you say is right then there is no hope for us is there? We are all dead"

Alan sighed "unfortunately yes but we don't know how long it will take to destroy it all. It may take a million years by then none of this will matter because it is highly unlikely the human race will last another million years. I could be wrong we may keep evolving, but we haven't evolved much since we have been top dogs on Earth and I don't think we will go much further. I think it will not only be survival of the fittest but I believe that it will very much matter where we live. This country is very old and reasonably stable. Certainly we have earthquakes but none so big that we can't survive them. Whereas Europe, North Africa, North America, South America, New Zealand, China, Russia, the Middle East even the Arctic circle are all unstable and not only suffer large 'quakes but have much volcanic activity. This mountain lake exploding is just one out of the box; we don't even have a true live volcano in this country. That is not to say we couldn't have."

Jim Milburn thought about it "so the fire in the sky and the splitting of the Earth was not just some fanciful prediction there really is a basis for it all"

"Who said that?" Alan asked.

"Nostredamus" Peter chimed in "but he wasn't the only one there was another who also predicted that as an end to the Earth."

"Peter have you any thoughts at all where this book may have come from?" Alan asked him.

"No sorry. I spent time in Europe just before Pinatubo went up, I was doing a study on the hot springs and other geothermal phenomena and got into a study group with a party Germans and Poles but that was all. I didn't really get to know anyone well enough for them to give up a secret treasure such as this."

"Hasn't it occurred to you that though the writing is difficult to understand it is in English?"

Peter stopped typing and stared off into space "actually it didn't occur to me, blatant arrogance on my part to assume it would be in English. Yet it is strange which means it has been transcribed or copied from something else."

"Very good Peter" his father said "now look at the writing it is positively archaic, lots of loops and whorls and some of the letters are written together as in the old Latin form."

"Well that doesn't tell us much, about all that says is that the scribe was from a region somewhere in Europe. All English languages are based on the old Latin forms."

"Not quite, some of the English language came from Cuneiform which was used in the Middle Eastern countries, Arab, Egyptian etc. travellers from around the world used a mixed form of language and when writing began used to use the easiest form to convey their meaning or intent. That meant a mix of old and new regardless of origin."

"So what we have come down to is, it could have been anyone who wrote the book" Peter sighed "we are back to square one Dad and I don't really think it matters where the book was written or by whom its contents are what we have to worry about."

"Actually I do think it matters where the person was when the book was written" ventured Jim Milburn "because where he was the person who wrote the original script survived. That's if the person who transcribed it into English found it in the area where it was written then it is a fair bet that whole area survived the holocaust."

"Jesus Jim you're bloody spot on why didn't I see that" Peter again started checking through his computer. Alan continued to read through the computer printouts.

"What we have to do" said Peter "is find out who wrote in this form and at what stage of humanity. We also have to realize that the person may have been a traveller and what was not necessarily in the place of his birth at the time.

The hours passed quickly the three of them pored over computer data looking for that elusive clue that would lead them to the transcriber. Every hour or so they would tune the radio for further updates from around the world trouble spots. Apart from the initial 'quakes and volcanic upheavals everything seemed to have settled down.

As dawn arrived Peter stretched and headed out the door for a breath of fresh air. He stared up at the mountain. The rain had cleared though the sky was still overcast, the light was low but the mountain was visible. Peter stared; the whole top of the mountain had gone. From a sharp peak the mountain was now almost flat on top. Around the base of the mountain huge new hills of rocks had formed. In time when the earth blew around and between them, new foothills would emerge, growing trees and grass as though they had always been there. The pyrocalstic cloud was long gone but here and there on the rocks traces of sulphorous rime was visible. He shivered in the cold morning air taking one last look before stepping back inside.

"No-one could have survived up there the whole top of the mountain fell off. Most of it probably landed on the poor souls who couldn't run fast enough."

As the three of them sipped coffee made from water drawn from the fire fighting truck they heard the first sounds of the rescue operation. The whop whop of the helicopter in the distance announced the first of the invaders. Peter had no doubt that the rest wouldn't be far behind.

As the sun rose barely visible through the veil of grey clouds the first of a great line of trucks ambulances and four wheel drives appeared on the road leading up to the Ranger station.

"Well here comes the cavalry" sighed Jim.

"Now this is where you get to be boss, it's your call Jim". Peter smiled and slapped him on the back. "Meanwhile I have to go I am heading for Dad's lab" he scribbled a number on a card handing it to the Ranger "if you need to contact me for any reason don't hesitate, okay?"

Jim Milburn shook the younger man's hand "thanks Peter I'll do that."

"I'll call you dad" he told his father.

They watched as he cranked up the very battered Toyota and left, the thick grey mud flying in all directions.

Alan Cashman bent down and examined some of the mud.

"You were very lucky here Jim this mountain really should have come down on top of you, I guess you were just far enough away."

"Bayley was the lucky place if it had been on the lake side of the mountain no-one would have survived" he answered.

The first of the trucks arrived. The coordinator of the operation jumped out his bright orange uniform was stark against the dullness of the day. He walked over to the two men and stuck out his hand.

"Reg. Hansen chief coordinator for the SES and Natural Disasters group. You'd be the ranger Jim Milburn?"

Jim shook his hand "that's me and this gentleman is Dr. Alan Cashman head of the seismic centre. His son Dr. Peter Cashman the vulcanologist, has just left he had some important work to attend to."

"That's a shame" the coordinator told him "because we were looking forward to having these experts here with us."

"Well I won't be remaining myself" Alan told him "I am expected back at the centre and there is nothing I can do to delay that. I originally only came here because my son was here. I will leave it to the experts and if there is anything I can assist you with you may call me or my son at anytime" he wrote the numbers down on a card shook the man's hand and gave it to him. Turning to Jim Milburn he said

"I have to go Jim call me if there is anything you need and thankyou for the hospitality." He smiled and shook the man's hand.

"Goodbye Alan I hope to be speaking to you soon." Jim watched as he jumped into the Nissan and sped off in the direction his son had taken not fifteen minutes before, waving as he went.

By the time he had left most of the SES and NADAS people had been disgorged from the trucks and were preparing to go up into the mountain.

"Do you know if we can get up the road?" asked one supervisor.

"Sorry I know nothing about what went on up there except for what young Dr. Cashman was able to tell us. He said the lake exploded, and we know the top of the mountain has come down. We don't know if there are any survivors Dr. Cashman didn't feel anyone else could have gotten out in time. We don't know about the road but all things considered I don't think it will be there I would suggest you go up as far as you can then you will have to climb the rest of the way. Several vehicles loaded with equipment and men headed for the road leading up to the Lake Marnie camping ground. The bright orange of SES, black and yellow of the fire-fighters and blue of NADAS stood out as men scrambled over rocks as the first of the climbers began their ascent. Jim watched them for a while but an insistently ringing phone took him back into office. Another day at work had begun.

"Lord Vulcan groaned in his sleep his dreams were vivid and filled with the bright beauty of his Idoli. He sometimes tossed and moaned disrupting the great Southern land he rested in. The wind roared its disapproval the sea heaved and lashed the coast with a fury that changed the shape of the great Southern land forever. New mountains were forced up into great peaks the huge rivers of lava poured into the sea and the ancient animals fled in terror."

Peter Cashman arrived at his father's lab his mind racing with new information and ideas. He had so much to do and the feeling of little time to do it in persisted. He didn't really know why he felt that something major was yet to develop and he didn't really understand the book that had been sent to him but he knew behind it all there was a reason; something he did not yet know.

CHAPTER 14

High on a mountain in a small stone tomb a young woman cried out as once again she stirred from her pain filled sleep. Erin Bannon was wet and cold her body hurt all over her lungs ached from breathing the deadly dust. She tried hard to focus her swollen red eyes on the small opening in front of her. As her vision became a little clearer she realized the smoke had gone she could no longer hear the crackling of the trees burning; it was daylight and she could see the sun.

Higher up in a tiny cave with only a now dead video camera for company Michael Bannon stirred from an uneasy sleep, a sleep filled with the sights of people running, burning, screaming. He shuddered as he suddenly came awake. He could not see, his eyes felt burnt, his chest hurt, his breathing was raspy he felt as though he had a bad case of flu'. The floor of his small cave was wet, he wet his hand and wiped it over his eyes; the dampness felt cool on his burnt face. As he tried to sit up the burns on his arm and shoulder made themselves felt; he cried out in pain. The tears stung his eyes. He blinked rapidly but still could see nothing; 'You're blind Michael' he told himself. He lay down again and wept.

Further down the mountain in a large dark cold cave six people lay silently shivering some silently praying.

Even further down the mountain the bright blue, orange and the more sober black suits with yellow stripes of the rescue teams were climbing steadily towards what was once Lake Marnie camping ground. They were not expecting to find survivors yet checked every crevice and small cave they found; so far no-one. It was eerily silent on the mountain, no cries, no calls for help no wind, no birds or animals. It was as though the whole mountain had died and taken everything with it.

In the large black cave three quarters of the way down the gully from the mountain road, Don Holman yawned and stretched. His back ached abominably and he had become cramped and stiff from trying to sleep on the cold damp rock. He stood up with great difficulty and tried to walk some looseness into his tired cramped legs. Young Tyrrel slept fitfully crying out in pain as he moved. His broken arm strapped against his body. Don Holman struck one of the three remaining matches to check him. The younger man's hand had swollen and discoloured, he felt that there was more than a break, perhaps his shoulder was also dislocated; it certainly didn't look right. He shook out the burnt match and stumbled toward the small opening to the outer cave no-one spoke to him; did they even know he had gone? Probably not, they probably couldn't even see him. As he squeezed through into the outer cave he realized it was daylight and the sun was crawling across the floor in small fingers of light. Just the sight of that made him feel better as he walked to the opening and looked out. All around and below him was devastation. Still some trees smouldered, huge boulders had rolled down the mountain like marbles looking as though they had been there forever. He realized they could not climb down any further, the boulders were balancing and unstable just one person stepping onto them and they could roll away.

He sat at the edge of the cave and stared down the gully looking for some way of climbing down. There was no way. Somewhere above him he heard a sound like a distant voice. A few small stones rolled down the hill past the cave; he strained to listen. There it was again a distinct voice. He leaned as far out as he could trying to look up but could see nothing over the overhang and the rocks above it. He started to shout,

"Hey! Hey! We are down here! Can you here me?"

He waited the voices stopped then a few more stones rolled past him, there was someone up there how could he make them hear?

He bent down and picked up a few small rocks and started throwing them one after the other over the overhang as far as his stiff muscles would allow him to. He kept up the barrage of rocks and stones in the hopes that one would go high enough to attract attention. Then he heard it a distant call,

"Can you hear me?"

"Yes! Yes!" he screamed in reply "I hear you I hear you!"

"Where are you?" came back faintly.

"We are over halfway down in a cave" he yelled back.

Suddenly a long red rope came snaking past the cave mouth but he couldn't reach it; he was almost weeping with fear that they would miss him. He grabbed a nearby branch and tried to snare the rope but it was just too far away. He sat back down on the ledge and stared at it, so near yet so far.

Suddenly a figure in a bright orange overall came rattling down the slope on the rope dislodging stones and bits of trees as he came. He looked over at Don Holman grinned touched his hat and said,

"Good morning".

Don Holman wept, great shuddering sobs wracked his body "thank god, thank god"

"How many are there?" his rescuer asked.

"There are six of us the others are in the inner cave. The younger man has a broken arm and maybe a dislocated shoulder he is in bad shape and will need a stretcher. The rest of us aren't too bad but none of us are young. We climbed down with difficulty I don't think we can climb back up again" Don Holman stared off across the gully "can you get us out?"

The rescuer nodded "yes but not straight away we'll send down some food and blankets and try to keep you warm until we can clear a pathway to get you all up. It's pretty tricky at the moment as there are downed trees and loose rocks everywhere."

Don nodded "yes we were very lucky we made it this far, we did it in the dark mostly."

He stood up then.

"I'll go and tell the others" he said quietly.

He squeezed back through the opening to the inner cave groping his way around the wall until he found some of the others.

"Come on now up you get" he shook them gently "we are going to be rescued".

Three of them stood without a word and stumbled toward the opening. The older man who had lost his wife on the mountain road, didn't move.

"Hey come on" Jim shook him again "we are going home".

When he didn't move Jim dragged him up and staggered over to the cave entrance pushing him through. As soon as he saw him in the daylight he knew he had been dead for some time.

"Oh god!" he said softly "why couldn't you have held on".

He laid the old man down on the floor of the cave and went back for Tyrrel. Helping the younger man to his feet his good arm around his shoulder Jim half dragged half carried him to the outer cave where the others now stood in the sun. He laid the younger man in the sun near the cave mouth sitting beside him cradling his head. They waited for rescue.

High up on the mountain in a tiny cave Michael Bannon had woken again he still could not see but he knew it was daylight. He felt around for the opening and leaned out as far as he dared feeling the warmth of the sun on his face. It stung him he put his hand up to feel his skin and the skin peeled away.

"You are not going to die Michael" he told himself "you have come this far someone will find you, you just have to stay alive long enough".

In another tiny cave the size of a stone tomb Erin Bannon had also regained consciousness. Her eyes though still swollen and very sore were at least functioning she could see the sun and feel the warmth on her hand outside of the small narrow opening in front of her. There had to be a way out but she didn't know where to begin. Once again she leaned back and placed her feet squarely on the rocks in front of her. Using her full body strength she pushed hard but nothing happened. Then she reversed trying to push the rocks with her shoulders but they were jammed tight. Her breathing was ragged and painful, the smallest amount of work made her exhausted. She stopped pushing and lay down breathing hard.

"Come on Erin think you can't give up now, you have survived, someone will come for you." she told herself. Yes they may come she thought but would they ever find her? She had run a long way, over two hills and down a small gully before she found the cave; any would be rescuers may not be able to find her, then she would die a horrible death of starvation.

The first of the rescuers were just reaching the wreckage of Lake Marnie camping ground as Erin was pondering her fate.

The sight that greeted them stunned them into silence. They gathered in a small group overlooking the Lake, it was not recognizable as having ever been a pretty lake surrounded by campers.

The water of course was gone all that remained was a huge spreading lake of bubbling mud rimmed with gigantic rocks. The once beautiful forest was gone the tree stumps still smouldered. Here and there remnants of burnt out cars were visible some could be seen crushed under huge rocks. There were no bodies, no tents or caravans. One side of the mountain on the opposite side of the lake was gone, blown out. The mud seemed to be flowing in that direction. Above them where the peak would have been there was nothing just a long jagged line like the edge of a huge crater. As they stood staring at the total devastation a small vibration ran through the mountain sending small rocks and shale sliding down the slope to land in the mud. It would flare up momentarily then be gone. There was no-one to rescue and no bodies to recover. The NADAS boss reached them and stared at the carnage,

"We still have to look someone may have survived there could be other caves. Just don't go down there" he pointed down to the camping ground "we can't afford to lose any more people"

In groups of threes the rescuers skirted the huge boulder rimmed mud lake and headed up the slope towards the top of the mountain. The going was hard and dangerous nothing was stable and a foot wrong sent tree trunks and rocks sliding down the slope. The rocks were covered in mud and rimed with sulphur, the smell was acrid. All of the rescuers wore breathing apparatus. The soft plop of the mud bubbling up was unnerving and all were very much on edge as they climbed slipped slid and crawled up the shattered slope.

Two hours of climbing brought them to the half way point just below a sheer rock wall. At sometime there would have been a walk path through the forest now it was an impossible climb. Half way up the rock wall two small caves were evident but they could not see any signs of life.

The NADAS boss searched along the face of the rock for hand holds or places where ropes may be used.

"It's no good" he said "we couldn't scale that not even a mountain goat could get up there. If there is anyone in those caves then they would have had to have been in them before the mountain came down and that's unlikely."

Even though he told the men this he still did not feel comfortable with not searching so he opted to call for a helicopter to transport a couple of men to the top and have them abseil down. Meanwhile they continued to search. Many of the remains of trees still smouldered and it was tricky knowing where to place feet without sinking into burning rubbish. On the west side of the lake where the greatest concentration of rocks had fallen they found the remnants of tent canvas and bits and pieces of burnt cookware. Then they found their first corpse.

One group searching for survivors stopped near a large burnt tree which was still standing. As one of the men leaned against it for balance something fell from it. He leaned over to check it and realized he was looking at a burnt human arm. He steadied himself and looked up. There in the fork of the tree were the remains of a corpse, blackened and in an impossibly torturous position.

They stood and stared at it. There was no point in getting it down and probably no way to identify it. He looked at the older man of the group, but he shook his head; the younger man felt ill.

The whop whop of the helicopter heralded its arrival the rotors stirring up ash and burnt material. The ladder was dropped and two men scrambled up with their equipment. Slowly the chopper lifted to the top of the mountain lowering the two men to the jagged edge. There they anchored themselves and prepared to head down the face of the rock.

In his dreams Michael heard a helicopter, it was so clear to him that he thought he heard the noise of people scrambling over the rocks nearby. He sat up and realized that he could hear something and he wasn't dreaming. He wriggled over to the opening and leaned out as far as he could. He opened his mouth to shout but nothing came out but a scratchy croak. He desperately tried to call he tried a gurgling growl to attract attention, but to no avail. Tears poured down his face his blind eyes turned upwards seeking a shadow or outline; but he could see nothing. He lay there sobs shuddering through his body his arm raised as if reaching for someone. Then the miracle happened someone grabbed his hand and a voice said,

"Easy lad I've got you we'll have you out of there in no time."

The rescuer who saw Michael couldn't believe his eyes. He was scrambling down the treacherous slope looking for toe holds, as he looked down and passed him to the next section he saw an arm come out of no-where.

"There's someone here" he yelled into his helmet radio "and they're alive."

Cautiously he came down to the small cave that was really nothing more than a rather large slit in the rocks. He saw the arm upraised as though reaching out for him then he saw the hideously burnt face of young Michael Bannon, it was obvious he couldn't see.

The rescuer could not even define his eyes himself. He reached out and grasped the hand holding it tight as he spoke soothingly. He stayed there for a long time just talking to the boy and holding his hand while the helicopter brought up the stretcher and two others to help him. It took nearly two hours of patience to get the stretcher in position and the boy onto it. But when he was finally drawn toward the helicopter a great cheer went up from those below watching the scene.

Down at the ranger station Jim Milburn heard the racket over the radio and smiled, he would ring Peter Cashman and tell him that someone did survive besides those in the cave. Perhaps there was hope now for others to be found. Though from what he heard he doubted they would be alive. At least they now had an eye witness and that would tell the Cashman's a lot about what happened on Boulder Mountain on that beautiful Easter Sunday.

Peter was bone weary when he pulled up in the underground parking lot. He took the lift down three floors to reach the lab and his father's overnight quarters. Once there he stripped off his clothing and stepped into a hot shower. It felt so good he had forgotten how tired hungry and dirty he was and had been for so long.

He threw on a terry cloth gown and fell into bed. His sleep was dreamless.

Nine hours later he awoke refreshed and starving. He rang his father's secretary to send him down food and organise a change of clothes from his apartment.

Once done he set to work in the lab with three of his father's scientists all experts in their own fields. He also brought in a computer specialist to try and decipher some of the writing that had faded or were almost illegible in the book of Vulcan. He began the long task of unravelling the book in a satellite link up to some of the best historical brains in the world. If it did prove to be a chronicle of events at the beginning of time and consequently the end of the world then he would find it. He may not be able do anything to stop it but at least he could let humanity know when their time was up. There was a good chance that some would survive just as the original writer must have done. Of course Peter did not know how long he survived he may only have lasted long enough to write the story and then succumbed; he didn't know he may never know.

CHAPTER 15

The restless earth continued to plague mankind for days afterwards. Aftershocks some big some mere ripples were felt around the world. Volcanoes, dormant for thousands of years continued to throw up magma, many of them distributing lava in huge rivers across the land. Mt. St. Helen's in Washington took on proportions of Mt. Kilauea in the Hawaiians. The sometimes shaky New York began to look remarkably like a large rubbish dump as continuing tremors rattled through the city bringing down the oldest areas and splitting many of the newer buildings. Subway and traffic tunnels caved in as the offshore volcanoes continued to erupt and grow. California launched a huge rescue mission for the people trapped on the now separated coast line. Slowly two of the great lakes emptied, their precious water running into the sea. In New Zealand a series of volcanic eruptions in the North Island took out the towns of Rotorua and Taupo, the Southern Alps exploded into life sending thousands running for their lives. Earthquakes rocked both islands regularly and White Island exploded, in a huge eruption, dropping enormous amounts of ash and cinders along the east coast of the north island.

In Australia, Perth, Adelaide, Alice Springs and Sydney all suffered major quakes. Sydney's famed Harbour Bridge buckled the huge pylons cracking as they took the strain of the violent shaking. Melbourne shuddered over three days opening up large cracks over the old underground river systems. Landslides and rock slides were common place in the Dandenongs and Blue Mountains of New South Wales.

Then a miracle!

As often happens when nature goes insane there was a miracle survival.

Nothing more was seen or heard of the "Dolphin". Though the Pacific Ocean was searched by plane and ship nothing was found. Occasionally debris would float up onto an island but that was all. Then during a pass by a RAAF plane over a few tiny islands heading toward Vanuatu, a small orange dot was seen in the now calm waters. After flying low for a closer inspection the captain decided to call in a helicopter. The orange dot proved to be that of a young girl who had been washed overboard from the Dolphin when the first wave hit. She had been caught in the wake of the ship and finished up many nautical miles away before the ship was brought to a halt.

She had been floating around the Pacific for nearly a week and had attempted to swim to the nearest islands. A life jacket had popped up not far from her she managed to struggle into it and had been hoping against hope of being found ever since. Apart from suffering from immersion and dehydration and the fact she had nothing to eat, she was in reasonably good shape; they flew her back to Sydney. The world would have to wait for the story of her terrifying ordeal though; she was incoherent when they found her.

On Boulder Mountain the rescuers continued their search for survivors.

Jim Milburn, ranger, rang Peter and gave him the news of a survivor, his voice was excited and he told him how and where he was found,

". . . . more than that though Peter it seems he had a video camera with him and filmed everything he could."

There was a note of triumph in Jim's voice that made Peter smile,

"Can you send the tape to me Jim or arrange to have it delivered to the lab? I'll give you the address perhaps a courier could get it here quickly."

Peter hung up, this video could tell them much and maybe they could work out exactly what did cause the pleasant cold and stable Lake Marnie to hiccup. The only worry he had was the heat, it could well have destroyed the film completely.

CHAPTER 16

In a small dark tomb of rock, cold wet burnt and in pain lay a young girl. By now Erin had cried herself out it hurt her chest to even breathe and crying made it worse. She had exhausted herself time and time again in and effort to dislodge the rock which had fallen over her tiny shelter. It was no good she could do nothing to budge it. She didn't want to give up she had survived so far and wanted desperately to live but she could see no way that would be possible. She would spend her remaining days going over her life remembering the good and the bad and making peace with the world. Her death would not be quick she knew, she would die of starvation unless she could will herself to die. She had heard people could do that and now that was what she would try and do. She prayed for her family, for those who died Jennifer and Michael, and for the safety of her parents and aunts and uncles. She prayed they would forgive her for giving up. She prayed for the strength to get through her death with dignity and hoped there was something "else" something beyond this earthly world. She would not die screaming and crying but peacefully quietly and alone.

Before she began the ritual of trying to will herself to die she decided to give it just a few more days until her strength started to fade. She would spend at least two hours per day or more if she could manage it lying against the covering rock with her arms pushed through the small space in front of her. She didn't think anyone would see her or if they were even looking anyway, but it gave her something to wish for. She tuned out all other thoughts and just listened to the bush surrounding her. Born and bred in the city she was never aware of noise as it was with her every day of her life. Now she had nothing but quiet and she had to strain to listen to noises without dismissing them as normal sounds. Her vigil began at the dawn of the new day four days after Lake Marnie blew itself into the history books.

The search for survivors and the tagging of the remains of the dead was grisly. The stench emanating from the camping ground was a mix of decay and sulphur, the searchers all wore breathing apparatus. Some days the lake would become restless sending the searchers into a run for cover as huge globs of hot mud shot high into the air followed by a tremor. The larger rocks were moved about like marbles. This happened many times as a body was found and they attempted excavation. It was nerve racking and dangerous work for those close to the lake. Those who walked the nearby hills searching in the remnants of a once beautiful forest, small caves and overhangs were at most risk. Each time a tremor rolled around the area more rocks would be dislodged from higher up to come tumbling down on them. Two men were injured this way, one with a broken leg and one knocked down by a rolling rock and suffered multiple fractures of ribs and shoulder. It was arduous; the heat radiating from the lake was quite extraordinary their face masks fogged up often forcing them to remove them rinse them in water before replacing them. Water was restricted to two litres per person for drinking purposes so the practice was frowned on.

Six days after the explosion Peter Cashman returned to the area with a very sophisticated monitoring device. A Seismologist working with his father had devised the instrument using all the monitoring systems they knew and used, encapsulating them within a tiny computer and enclosed the whole lot within a small hand held instrument that was both heat proof and hopefully lava proof and could also be left on the ground.

Peter had received the film from the Ranger and began down loading it. The first part was quite clear showing the missing lake, the mud bubbles and steam rising from the lake. When all hell broke loose it was obvious the boy had been running with the camera still on and much of what was happening was a whirl of different views which had to be brought into focus. From the cave they were able to discern some of what was happening but as the heat grew the film started to fade. Peter left the film to the experts and decided to head back to the lake to see first hand the damage. He would never have believed it if he hadn't seen it with his own eyes. There was simply nothing left.

Staying well away from the lake and encased in a protective suit and breathing apparatus, Peter walked the perimeters of the camping ground. He couldn't get near where the cabin had been, huge boulders blocked his way, puddles of thick grey mud and still hot magma covered everything. He kept to the west and north west sides where the mountain had sloped upwards into beautiful forested walks. Above him was the sheer rock wall that had been left behind after the peak came down. The two tiny caves were just visible; the one where young Michael Bannon had been rescued from was marked with a large cross. He went on past the wall and two hours later after much clambering over burnt tree trunks and still smouldering rubbish he came to a small stream. He sampled the water in a small vial; he would test this and other liquids including the now cooling magma and mud. He looked up from where he stood, above him was a huge tumble of rocks that looked as though they had always been there but he knew they hadn't they had roared down from the peak when the mountain shook. ("Lord Vulcan shook his fist") he was moving away from the area when he caught a small movement just briefly, he shook his head sure that his peripheral vision played tricks on him. He turned to walk away when he caught the movement again from the corner of his eye. This time he turned and looked up straining his vision for some movement along the line of rocks above him . . . nothing! He stood dead still focused his eyes and waited he felt there had been a movement and it had him curious. There! He saw it again, there was something up there. Keeping his eyes fixed firmly on the position of the movement called through to rescue headquarters.

"I don't know what I am looking at" he told them "but there is a movement up there".

He wanted to climb up and have a closer look but the SES captain asked him not to,

"Wait until we can get there" he told him "we can't afford to lose our experts"

Peter waited for an hour then began to climb. He knew how long it had taken him to get to this place and he didn't think that anyone else could get here any sooner. If there was someone up there he wanted to satisfy himself he done everything possible for them. Of course it was entirely possible what he was seeing was just a piece of clothing or something similar that had been caught on the rocks. Or maybe it was an animal, whatever, he had to know for himself.

He couldn't rope himself to anything and all of the rocks were large and smooth. He knew many of them were balancing and there was a good chance that another tremor could set them rolling and he would be crushed. Still he pushed on sometimes climbing between massive boulders, the gaps between them filled with the deceitful and dangerous shale. The appearance of firm ground was an illusion and Peter found himself sliding dangerously into rocks as shale slid and clattered away under his boots. He cannoned off many a rock each time expecting that his body weight would be enough to start it rolling. He held his breath for so long waiting for this to happen his chest ached. The last few metres were the most exhausting with rocks piled one on top of the other at times making his passage impossible. By the time he was within striking distance of the target the other rescuers had arrived at the base and were yelling at him through his head phones not to try and go further. Peter turned off his radio and continued to climb. As he clambered over a large reasonably flat rock, his breath coming in short painful pants, he saw something he never believed he would, an arm, no, two arms through a tiny gap in a very large rock. How on earth did someone get there! He was amazed. He turned on his radio and in a voice far more controlled than he felt he told them,

"I think we have a live one, I repeat I think we have a live one."

He reached over and touched the arm closest to him, stroking it softly. There was a small movement of the hand he reached for the hand and held it gently. It was a small hand a young woman's hand, torn burnt and bleeding but the movement said she was alive. Suddenly both hands twitched as though the person were asleep and just coming awake.

Peter held it and spoke softly,

"Can you hear me?"

From inside the tiny narrow slit came a gurgling croak.

"Don't try to talk just squeeze my hand if you can".

He was elated as just the tiniest amount of pressure was put on his hand.

He looked around, how on earth were they going to get her out, one wrong move and the whole lot could come down on all of them. Peter climbed closer to the tiny cave, directly in front of it was a ledge, it was narrow with no room for error but he stepped onto it and sat down. He held her hand and searched for a way in. The lie of the boulders told him that the big rock that covered the front of the cave had slid there; it rested on the small overhang that had once been all the cave was. Below where Peter sat, another rock, not very big, had filled in the front leaving the tiny gap between them that had been this girl's only access to the outside world. If the bigger rock had slid just a few centimetres further the cave would have become a sealed tomb. How they would get her out was anybody's guess, perhaps a charge in the right place could force the bigger rock to slide further down the mountain there wasn't much above it just some small stuff and shale, and they could dig her out of that if they had to. The whop whop of the chopper told him that a medic team was being sent in he guessed that after six days this girl would be starving and thirsty and quite probably freezing cold. Their first aid needed to be food water and blankets if she was able to take them.

"We are going to try and get you out of there do you understand me?"

Again the small pressure on his hand.

"Can you speak? If you can squeeze my hand if you can't don't move"

The hand did not move.

"Okay, I am just going to move away for a little while now to guide in your rescuers."

Erin panicked, she could hear him and feel him she felt sure she wasn't dreaming it seemed so real and now he was leaving her. She drew on all her failing strength and grasped his hand as tightly as she could. She couldn't let go because he might not come back and even if it was a dream she needed that hand to hold when she died. Peter was surprised by the sudden grip he felt.

"It's okay love I won't leave you I'll stay here until they get here okay?"

She squeezed his hand in response.

The blue uniform of the NADAS came into view.

"You shouldn't be here Sir" he called

"I can't leave now I am holding her hand and she needs me." Peter said.

"She's conscious?" his voice filled with surprise "my god how did she survive this long?".

"The will to live in people is very strong even the frailest of us will strive to continue life under the most extreme circumstances. I don't think she would have lasted much longer but for now she is with us and if possible I am going to keep it that way."

The NADAS chief looked at him with a new respect,

"Of course Doctor I wouldn't want you to leave in those circumstances as long as you understand the risks you are taking."

Peter grinned

"The risks chief? I am a Vulcanologist you don't think that is a risky enough job?"

The NADAS chief grinned back at him,

"Yeah I guess."

The Medical team stood on the top of the ridge above the tiny cave that was Erin's tomb. Peter sent a message up the line to tell them that medication was a prime importance then to get her out. They sent down morphine.

Peter told Erin he would help ease her pain with a small injection and did she mind.

At first she made no response, she was afraid, what if she was dreaming and this man telling her he was going to ease her pain was really god telling her she was going to die now, how did she know? Did it matter anyway? Death was preferable to the pain, distress fear and hunger she had experienced over the past week. She reluctantly squeezed his hand. For a moment he stroked the hand and spoke softly to her almost crooning as you do to a baby when it is distressed. She began to relax at the sound of his soft voice then she felt a small prick in her arm. Within minutes a warm feeling flooded her system and everything seemed to drift away. She felt herself floating free, free of the rock tomb that held her, free of the world that had taken her cousins from her, free of the horror and carnage she had witnessed. The message from the medic said not too much as in her starved state she could easily be overdosed. Peter gave her just enough to ease her pain.

The first medic arrived on an anchored rope from the top of the ridge.

"God the poor little thing how are we going to get her out?"

Peter shook his head scanning the surrounding area,

"I have no idea, perhaps they could blow it".

An engineer slid and rattled down the slope inspecting the rock fall as he came.

"Who said blow it?" he asked.

"I did" answered Peter, "I don't see any other way do you?"

The Engineer scanned the huge rock resting above them,

"I think you have a point there, there isn't much above it and we could dig through any of that coming down. As long as she has enough room in there to get away from the entrance other wise we may kill her."

"She will die anyway if we don't get her out" Peter said quietly.

The Engineer looked grim,

"Yeah I guess. Well let's do it!"

Peter, the NADAS chief, engineer and medic began the job of getting back up the slope above them while the ground was cleared for a radius of 2 kilometres. Before she left the medic gave Erin two more shots one was vitamins and minerals the other was penicillin to begin the fight against the infections that would be rampaging through her system. She knew the morphine injection would keep her out of it for about two hours; it would be enough time to get set up.

As Peter was leaving he reached over and grasped her other hand gently pushing her arms through the slit.

"If you can hear me I want you to do something for me I want you to slide back as far as you can and face the wall. If you have a jacket or something pull it over your head and face and don't worry I will be back for you."

In her dream Erin heard the soft voice again, this time it was urging her to move back away from the small opening. He told her to face the wall and cover herself. At first she didn't understand and though she wanted to do as she was told her body did not want to move. The freedom of floating was so comforting she did not want to give it up. When she realized he wanted her to do this for a reason and that he would be back for her, she made a superhuman effort to force her unwilling body to move. She rolled and slid over to the back wall lying with her face against the cool dampness of it no longer concerned with the smell nor the taste. Blackness began to take over her, firstly at the edges of her mind then slowly it spread until there was nothing but blackness, a long deep void which Erin gratefully slipped into.

The charges were laid under the top of the rock. They couldn't drill into it so they scraped away the shale and made a small basin which was packed with explosive. The charge didn't need to be big just enough to get the rock to move. Scrambling back up the slope on the end of the rope the engineer set up the electronic mechanism then everyone went running for cover on the other side of the ridge. The explosion seemed unnaturally loud in the stillness of the mountain, the echo repeated throughout the area, the vibrations sending rocks and rubble tumbling into the hot mud pool of the Lake.

As the dust subsided the engineer looked over the side. What he saw dismayed him.

"I don't think it moved" he told those waiting behind the ridge "I am going to have to go down."

He slid down the slope toward the big rock. As he neared it he saw that it had moved, in fact it had slid downward by a few centimetres completely enclosing Erin in a rock tomb. He got back up as fast as he could.

"She's locked in and we have to do this again or she will run out of air."

Again he went down on the rope scraping away shale and rocks that had come down after the first explosion. This time he added more explosive pushing it in as far as he could under the edge of the big rock, 'we just need a bit of luck,' he thought, 'just enough to flip the rock away from the cave and send it down it didn't matter if the front one didn't move they could pull her out through the gap it would leave.' Again he set the charge and pulled himself back up to the top,.

"Here goes nothing" he said and hit the button.

The report was deafening, the mountain shook and the ominous rumble of rocks sliding filled the air along with thick grey dust and debris.

When it had settled he peered over the side, the big rock had gone. He jumped up and screamed,

"We did it!"

The others rushed to the edge of the ridge and looked down, in the settling dust there was no sign of the rock. Well below them small rocks continued to slide.

"We must have blown it to bits" he said "I didn't expect that, I hope the girl's okay."

Peter and the medic quickly lowered themselves down to the cave mouth, followed by two men with shovels. The small cave, and Peter marvelled at how small it was, was filled with dust rubble and shale he could not see the girl, for an instant he panicked. Then he heard a small noise almost a groan, and he realized that the heap of rubble they were looking at was Erin covered in dirt and dust. He wriggled himself onto the cave floor and dragged the unconscious girl out of the mess cradling her in his arms. She was so thin so tiny as he held her feeling her heart beating and noting her shallow breathing; he wanted to cry.

"She is alive" he told himself "that's a start."

CHAPTER 17

Dr. Alan Cashman had been called away to Northern Territory where there were reports of huge holes opening up outside of Alice Springs and Katherine after the most recent 'quake.

He had seen this happen in other parts of the world where cave systems and old lava bubbles broke open during and after Earthquakes. The soil above them would gradually pour into the caves leaving huge holes. They couldn't be filled and generally were fenced off to become a tourist attraction. However in this case some of the holes were appearing in unlikely places, though not unlikely for nature. Part of the Stuart Highway had collapsed into one of them unfortunately taking a semi trailer, its load and driver with it. The Rig had not burned and though the driver was trapped he was alive and had answered his radio. Alan was going to see if it was stable enough to send people down inside to try and get the driver out. Sometimes further 'quakes caused the collapse of these caves.

From there he needed to get to New Guinea where a large land subsidence had dropped an entire village some 15 metres below ground. This was a frequent occurrence in Japan but he had not heard of it in New Guinea then again nothing that was happening was predictable.

A new tsunami had swept across the Pacific from West to East and again Vanuatu was in its path. Again the once tropical paradise was wiped clean of all but those living in the northern sector. The deaths were inestimable as no-one knew where people were after the last one. Again the broken ridges and reefs slowed the pace of the water and on reaching Fiji it was minimal more a high surge tide.

New Zealand's volcanoes continued to erupt sending lava streams into both the Southern ocean and the Pacific. Storms in the Pacific regions became violent as though the rain was determined to put out all the fires and volcanoes. (The Lord of The Wind and Air made clouds and it rained on the earth, filling the lakes and streams and all manner of life began)

Elsewhere around the world the human race suffered at the hands of the ficklest of the fickle, nature; or was it?

CHAPTER 18

Back at the lab after seeing Erin taken to hospital, the same hospital where her unknown cousin Michael was, Peter started receiving information regarding the state of the Earth at the time of the Ice age and just prior. As expected the carbon dating showed that there had been many upheavals and volcanoes in the period preceding the last ice age. Many areas that are now desert showed signs of heavy vegetation in those years, these were obtained by using the huge mining core drills now set up at various places around the globe. Peter was delighted with the results but knew that most of this knowledge had been retrieved years before and was being constantly updated.

He needed more he needed to know if these things happened simply because the Earth was still forming or did they happen because there was an outside influence.

How could he find out? He could not go back in time to see for himself so the world had to tell him. Somewhere in the world was a cold stable place that for no particular reason that could be found suddenly blew up. That would then give Peter a reason to believe that something other than nature had had a hand in it. If there was a wandering star or planet out there in the blackness of space exerting this enormous influence on the Earth then it had to be found and quickly, humanity need time to get used to the fact that "time's up" and "only the fittest will survive" This is as it had been in the animal kingdom from the very dawn of time and human beings were the longest survivors in the prime position. He always knew the Human race could not go on ad infinitum something had to come along, bigger stronger more powerful to pull that smart capable animal off his throne, even if it was something not of this Earth. In the next few weeks Peter would work 18 hours a day collating and sifting through every scrap of information that came in. He took breaks to discuss the possibilities of the book of Vulcan being the prophetic work as proposed. No-one had been able to link the story to a true happening yet jangling away in Peters' mind was that elusive thought that he couldn't quite grasp, a feeling more than anything of a truth waiting to be happened upon.

Then suddenly an e-mail landed in his mail box early one morning about three months after the Lake Marnie explosion.

"Peter Cashman, need to speak to you regarding core drills taken from various parts of Central Europe, similarities to other parts of the world that you would not believe.

Cold stable area found may yield the knowledge we seek.

John Craznow.

Peter was excited surely this was it, this was the beginning of the answers they needed. Someone at last had found something to prove that all that happened in the long past years was not just a natural happening. At least this is what he hoped it was. He didn't know John Craznow he hadn't even heard of him, was he a scientist? a driller? No doubt whatever he was he had the experience to know what he found was genuine or not.

Peter's meeting with John Craznow took place in a video link hook up.

He was at present at a site on the border of northern Italy and Switzerland. During a deep core drill they had brought up bones and vegetation that had never been seen before. The area had been cold and stable although Italy itself is not stable. That was not the surprise of it all though the surprise was that in the north of Western Australia similar vegetation had been found, vegetation that almost matched that found in the core drills of Italy.

Peter was amazed, how could this be, the two places were so far removed. He knew of course that Australia was once covered in thick lush vegetation, but that was presumed to have been millions of years prior.

"Yes" Craznow agreed "it was and that is how old these core drills were, millions of years."

Peter was still puzzled he could not find the connection with the Book of Vulcan.

"I guess your wondering where all this is leading" Craznow asked him

Peter only nodded.

"Well the bone samples we brought up were compressed, no not compressed, crushed."

Peter suddenly began to see.

"Go on go on" he said.

"The area had been cold and stable in the core sample before the bones were found and after, yet at sometime in that period there was a very big earthquake big enough to split open the ground and close it again compressing or crushing those who fell into it. After that sample of vegetation and bone there is no more of that vegetation the samples we brought up were devoid of vegetation, in the large varieties, trees etc. only grasses and low plants. The next layer showed the presence of ice and large amounts of water, also not seen previously. I made some comparisons to various core drills taken from around the world it's taken me two months to work them all out and the only one that comes close to this Italian drill is in Australia up in the North West just inland. The vegetation is similar though no bones were found but both areas were stable before and after and both lost their vegetation. I believe that instead of looking all over the world you have the answer right there in your own backyard. Set up a dig and start looking for the answers, I will almost bet my pension you will find them there.

"Are you saying we are looking at a race of people? A population of the Earth all those years ago?"

"Yep that's what I am saying. I, we, believe that this present population on Earth could be the second or third time that man has populated this planet and each time has been wiped off the face by an unusual occurrence. I believe that because Australia is the oldest piece of land it holds the key and I think if you go to where those core drills were taken you will find evidence of previous population."

"Well done John I look forward to meeting you in person would you be able to come here and help start the excavation?"

Craznow nodded,

"I'll be there as soon as possible. We'll wind up here then I am on my way, I look forward to meeting you."

Peter broke the link and turned to his lab crew,

"I believe we are on to something here if anyone has any ideas to help push this theory along I would love to hear them. Meanwhile I must contact my father I think we need him here he is the best I know of when it comes to earthquakes."

Peter's excitement continued to grow, 'is it possible have they found the key to the Book of Vulcan, could his father have been right that an external force caused these huge upheavals then left the area and allowed the Earth to begin anew? If so is that what is happening now? Is it on its way back? This time humanity was more vulnerable with its buildings and computers, satellites, electricity, dams, penchant for building in high places and its need for combustible materials, petrol oil diesel and explosives. If the populations of previous times had been wiped out surely they would not have had these things that the human race now needs to survive? These things that will make it worse for them when the time comes. If there is such a thing out there then we are all doomed how many places on this Earth could you hide from such devastation. The old ones had caves, and flimsy shelters didn't they? Or were they adept with stone and wood? We have glass steel concrete and everything in between.'

Peter mulled over the information he had been given, time was a wasting and he still felt they had precious little of that very commodity. He got to his feet and made a few phone calls, he had to find the right people.

In Windsor Private Hospital, Erin continued to improve. She suffered appalling burns to her arms legs and face all of which, with the aid of laser, were beginning to heal well. Her lungs were different though, she had sustained burns to at least 30% of her lungs diminishing their capacity by over one third. Her voice box though damaged was slowly beginning to heal, and her speech scratchy and rough was at least understandable.

Her first weeks were in intensive care where she lay on a wide water mattress. She was fed intravenously, her body dangerously thin, her blood pressure low from the starvation and the ingestion of gases from the eruption. Doctors feared she would not survive yet survive she did her body gradually responding to the intensive treatment. After eight weeks they moved her into a single room with a specialist nurse who attended her every need. It was after she was moved that a social worker came to see her to ask for some of her family history so they could contact relatives. Until that happened they had no idea who she was or where she came from.

Erin wrote short notes willing her burnt hands to work for her. At times trying to tell them what they wanted to know crying often when her voice failed her. It was all she could do to tell them her first name. She became exhausted easily.

Then they found the name tag inside her jacket that she wore when they rescued her. The social worker stared at the name tag; she knew that name could it be a coincidence or could they be related? On the floor above a blind boy had been brought in for surgery after also being rescued from Lake Marnie, certainly they were far removed from each other in area but that meant nothing, two young people named Bannon? They had to be related.

The social worker held Erin's hand just as Peter had done before she was rescued,

"Do you have a brother?" she asked.

Erin shook her head.

"Do you know Michael Bannon?"

Erin stared at her, picking up the pen in a trembling hand she wrote,

"Michael . . . cousin . . . dead."

The social worker smiled,

"I don't think so but I would have to take you to see him he is blind and in a very bad state." She smiled as the tears started down Erin's burnt cheeks.

"It's okay Erin, it's okay".

The social worker arranged a wheelchair and took Erin to the Surgical ward where Michael Bannon lay swathed in bandages. For all that Erin could still see her cousins features.

She reached out to touch him and whisper his name . . . "Michael".

He responded with a small moan.

She sat for a long time by his bed marvelling at his survival; how did he?

She would come again tomorrow and every day until he was well enough to talk to her if he ever was. He had suffered badly from breathing in the gases and sulphur, his lungs burnt and scarred, third degree burns on his arms, back and face. Doctor's feared for his survival yet felt he just might make it. Erin knew he would she wrote "he will live."

That night the social worker made contact with Erin's and Michael's families for the first time since that dreadful explosion.

PART 2

CHAPTER 19

The meeting between John Craznow and Peter Cashman finally took place in the town of Broome on the far North West coast of Western Australia. It was a warm greeting like the reuniting of old friends.

"We have much work to do John" Peter said "my father will be arriving from New Guinea tomorrow then we will go out to the drill site. I have been able to get the services of a man called Mungaway, he knows the country well and has heard stories from the old ones of the rivers of fire. I don't know just what that means to us, but I do know that he will be invaluable in determining the nature of whatever we find. At least he knows where to get further information if we get stuck."

"I am looking forward to it Peter I would have been happy to go straight out there I feel the need to get this done quickly".

Peter understood what he was saying he also felt time was short but they could achieve nothing if they went stumbling around not knowing where to look or what to look for. They needed the complete team and Mungaway and his father could not meet them until tomorrow; they would have to wait.

The alarm buzzed at 5.30am but Peter was already awake and eager to go. The sound of a small plane coming over the town heralded the arrival of his father. Outside in a truck on the seat asleep was an aboriginal with white hair and beard.

Peter tapped on the window,

"Mungaway? Peter Cashman, pleased to meet you" he offered the older man his hand.

Mungaway sat up smiled and shook his hand,

"And I you" he said in an almost clipped accent.

They drove out to the airport to meet Alan Cashman. Mungaway's truck left behind for the comfort of a new 4 WD. Peters' old Toyota finally giving up the fight and falling to bits.

He greeted his father warmly and introduced him to John Craznow and Mungaway.

"Now we are a formidable team let's get this show on the road. Peter you lead off in your vehicle, Mungaway you follow in the truck with our equipment".

They piled into the 4wd and headed off into the red outback of Western Australia.

Even though it was late winter the air was hot and dry, though they were assured the nights could be very cold. The scenery was extravagant, more colours than any country they had ever seen. Small pockets of beautiful trees and water holes dotted the landscape. Kangaroo and Wallaby were sleeping under shade near the water. Lizards and Goanna sunned themselves on rocks absorbing the heat of the early morning before heading into the shade later. Cockatoos screamed and screeched their way across the sky landing on a gum tree in blossom covering it in white. Eagles cut the sky riding the thermals in their never ending quest for food. Huge cliffs impossibly red reared high above them as they wound their way through gorges and tracks. The river gums with their great spreading tops and beautiful white trunks relieved the redness, softening a sometimes harsh landscape.

They stopped for a break at 10am. checked their maps discussed the best ways to get around obstacles then drove on. The Edgar ranges proved to be daunting in places and for all the power of their vehicles they still had problems getting over them. At times they were forced to unload vehicles and trailer, get them over a particular area then reload. It was hard manual work the temperature soaring as the day progressed. Over the range they traversed the northern end of the Great Sandy Desert before arriving at a point near the drill site; this would be their permanent camp. The sun was fast heading west as they pulled up.

"Get the tents up first before we unload" Mungaway told them "it will be too dark otherwise."

By the time the tents were up it was pitch black and moonless. Fires were lit bed rolls dragged out and instant meals readied along with some of Mungaway's delicious damper.

"Tomorrow first light we will head into those hills behind us. The drill team there have found another site that is proving as good as the desert site and easier to work on. The team will also come back here at night and set their camp up with us taking in turns only to leave a night watchman. Many people know about what we have been doing we don't want people here in their droves tramping all over the place. This is one reason why we camp so far from the actual sites, we will be the only ones who know exactly where they are." John Craznow continued to fill them in on the drill site and what to expect the next day, as interested as Peter was he couldn't keep his eyes open, his next memory was early dawn just before the sun rose. A grinning Mungaway was handing him a cup of coffee,

"Did you sleep well Peter?" he asked.

Peter shifted uncomfortably,

"I think I er . . . fell asleep during the briefing."

Mungaway laughed,

"You did that alright, but it doesn't matter you didn't miss much."

The others came awake stretching and walking out the stiffness of sleeping in a bedroll.

The morning was glorious, the air was cool no wind and the ever changing landscape now clothed in deep purple. Peter breathed deeply and stretched his body doing ten minutes exercise before joining the others for breakfast.

Just as the sun rose they set off for the first drill site. It was hard going the sand was soft and the track often disappeared. There was no-one at the site now but the core samples were still there laid on a bench in a permanent hut surrounding the actual drill hole where the samples were found.

The shed was hot and stuffy inside but the glare of the sun made it difficult to see the vegetation. Peter and two of the scientists stayed inside the hut to examine the particles. Satisfied that they had vegetation and proof that the area was once a living jungle they moved on to the next site in the foot hills behind their camp taking one of the core samples with them.

The next drill site was a hive of activity. The clank clank of the drill sounded loud in the still morning air. Peter strolled over to the nearest driller and introduced everyone,

"Have you found any vegetation particularly that type of the last drill hole? He asked.

The driller grinned at him

"We've got better than that Dr. Cashman we've got proof that something really strange happened here and . . . and . . ." he dragged out "when I show you the core samples I've got another surprise for you."

Still grinning the man marched off to the small shed bringing back with him a core sample that was still showing flecks of bone, Peter was astonished,

"When did this come up"?

"Just last night just before we shut down" the driller was still grinning "are you ready for something else"?

Peter was beginning to feel excitement, he knew that the others felt the same way; his father gripped his arm,

"Peter we could have something here, real proof, perhaps Lord Vulcan is not the myth we thought."

The driller lead the way walking behind the small hill down into a narrow gully which sloped rather steeply toward the base of another hill. He followed the line of the hill then disappeared out of sight. Peter followed him and stood open-mouthed, there in front of them was a cave and inside the cave were small frondy palms. The distinct sound of water came to them.

"It's permanent water? Out here?" Peter asked.

"Oh yes sir but it's more than that" answered the driller.

Mungaway stepped forward and examined the ground the plants and the rocks. He turned to Peter and shook his head,

"Not my people Peter, not my people."

The driller continued into the cave until he was lost in the gloom. Peter followed.

Ahead of him a brush torch had been lit and place wedged in rocks. The driller told him that torches were fine but they needed really strong lights where the brush torches could be placed all the way down and gave off more light.

Peter repeated the last bit to himself 'all the way down?'

They continued into the cave the sloping floor continued downwards, the sound of water ever present, the walls narrowed occasionally but all could get through easily. After some time the floor levelled off that was when the driller threw the switch to a series of battery driven arc lights.

"We didn't have enough lights for all of it but you can see a lot I think you'll be amazed".

Peter was not only amazed he was awe struck. No-one said anything, they were all dumbfounded. The small passage opened into a huge cavern, the air was fresh so it was obviously coming in from somewhere; the walls were adorned with paintings. Fierce battles, building huts, growing food, drawing water, and the stars in the sky.

It was this section that had Peter riveted to the spot. There in the middle of the star painting was a huge white object. It wasn't the moon as the moon was also visible, it didn't look like a space ship, it certainly wasn't the sun; so what was it? Peter turned to stare at his father, they spoke in unison,

"Our wandering star"!

They walked closer to the wall skirting the small but apparently deep pool in the middle of the cave. The paintings were as bright as new, the cave temperature and lack of visitors ensured their brightness. The painting of the stars showed the southern constellations; in the background was a distinct comet complete with long sweeping tail. The sun was rising over the horizon the moon to the left was waning in crescent and there in the middle of it all was a huge white object. It was round, more of a sphere and it didn't have definite outside lines as the stars did it was misty the white paint smeared slightly as though they were trying to portray misted outlines as with the comet. It size in relationship to the moon was huge at least ten times the size maybe even more.

"This would have been millions of kilometres away when it was drawn and look at the size of it!" exclaimed Peter.

The other scientists stood in awe of the huge paintings, particularly the star painting.

Mungaway was entranced,

"These were the old ones we were told about. But they were not my people they were the people before time"

"You mean you were told the stories of the old ones Mungaway?" Alan asked him.

Mungaway nodded,

"Yes, my people lived in caves where the old ones left their stories but I have not seen stories like this."

The paintings were the height of the wall going right up into the gloom above them at least 20 meters high.

"How do you think they got up there?" Alan asked no-one in particular.

"Vines, ropes made of reeds; this after all would have been in the middle of a jungle then." Mungaway answered.

"If that is so" ventured John Craznow "then the fresh air we can feel coming into the cave must mean there is another exit or entrance as the case may be."

Peter nodded assent,

"You're right John, also somewhere in here will be the original entrance as it was at the level of the ground all those millions of years ago. I don't expect we are going to walk through it into a jungle, but it may give us some more answers."

Taj Maranesh, the scientist brought in who was an expert in all things strange and wonderful, different and unexplained, had wandered off to look further, he called them now,

"Peter, come and have a look at this."

Peter and the others walked over to where he was standing, they could just make out another small entry to something beyond the cave.

He spoke to all of them,

"Hasn't anyone wondered why there are no bones? People lived here they painted these walls, they obviously lived outside but wouldn't you think we would at least find some bones.?"

No-one answered him; he clicked on his torch and shone it into the entrance,

"There look!" he pointed.

They crowded forward and there in the torch light were the remains of a skeleton of an apparently very small adult or child. Mungaway stepped forward and examined the bones,

"They are not of our race Peter" he said "and this person did not have even a resemblance to our bone structure."

"I am going down there" Peter told them "can I have some ropes and lights please" he asked the driller.

"I wish to go with you Peter" Mungaway said.

"You are welcome I think I need the company."

The driller was gone for some time before returning with ropes and torches.

Mungaway removed his shoes and insisted on going first. The passage was narrow and steep and led almost directly downward without a curve. The floor was slippery with moisture the going was slow as they slipped and slid their way down. They finally stopped on a ledge where they rested fanning the torches around. Mungaway shouted,

"There Peter, over there"

Peter pointed the torch and switched on another for added light. A set of steps carved into the rock led downwards into the blackness below them. Peter shouted up to the others,

"We've found steps come on down as far as the ledge, but it's slippery be careful."

Peter and Mungaway continued along the ledge to the steps, they edged their way down feeling along the rocks for hand supports torches pushing into the complete darkness in front of them.

After what seemed like an eternity they suddenly touched bottom. A fan of the torches showed they were on the floor of another cave the ever present sound of running water was the only sound besides their laboured breathing. Mungaway stepped forward yelped then disappeared out of sight. The random pattern of light from his torches the only indication of the direction he had gone. There was a slithering sound then a splash then silence.

"Mungaway?" Peter called "where the hell are you".

He heard a laugh then,

"I'm down here" he called "it seems that floor goes into a ramp and I came down it and finished up in the pool. Bloody cold it is too."

Peter eased his way forward taking small tentative steps in an effort not to repeat Mungaway's ungainly entrance into the cave. He gradually worked his way down the ramp and onto the floor of the cave. It was not as big as the upper chamber but it was high and again the walls were adorned with paintings. The air was still fresh but they could no longer feel a breeze. As they played the torches over the walls they came to a pile of bones on the far side of the pool. The others by now had reached the ledge and were shining their torches down. The driller had lowered down an arc light from the upper chamber and it was now positioned on the ledge to shine down into the cave. The switching on of the huge white light brought gasps of wonder. The walls were completely painted but this time not with the everyday things of life but with visions of violence. Volcanoes reared high spewing magma and lava, the jungle paintings showed trees flattened and long splits appearing. The rivers spilled out across the land. The animals were depicted in full flight; running from what? Then in another painting the huge white sphere this time appearing to be twice as big, was in the sky.

There was no need for words they all knew they had found what they had been looking for. The core drills would have drawn up earth from this era; they were now standing in a place older than time itself. One of the scientists edged his way down to the cave floor crossing to the pile of bones he began to examine them.

"Hmm no trauma on these bodies I would say they either asphyxiated or died of starvation. They are in very good condition probably due to the controlled temperature of the cave. I would say these people took refuge in the big cave at first then were driven downwards as the conditions outside deteriorated. They obviously lived here for a long time and there must have been many more of them at some time because these painting would have taken quite a while to do.

Mungaway examined the wall paintings.

"They used natural dyes from plants and grasses to do these; it would not have taken them long really. Three painters could complete these walls in about a month maybe two at the most. They, like my people, only painted what they saw and as it happened so each painting was representative of a happening at the time; this would have been done as soon as they saw it occur. They did not commit it to memory. The fact that none of the colours have faded more than others also shows that they did them quickly possibly two to three people working at all times together."

"Is there any signs of death there Mungaway?" Peter asked.

"Yes Peter if you look closely you can see small figures amongst the jungle plants and in the river. These would be the bodies of those caught outside. They were not a very big race though which was probably fortunate because these caves, though high would not have housed a large tribe."

Then another discovery! Mungaway searched the walls for other signs things that could tell them more about the people and the times they lived in. On the far side of the pool where small cooking pots and other pieces of implements were found Mungaway found another smaller painting. In the painting was a volcanic cone, smoking and in the smoke curling towards the sky with his hands outstretched toward a large white sphere was a dark almost non-human figure.

"Peter!" his voice sounded unnaturally loud in the small cave "is this what you're looking for."

Peter Cashman eased his way around the pool and bent to look at the small painting, everyone heard his gasp of surprise.

"Peter? What is it?" asked Alan Cashman.

"You all need to see this" Peter told them "we've found Lord Vulcan and Idoli!".

Remarkable though their finds were they could not tell the world. One word outside their group and the world would come tramping through these caves and destroy them. Besides that Peter Cashman was fairly sure that not too many people would give any credibility to the Book of Lord Vulcan nor to the painting as being representative of it. Finding the painting only proved one thing, that whoever wrote the book transcribed what happened from paintings done by such people as these. It didn't necessarily follow that the person had actually transcribed **these** paintings into a written book. For several reasons but certainly the first one being because these paintings were not the complete story as was written in the book. Maybe somewhere else in the world was another place like this that had the full story of Lord Vulcan.

As though reading his mind Alan said,

"Just because the whole story isn't here Peter doesn't mean it wasn't written in Australia. After all if these people survived long enough to record this much there may well be other caves where they survived even longer and **did** paint the whole picture."

"I agree" Taj added "and if you look very carefully over by the cooking area there is a large crack running the length of the rock. Some of the painting there is disjointed so I would say that at sometime there has been another opening there possibly closed by tremors. I think if we really put our minds to it we would find a whole cave system throughout these hills and mountains and I believe that given what we have seen, others could have survived longer or at least have written far more than these people. These people were land dwellers and farmers, but their society must have had its scholars and scribes, in some form, we are looking for where they lived."

Peter nodded his assent,

"Okay Taj I think you have something there. So I guess what we have to do now is move the drill and keep moving it until we come up with something more. We also have to start looking for cave systems and for that we need sonar. Something we can bounce around inside the earth, it will make our job easier.

Peter and Alan Cashman along with Rob Newcraft one of Alan Cashman's closest colleagues, headed back to Broome. They would fly to Perth to visit the seismic centre and hopefully beg or borrow their most up—to—date sounding equipment. It meant telling more people what they were up to but another one or two shouldn't really matter as long as none of it became general knowledge. They had much work to do and they needed to get it done quickly if humanity was to have a chance of survival. The drilling crew, two scientists and Mungaway would remain at the site and continue to look for further openings and core samples of vegetation.

All were excited at the prospect of the hunt, Peter and his father pored over the maps as their plane carried them to the Capital. Geographical maps showed nothing of the caves, it was obvious that not even the rangers in the area had knowledge of them or there would have been a reference to them somewhere.

"Of course it is entirely possible that the caves have never been visible because they simply weren't there." Alan Cashman opined.

"You mean they may have only come to light because of the earthquakes in other parts of the country?" asked Peter.

Alan nodded,

"I was thinking about the holes in the Northern Territory. All of these large holes were caused by the cave systems collapsing during 'quakes. The Great Sandy Desert is in line with Tennant Creek in the Territory. Tennant Creek has had a series of 'quakes that have caused damage as far out as the Tanami Desert, which in turn has it's western edge against the Lewis Range on the West Australian side. The Great Sandy is slightly below and to the west of that but the Lewis Range runs right up to the door step of the Edgar Range and the hills surrounding it. There is no reason at all why a good sized temblor could not cause damage as far away as the Edgar Range. I believe those caves have been sealed since those upheavals and the movement of the earth has opened them up again."

"But how do you account for the ferns growing in them?" Peter asked.

"This again is not unusual. In parts of the Northern Territory there are a lot of small palms and ferns that have grown in caves where there is a lot of water and sometimes very little or no light. They do grow towards the openings as though they know the light is there and at times with earth movement they may actually have some light on them. But the thing is Peter they do grow like that."

The trip to Perth was uneventful; as soon as they arrived they arranged for a hire car and headed for the seismic centre.

"I guess we'll have to consider the possibility that the centre won't let us have their equipment unless we have one of their chaps along." Peter sighed he really didn't want anymore people in on the hunt.

"Oh well if we must we must I suppose" said his father "what do you think Rob?" he asked of his friend and colleague.

Rob Newcraft thought about it for a while,

"It may just be to our advantage to have one of their specialists with us. Not because we need him but he could run the equipment leaving the rest of us free to do what we want without anything interfering."

Peter and Alan both nodded agreement.

"Good point there Rob" said Peter.

As though greeting them on their arrival at the centre a small tremor ran through the area. It only registered 3 on the Richter but it was big enough to get everything rattling for a few seconds. The guard at the gate looked quite worried,

"I hate it when it does that" he said to them

"Well prepare yourself" Alan told him "we are going to get a lot more of them".

They were guided into a parking space and met at the door.

"Did I hear you tell our guard we are going to get a lot more 'quakes?" asked the white coated assistant who ushered them into the building "do you know something we don't?"

Alan laughed,

"I am a seismologist it is my job to be pessimistic".

CHAPTER 20

In the weeks and months after the initial eruptions around the Pacific Rim of Fire, followed by earthquakes, tsunami's and tremendous storms, many who had survived the initial upheavals, succumbed to disease starvation and their injuries. The death toll was huge and for the most part inestimable. Whole towns were gone, villages wiped out, islands disappeared forever from the surface of the oceans drawn down into the depths by the implosions of the undersea mountain ranges.

Huge openings like giant zippers ran across the land taking people homes and animals. Many closed afterwards leaving no trace of what had been before. Without knowing how many had died some people were betting that one quarter of the world's population was now either gone forever, missing or dying. India, though it had survived the initial 'quakes, it was now discovered, was sinking. Already parts of the coast line were becoming inundated by the sea. The entire population along the southern coast line on the Indian Ocean was on the move north searching for higher ground. Overnight Bangalore doubled it's population. People slept on the streets and begged for food. Rumours swept the country that the Poles had started to melt causing a rise in the oceans. This led to panic many people dying unnecessarily as they were trampled in the rush to get away. Turkey, Azerbaijan and Iran all shuddered and collapsed after a series of violent 'quakes between 8 & 9 on the Richter. Stores of arms and weaponry exploded killing many. Fears of a highly toxic gas leak in Iraq saw people trying to cross the borders into neighbouring countries and being sent back or shot. Chaos reigned.

Then as suddenly as it all started it stopped. The volcanoes continued to spew ash and gas into the air but the tremors stopped. You could almost hear a collective sigh of relief.

Out on the edge of Western Australia's Great Sandy Desert where the Edgar range meets the hills then the Lewis Range, Peter Cashman, his father, their team including Mungaway, and a new member from the Seismic centre, Dr. Merilyn Ross, searched and drilled into the night looking for the elusive cave systems that would give them the answers. They had not turned up one core sample with any vegetation. Certainly they found remnants of water and grass but not the jungle type vegetation that had been found to the east of them. It was hot difficult and frustrating for all of them and many times they would spend their nights after a late meal, arguing fiercely about where they should try next and why. Peter and Mungaway often visited the first cave site to try and find openings into other caves. Even setting up the equipment and sonar did nothing to give them any reason to believe there were other caves in that area. Taj continued to exhort them to try and force the large rock crack in the lower cave further open, even at the expense of losing the painting. Peter and Rob Newcraft would have none of it the paintings must be preserved. And had the sonar shown any reason to believe there was another cave behind the crack? No!

Merilyn Ross tired of the continued arguments, after one particularly heated session decided to go for a walk to the caves and consider the paintings. They were beautiful beyond belief it was awesome to stand in the caves and look at something so old, yet as bright and as beautiful as the day they were done. With her she took a small echo sounder a hand held but a more sensitive version of the big sonar they were using. She strolled to the caves watched by Mungaway who followed her at a distance. Inside the big cave she walked around the walls trying to locate the tiniest ping that would tell her there was a space behind them. Nothing! Lowering herself into the smaller chamber she switched on the permanently set up arc light and let herself carefully down the steps and ramp to the floor. Standing on the edge of the pool she stared down at the dancing reflection of the arc light, 'why were there no more caves' she thought, 'it just didn't seem possible. There were so few bones found no more than ten people including children there had to be another system somewhere'. She dropped her hand to her side making a small exasperated sound.

From the darkness above Mungaway watched her, he felt that if anyone was going to find something it would be her she had the dedication they needed and was tireless. Never satisfied she had gone over every inch of ground that looked promising. It was hot and difficult work and after the first two days even though she had covered up and taken care she had still gotten burnt on the hands arms and face and suffered mild sunstroke. He admired her even Peter had to admit she was, in his words "gutsy" As she stared at the water suddenly Mungaway heard her say

"Yes!"

He couldn't see anything different yet she continued to stare into the water. What had she suddenly found or realized? Whatever it was he doubted she would share it with him if he asked her. He stayed where he was as she came back up the rope and headed into the upper chamber. She had walked right past him in the dark neither seeing him nor expecting to.

Mungaway followed her back to her tent. Her light came on and the shadows told him she was about to settle in for a bit of reading. Still sure she had found something he left her and went to his own tent. It was late and their working days were long he needed sleep yet he wasn't tired. When he was young his grandfather had taught him to stay awake for up to three days and stay alert. Sometimes when food was scarce or big storms were coming it was necessary to do this in order to survive. To go to sleep might have meant an animal may have gone past without being seen and to a hungry tribe that was a tragedy. He walked to the first sandhill and sat on the top staring out over the moonlit desert. He looked at the stars and watched the satellites zooming from west to east and north to south. He was intelligent and well educated and liked being able to live in both worlds, his tribe and the modern world. He owned a small sedan and of course his truck, and his job was varied from public relations, to translator, to tracker to teacher. He was capable and experienced in all of it but this was by far the most interesting job he had ever done. His wife and two children whom he adored did not like the tribal life although they did spend their holidays with his people. His wife Linda was a University lecturer in art and was a talented painter in her own right. His people and their way of life being her greatest inspiration. She was also white and though that had been a problem in the beginning with his people they had come to accept her and loved her as he did. His two children had the best of both worlds; both tall and good looking. His son had the darker colouring but Linda's striking blue eyes. His daughter lighter in colouring but with reddish brown curly hair and almost black eyes. He missed them so much when he was away but they had busy lives and he was sure they didn't miss him. Still it would be nice to get a break and go home to see them. He sighed, decided to go to bed then suddenly a thought hit him, he knew what Merilyn Ross had found.

CHAPTER 21

In Italy at the drill site on the Swiss border, further drill samples show more promise. Further bones were brought to the surface of a race that matched nothing on Earth. Their bone structure was small and had no apparent diseases like arthritis or similar. The much smaller bones were of children according to the experts, well formed children not babies so the race had to be quite small.

Peter Cashman received an e-mail from Italy a year after the drilling had been started stating they had now recovered a large portion of bone that almost made up a skeleton and would he be interested in coming to Italy to see it. If not they would arrange shipment to Australia. With the disappointments of not finding a further cave after the initial finds a rather disillusioned Peter Cashman decided to go to Italy examine the bones and stay on the drill site for some time. He had recently returned to Sydney to present his final paper, and with the advent of Lake Marnie and other volcanic phenomena he was able to present a good paper, one that brought praise from his examiners. He was awarded his second Doctorate in Earth Sciences. The only thing he needed now was two more years in the field and a Professorship was his. That was his ultimate aim, unless of course the mark he received and the final examiners appraisal of his work was such that he would be offered a Professorship.

He left Sydney two days after receiving the e-mail, leaving the drill sites and cave searching in the capable hands of his father, Merilyn Ross and Mungaway.

'Somewhere' he thought 'there is an answer, a truth waiting to be found'. Though they knew that there had to be other places where the tribe in Western Australia lived out their last days, finding them was the proverbial needle in a haystack. Merilyn Ross had spent long nights in her tent reading on cave systems and how they are formed. Though her expertise was Seismology, rock formations didn't always fit into that category and she had an idea which she refused to share until she was sure of herself. Mungaway had often seen her pacing in the moonlight talking to herself going over things she had read. Sometimes he walked with her and they talked about the cave systems. Mungaway was aware she was onto something and he probably knew what it was but it was up to her to tell him, if he mentioned it she would feel cheated as others had not worked it out. So he walked with her and talked with her and waited.

Peter flew to Italy first class he needed the space and the relaxed atmosphere to marshal his thoughts and make decisions regarding the drill sites. He could not give up on them because he still believed they held the key to all of it, yet he knew if they didn't get some answers soon humanity would run out of time. After months of relative peace around the Earth, the rumblings had started again. The Astronomers scanned the skies seeking the object Peter had described to them. Hubbell telescope, though finely tuned was picking up nothing like it. Scientists in Germany Australia and America were working on a new telescope that was larger more powerful and more sensitive to change; it was hoped it would be up within the next year. The problem as Peter saw it, was that in the event of the book being right, by the time the sphere came into view it would be too late for everyone. They had to find something now and make plans for survival if it was possible. The longer it was left the more would die. Even so the chance of anyone surviving was slim anyway. They had no proof that anyone had survived the last catastrophe and unless they found something to go on it would have to be assumed that the next one would be total annihilation. Hadn't some of the Dinosaurs survived? The crocodile, the Rhino, the Monitor Lizard, the Dragons the Whales, weren't they all millions of years old? Or had they in fact come after the last upheaval were they also a **new** race of animals. Everything that pointed to the old race was buried, millions of years of earth changes had covered the traces. And what if these people were only another race, as his father suspected along with others, the second race, they would probably have to go too deep to try to find the maybe first race. The whole situation was becoming confusing even to Peter's analytical mind.

The trip to Italy was eventful, the 'plane having to change course several times to avoid smoking volcanoes. Peter was able to see them from the great height they flew at, the clear view of them showed him how big they must have been up close. He knew that if this continued the earth would eventually be covered by ash and smoke and it could do untold damage to all of the forests farms and animals. There was nothing they could do about it, there was no way to blow up a volcano it was up to the movement of the earth to change a smoker to dormant.

He landed in Rome and was picked up for the journey to the border. They spent one night in Bologna, then finished the journey at a tiny place called Chavenna. From there he was transferred to a 4WD to take him into the mountains to the drill site. They arrived late, summer had rolled into Autumn and the night was cold. Peter had little warm clothing with him, his sheepskin left with his father for the cold desert nights. The tents were set up in a circle around two large fire pits one for cooking and one for heat. He was introduced to Ramono Parvon by his driver. Peter had heard John Craznow mention this man on several occasions, saying he had the best "finder's nose" in the business, he just knew when things were right. He was ushered to a single tent. He had a good sized bed plenty of blankets a desk and lamp and his own utensils. On the end of the bed was a long padded parka, Ramono stuck his head in the flap,

"You will need that Doctor Cashman the night's here are freezing" he grinned.

"Thank you I don't have a good jacket with me" Peter smiled back he liked this man.

CHAPTER 22

As the rumblings and 'quakes continued around the Earth, coastlines changed forever. Verdant pastures and rain forests disappeared, the gorges in Australia and the Americas either widened and deepened to tremendous size rivalling the grand canyon or collapsed inward covering waterways and leaving nothing more than desert. The Himalayas, Andes, Urals, Swiss Alps, Southern Alps, and Blue Mountains all suffered rock and landslides changing their shape forever. The Geysers of the national parks in America and New Zealand and Canada, either became monstrous along with hot mud pools and boiling rivers or they closed over and never blew again. Some land, on the West. Australian coast, the East coast of Africa and the coast of Patagonia rose out of the sea as the undersea volcanoes in the Indian Ocean forced the land upwards. The one thing that all had expected had not as yet happened. There was no Polar melting. Certainly the ice shelves had broken up particularly in the Northern regions as Alaska shook and shuddered, but with the onset of Autumn and then winter in the Northern hemisphere it was expected it would refreeze. It was hoped! Another strange occurrence had the scientists scratching their collective heads, the hole in the ozone layer above the North Pole was considerably smaller than it had been in many years. Now they would have to take a wait and see if the hole above the Antarctica would also show this in summer. People continued to die in their thousands. Sudden temblors brought down makeshift shelters and newly built houses. A huge tearing noise would herald yet another land subsidence or split which people got caught in. The Japan Islands were only half their usual size, subsiding land and land splits that filled with the sea water caused whole small islands to disappear. Some resurfaced days later wiped clean, the fishing villages gone the people no more.

Some areas of the world were more stable than others and that was where a panicked people headed to. Many who survived just stayed where they were and hoped the next one would miss them. Affluence had gone out the window influence was the key word; if you knew someone or had money or had a profitable business that was still trading you got information, food and anything else necessary. The biggest trade came to be clean drinking water. Those who lived in the colder areas had plenty those who lived in the 'quake prone areas or the dry areas of the Earth, had none. It was a sellers market. Food was also becoming scarce in certain areas as the land was degraded by sea water or the pastures collapsed inwards taking farm produce and animals with it. Australia continued to cope well, many of the farming areas had not been touched. Once it was determined what the people needed any excess was sold to countries in need. In certain cases food aid shipments were organized with Australia being one of the biggest contributors. The lack of volcanoes in Australia put the country in a better position. Apart from the explosion at Lake Marnie some smoking areas within the Blue Mountains and the Great Diving Range and various vents that had opened up around the country, the continent stayed free of the catastrophic horror that went with an erupting volcano. The biggest worry for this part of the southern hemisphere was Mt. Erebus in the Antarctic. Monitoring had shown it to be rumbling with and average of four 'quakes a day breaking up the ice shelves. Up until this time the 'quakes had not been large enough to do major damage that didn't mean it wasn't building up for a big one. If Mt. Erebus blew its top the pole would melt, there was nothing surer, that would be bad for Australia especially the low lying areas in the south the eastern seaboard and the islands off the coast.

The Astronomers worked around the clock searching the skies for any movement that could lead them to find the sphere. But they found nothing! Talk began amongst scientific circles that Peter Cashman had become fixated and that the problems Earth was experiencing were natural occurrences that would eventually settle down and had nothing to do with a Comet, a wandering star or some sort of sphere that was just going to arrive one day. Even those within his father's circle began to ridicule his ideas. His father was appalled, he also believed in the Book of Vulcan and had been the one to start Peter on his quest. He asked his colleagues for patience to just believe for a little longer somewhere out there was something and they would find it! It was very hard to make his argument convincing without telling them about the caves they had found and the wall paintings in them. He could not do that, he and Peter and the rest of the crew were sworn to silence on the caves it would all be destroyed if others were to know and come looking. He just had to try to keep his arguments within the bounds of science, and without proof it wasn't easy. His best allies were those who also believed that there had been one maybe two races of man already on the Earth each time wiped out by some extraordinary event. These people believed that whatever did it came from somewhere else, maybe as had been put forward for years, a comet! or an asteroid! So to them the sphere story was not so fanciful it could well be true; something caused the disappearance of the Dinosaurs.

Back on the edge of the Great Sandy Desert Merilyn Ross remained at the caves site. Others had come and gone and those who stayed usually took breaks to the coast or a week in Perth to refresh themselves but not her she chose to stay. Mungaway had taken a short two week break during his wife's leave from University and another over the following Christmas New Year. Merilyn Ross celebrated on site with the drilling team and John Craznow, who had again visited the site and found her a most interesting woman. He had remained for some time and their animated conversations drifted across the desert throughout the night and into the small hours of the morning. When he again left for further sites he did so reluctantly, he enjoyed her company and was fascinated by her ability discuss the subject without returning to the same old ground. Her approach was always fresh and new. He felt more than admiration for her he was also developing a need for her.

As the plane took off carrying John Craznow back to Broome the lonely figure of Merilyn Ross continued standing on the broad red expanse arm still raised as though reaching out for him. She sighed noisily, and wished she had reached out for him.

She had not had a break from site because she had no-one to go home to yet if John had asked her to go to Broome with him she would have gone. She sighed again as she watched the tiny speck of a 'plane disappear into the distance. Striding back to her tent she heard the rumble of an approaching vehicle, Mungaway had returned and she was never so pleased to see anyone, with one exception of course. They had become great friends; he was so honest in his approach that she felt he was the only one who really understood. She knew that he had it worked out she was onto something but he did not pressure her into divulging her thoughts. She wanted to in fact she desperately needed to tell someone, perhaps this time she would take him into her confidence. She threw her arms around him as he jumped out of the truck handing him a cold flask of water.

"Hmm genuine cave mineral spring water, we should bottle this Merry" he laughed.

"Are you here for long we have so much to talk about Mungaway" she smiled at him.

"Yes for the duration, my wife is back at work the kids are back at their respective professions or whatever it is they do and I have returned to my beginnings". He smiled his dazzling broad smile that Merilyn loved.

"We had a visitor I have not been so alone" she told him "John Craznow came over for a time and we got on so well Mungaway he is so refreshingly honest calls a spade a spade. He still thinks this is the site for the answers and I agree with him." she tucked her arm through his as they walked toward the cave site.

He detected excitement in her voice it was more than a professional admiration he could hear, he detected love perhaps? He didn't know anything about Merilyn Ross but he did know she was alone in the world with the exception of a small circle of friends, and the idea of her becoming involved with someone like John Craznow was nice. John was a good man and dedicated to his work the Cashman's relied on him so much he was in essence their right hand man. He hoped Merry would become involved she really needed someone in her life who understood what she did and why. He Mungaway, would do everything he could to bring them together when next John Craznow called.

CHAPTER 23

Peter Cashman flew back from Italy two weeks after visiting the site. The biggest problem with this site was the water. The snow and ice made it difficult to get a clear drill with the holes often filling overnight when the weather was too bad to drill all night. The results had been good and although the bone fragments were small and difficult to extract the scientists there had managed to assemble quite a lot of a skeleton. The race was small like those in Australia with fine bones almost like a child's structure. He estimated they would not have reached any more than 160 cms at the tallest. It was a remarkable find and although they continued to bring up good core samples from unimaginable depths and they had drilled through cave systems which had been excavated, they found no sign of where these people lived or how. The Australian site was unique in the world and Peter was beginning to agree with John Craznow that that particular site held the answers. He landed in Sydney and went directly to an apartment he and his parents shared when there. He checked his mail and his e-mail found nothing that was of extraordinary interest and went off to shower and change. He ordered a meal from the restaurant next door taking his time with a bottle of wine on the balcony overlooking the most beautiful harbour in the world. A beep from his computer followed by his flag man indicated incoming e-mail normally he would let it go until he felt like working but decided this time to print it out and read it at leisure. Having instructed the printer, he returned to his bottle and view. As he relaxed his mind began to wander to the site in Western Australia. What treasures must be there if only they could find them. John Craznow had been very positive about the site at their last meeting he had told Peter that he felt Merilyn Ross may well be working on something that may surprise. No she had not said anything nor given any clues as to what it was but he thought there was something she wasn't telling him. Peter considered it, she was a smart woman and very good at her job she had adapted very well to harsh environment and seemed to revel in the challenge offered her. Peter was glad she was on the team, she was often the soothing voice when the arguments became too heated and continued to rehash old ideas.

With this in mind he was drawn back to his e-mail, 'perhaps she has found something' he wondered.

He picked the e-mail up off the tray and carried it back to his balcony chair; it was from Taj Maranesh. He had recently flown to Darwin and Indonesia to look at skeletal remains found over one hundred years before. He felt they may have some likeness to the bones they had in the caves. Finding nothing that was even remotely like what they had on site he flew back to Sydney and spent some time with Con Stratkos one of the computer wizards who was trying to decipher the Book of Vulcan. That day Con had been able to bring one illegible page up to reasonable clarity piece by tiny piece then assembled it until they were able to read some of the text.

. . . . "and the people cried in fear as the Lords of the Earth Wind and Fire devastated their world. And the leader said 'let the darkness become our light (?) life (?) and the water protect us . . . ." Peter puzzled over it no doubt the author was referring to caves or something similar, it did make it seem as though the tribe had moved underground but it was no proof of where this took place. As the rest of the page was not yet legible it was simply a line taken out of context and may mean nothing more than a saying by a sage or scholar of the tribe. There was no guarantee either that the word they couldn't complete would have been life or light, whatever it was would put a completely different slant on the whole thing.

Still he was pleased with the work they were doing and at last they had hit on a method of reading some of the more badly damaged pages. It would all take time but ultimately most of the story would be readable. Of course time was something Peter still earnestly believed they had very little of, so it may just come all too late.

He decided that he would only have overnight in Sydney then head back out to W.A. he wanted to get back on site, he longed to see the caves again, he felt like a child with a cherished secret.

CHAPTER 24

Merilyn Ross and Mungaway spent most of his first night back discussing some of the thoughts John Craznow had put forward. Merilyn became animated when she spoke of John and often Mungaway would catch her staring off into the distance as though searching for the 'plane that would bring him back. The second day they went to the caves. Since the last time Mungaway had seen them Alan Cashman had sent an electrician from the lab. who had wired the upper walls, stairways and ramps with soft offset lighting. This allowed people to see where they were going without the harsh white light of the huge spots damaging the wall paintings. The paintings took on an eerie life like quality when viewed in such subdued lighting. They sat together in the lower cave the sound of running water ever present, a source they had not yet found. They sat without speaking staring at the stunning paintings almost believing they could hear the cries of the dying all those millennia ago. After some time of saying nothing Merilyn Ross started to speak slowly, haltingly at first as though afraid to share her views with anyone.

"Mungaway I would like to discuss my thoughts on the cave systems that may have housed the scholars painters and scribes of this time."

Mungaway sat quietly not speaking waiting for her to at last tell him the secrets he believed she had harboured for so long.

She stood up then and walked to the edge of the pool and looked down,

"Tell me what you see Mungaway, look."

Mungaway joined her at the pools edge and looked down it was exactly as he expected tiny points of light danced in the water, the reflections of the lights softening and dancing.

"Yes I see Merry now are you going to tell me what you see?"

"You know what I see Mungaway you have known for a very long time haven't you."

He nodded "yes Merry I suspected it. So where do we go from here?"

"Scuba gear long lines the type of gear they use in cave diving out on the Nullabor I should think. And of course people who are within our group and can be trusted as they do have to take people there who have had little if any, scuba training."

"Yes we will have to get Alan Cashman on to it straight away and try to find out where in the world Peter is."

"I wonder" mused Merilyn "if it goes far or anywhere for that matter we could come up against a wall yet."

Mungaway shook his head "No I don't think so I think it will go just where we think it will and maybe even further than we ever imagined."

Peter Cashman arrived by light plane on the third day after returning from Italy. With him came a load of Scuba gear and lines and a Scuba expert from the Seismology centre in Melbourne.

"Do you know what all this is for?" Peter asked him genuinely puzzled.

"No Dr. Cashman I only know the gear was requested by Dr. Alan Cashman and I was requested to go with it."

They arrived at the site and were greeted by the drilling team Merilyn Ross and Mungaway. The instructor was introduced as Dave Madden. Everyone pitched in to unload the gear, there was enough for six people to use; then a conference in Peter's tent to bring him up to scratch.

"What did you request this gear for Merilyn, are you going diving in the pool?"

Merilyn nodded her face alive,

"Yes Peter we are going diving but first I want to show you something"

With that they all walked to the caves. Peter marvelled at the lighting and the amazing life like appearance now given to the paintings. In the lowest cave he stood at the pools' edge with the others, looking down.

"What do you see Peter?" asked Merilyn barely able to hide the excitement in her voice.

"Water of course what else should I see?" he looked at her for a moment then returned his gaze to the water. Merilyn said nothing just stood and watched his features, 'he must work it out' she thought. Then a change came over him he leaned forward then glanced at the lights he stood back and looked at the pool from different angles each time returning to the pools edge to look straight down.

"Is this so" he said softly to no-one in particular "how could I have missed it?" he asked of himself.

"You know then Peter"? She asked

"I think so Merilyn, I think so."

"Then will someone please explain it all to me please?" asked the head driller.

"Simple" said Merilyn "in a cave such as these caves are, most water comes from seepage and the seepage continues over eons wearing away huge basins that constantly fill with water no matter how far underground. Now ever since we have been here we have heard running water but could not find the source we all thought it was a rivulet behind the rocks somewhere it's sound magnified by the cave." No-one spoke. "In essence that is right but it is bigger than a rivulet it is probably a stream or part of an old underground river that has branched around these hills. This pool, if it were just a seepage basin, would be dead still, so still that you would not be able to clearly discern the water's surface, light would reflect straight down in a steady light giving an illusion of the bottom being quite close. But this pool does not do that if you look straight down you will see the pin points of light and reflections from the wall lights are dancing, constantly moving, even though the surface isn't. This can only indicate one thing this water is constantly being replenished from below, from a stream or a river. I believe if we go down there we will find more caves and the answer to the scholars and scribes of this tribe. She smiled triumphantly at Peter.

He threw his arms around her "Merilyn I think you've done it, it might be tricky but I think you have the answer. What would we do without you on the team? You have earned yourself a paid holiday to anywhere you want to go just name the place and the time and it's yours."

She smiled at him "Not yet Peter I want to see this through we may not have much time and this must be found and worked on. When it's all over and we have done all we can then offer it to me again and if there is time left for us I will go." She smiled at him again.

"It's a deal" he told her.

That night they made plans for the dive for the following day. During a spell in the caves just before bed Merilyn met the Scuba instructor again. He was just sitting staring in wonderment at the paintings.

"They are so beautiful" his voice barely a whisper.

"Yes they are I never tire of them." She answered.

"Does anyone else know about them?" he asked her.

"No just our team and now you, you have been sworn to secrecy haven't you?

He nodded "Uhuh Dr. Cashman Senior told me he would draw and quarter me if I didn't keep my word on this and now I can understand why, tell the world and these caves would be ruined forever."

"Well you've got that right" she agreed "I want to go down first with you and Peter of course, I have already had some experience diving around Rottnest Island and I do understand how line diving works. So I would appreciate it if you would organise for me to go down there. I've no doubt Mungaway, being our resident specialist in tribes would also appreciate being able to go down with us."

"I don't see the problem Dr. Cashman Senior told me to do whatever you wanted me to I guess he has a lot of time for you."

Merilyn flushed a little she wasn't aware she was held in such high esteem by either of the Cashman's.

CHAPTER 25

The morning dawned hot and bright the sun just peeping over the eastern edge of the desert when four of them emerged from their respective tents and headed for the caves. When they got there the drillers were already fixing lines. Red coils of line were set up all over the floor of the cave. No-one knew exactly what they would be up against; beneath them could be a raging river that could sweep them into the bowels of the earth. Or it could be nothing more than a stream that ran through rocks and there were no caves. Each dragged wet suits on over under wear helping each other to adjust the fit. Then came the tanks, they were using flat silver packs in the event of having to crawl through tight spaces. When ready they solemnly shook hands all round, they tested their radio equipment and then finally the instructor slipped into the water. He dived then resurfaced, took the light from the edge and dived again he seemed to be gone for a long time then he resurfaced.

"Okay it's a fairly long swim, straight down then there are some rocks and what is beyond them I don't know. Switch on your head lights and the light you are carrying and leave them on at all times if you get into trouble yell through your radio and follow your line back; the drillers will pull you up if they have to."

They slid into the pool sinking slowly with the weights around their waists.

Then head first they turned and swam down pushing with their fins until they reached the rocks. They manoeuvered around the rocks the instructor and Peter going together, then they were gone. Merilyn and Mungaway followed them and as they came around the rocks they were caught by a huge rush of water. They were dragged along forever before they could find their way to the surface. As Merilyn surfaced she saw a light on a ledge ahead of her and to her right, on the ledge stood Peter, opposite him stood the instructor between them was some sort of a net like a construction net. Merilyn and Mungaway headed for the ledge swimming strongly against the current that was pushing them along. Peter helped pull them out of the water.

"Wow what a ride" he enthused "there is only one problem how in hell's name are we going to swim against it to get back to the cave?"

"We may have to get the drillers to set up winches and winch us back." said Dave "I have been winched out of heavy rapids travelling much stronger than this it does work so we'll worry about it when the time comes."

"Why the net?" asked Merilyn

"Come and see for yourself" said Peter.

She walked to the edge of the ledge and peered over shining her light down as she did. The water poured in a black torrent straight down it was impossible to estimate the drop and impossible to know where it went. Merilyn felt defeated.

"I think it's lucky for us that I went first and always carry the net in my equipment" Dave told her "otherwise we would have all gone over the side to god knows where."

"Well I guess that's that Peter we can't go down there and there are no caves here so we go back to the drawing board." she said.

"Not exactly Merilyn I want to show you something." he smiled.

He walked to the net and slowly made his way across to the other side.

"Come on it's easy."

Merilyn eased her way across followed by Mungaway. On the other side she was shown a small slit in the rocks just big enough for someone to squeeze through.

"Dave found it as he landed on the ledge we think it leads to a cave. You're smaller than us so you go through, but be careful we don't want you falling into another river."

She got through it and shone her torch around; what she saw took her breath away. The walls were covered in paintings, and symbols. The paintings were all representative of what had been happening outside their cave environment. The cave was large and there was evidence of cooking fires and many implements; all intact. Then there were the piles of bones. At least forty people had lived here. The others squeezed in behind her, staring in amazement.

"But they couldn't have got in this way" Merilyn exclaimed "it wouldn't have been possible to come down that river and survive."

"The river then was probably only a stream and quite possibly on a different course, for people who live near or on river systems they must have fished and swum. Coming down through that pool would only have meant holding their breath for a short period of time then they would have been into a small underground river that was probably only half the width and no-where near as fast as it is now. The water seeping down through the ground and the rocks plus the eons that have passed have created a huge river that probably feeds into an even bigger artesian basin. If we had continued down there we would have died. Dave got his rope hooked on a rock on that side that is why he finished over here and I finished on the other side. And of course there is also Taj's theory that the split in the rocks above us may lead to another passage down is probably right. There may be another way out of here without swimming".

The four of them stood in the lowest cave playing their torches over the walls. The history of the race and the turbulent times that led to their death was there for all to see in the brilliant paintings. The sphere was there still looking large in the night sky, the volcanoes seemed larger and more menacing, the very top of the cave was depicted with people crowded together watching the horror outside. There were bodies everywhere inside and outside the cave. Again the ancient, unbelievable animals, never found before, never catalogued, with no names, fled in terror, falling into the abysses as they were created, burning as the hot ejection's landed on them.

Then the most amazing discovery of all! As Peter and Mungaway toured the walls peering into every dark corner they found a small niche in the far reaches of the cave on the walls were symbols, line after line reaching from way above their heads all the way to the floor. Two walls almost facing each other completely covered in the symbols.

"Peter this is writing, nothing like I have ever seen but it is writing." Mungaway was entranced by it.

Peter was so excited he could barely control himself,

"Mungaway we've found it we've found the writing and the original writer of the Book of Vulcan" He yelled to the others "come and see this and prepare to be amazed."

All four lights were trained on the walls nobody spoke, there were no words to define the feeling of having found something so extraordinary, so old.

Some of the symbols were written in blue and highlighted with red. Some were written in black like charcoal with small white curls on the (?) letters.

"I suppose each different colour is representative of the way the word is pronounced or it may well denote a whole sentence or description in just one set of symbols. Considering only two walls are covered like this I would suggest the latter to be closer to the point" said Peter.

Merilyn was nodding "there is a tribal history written here and I think it includes all of the comings and unknown goings of the sphere and how it affected their lives and what they believed it was."

To one side of the niche was a huge smoking cone and curling up from the cone was a black semi transparent figure holding his arms up to the sky; above him was the sphere.

"I think we just found Lord Vulcan and if I am not mistaken the sphere is Idoli" Peter said "yet we can not actually find a reference to that name being given to the sphere. I think we would have to record all the symbols and see if we can't break their code.

Mungaway had been poring over the symbols around floor level as there were some differences to those further up. There were some pictogram and sciagram style symbols and he found that the same set kept appearing along this one section of wall.

"Peter" he called "I think I have found Idoli. Look!"

Peter got down on his hands and knees and studied the symbols Mungaway had pointed to; there were whole sections where the same set kept appearing.

"Look Peter the black symbol there is very similar to the curl of the smoke from the volcano around that black figure, suggestion being that is the name they have given it. Now if you look a little further along you will see a set of round symbols and each one contains white circles, I may be wrong but to me that says that is the name they gave the sphere. I bet if you could break this down you would find that one would translate to Lord Vulcan and the other to Idoli. I have not studied Hieroglyphics but I did a study course in Epistemology and we often had to translate from pictograms and sciagrams, to give us insight to where knowledge all began. What do you think?"

"I think" said Peter "that you are a genius Mungaway a genius and you shall be rewarded fittingly" he grinned slapping Mungaway on the back "now we have to find our way out of here and get some light down here so that we can start translating. We need for one to go back and ask the drill team to start moving that big rock at the back of the cave to see if there is anything behind it the rest of us will stay here and search for a gap or opening down here."

"I'll go" said Dave "I have the most experience here and I wouldn't like anyone else to get into trouble I may not be able to get them out of."

Peter called the drill team on the radio telling them that Dave was coming back and as soon as they felt the rope go taut to start winching. Dave moved out of the cave crossing the net to the ledge so that the rope had a fairly straight line to him. The others watched as the rope slowly tightened then Dave was in the water and within seconds had disappeared into the gloom of the rushing river. They waited for what seemed like an eternity before they heard one of the drillers saying,

"We've got him in the pool he is rising now."

The others immediately set to finding an opening or gap it had to be above their heads somewhere up in the gloomy reaches of the cave. Finding it was one thing reaching it was going to be difficult.

CHAPTER 26

The world reeled as yet another onslaught of Earthquakes shook those areas already devastated. The authorities stopped counting the dead it was all they could do to keep up with the living that were surviving, in many instances just surviving. The Volcanoes around the Pacific Rim of Fire spewed lava and rocks though very little ash, this was a blessing, at least areas that many did not have to evacuate because of lava did not have to worry about ash. Teams of shooters throughout the world were on standby. The animals that they couldn't save had to be shot, many were found to be terribly burnt but alive amongst the debris of forest fires. Africa shuddered many times. Ethiopia's lines of mountain ranges split in places causing huge rock and landslides. The string of lakes, more often than not dry, outside the town of Nazret, had filled then overflowed, and continued all the way across the border into Kenya, where Lake Rudolf, unable to cope with the water pouring into it spilled into the desert. The Chalbi became a huge lake overnight. In the west the Atlantic rolled over the land as undersea cones pushed their way to the surface. Senegal, Ivory Coast, Liberia, Ghana and Nigeria took the brunt of it. Towns and cities were washed away the people going with them In Namibia the mountains became the refuge of those left though the country suffered continuous tremors for sometimes days on end as the mountains changed their shape. South Africa suffered major casualties on both its west and south coasts as the Indian and Atlantic Oceans clashed violently across land. All but the tops of the mountains in Madagascar were inundated. Tsunami's created by the disturbances under the Indian and Atlantic Oceans were sent across the Indian Ocean to crash onto West. Australia's shores. The small and very scattered population of the state meant few died and loss was minimal; however West. Australia continued to shudder under a series of tremors reaching 5 on the Richter many of them in outlying areas. Areas such as Meckering and Cadoux, Geraldton, Northhampton and Perth itself all suffered. The smaller towns lost most of their bigger buildings while Perth suffered major cracking to bridges and some of the older buildings. Ferry services across the Swan were at a premium as no-one dared use the main bridge systems.

Melbourne was rocked frequently sending shock waves to the larger towns of Ballarat and Geelong. Sydney suffered many small tremors since the major 'quake which took out the Harbour Bridge, leaving it in place but buckled with cracked pylons. Adelaide and the surrounding hills were shaken violently and frequently. Older stone homes and buildings falling like packs of cards. The hills split sending great rock slides crashing down onto the main highway often sending cars and trucks over the side to crash and burn in turn starting bush fires. These were often followed by huge rainstorms that finished what the rock slides could not do, sending rivers of mud and more rocks down the hills into the outlying suburbs.

Across the world people cowered and wept in fear at the might of nature being thrown against them. At the end of the second year after it all began it was estimated that just over half of the world's population were still able to continue, the other half being either dead, missing, or injured.

CHAPTER 27

In a cave way below the hills on the edge of the Great Sandy Desert in Western Australia three people sat copying symbols and pictograms. After finding the lower cave, the drillers had moved into high gear and gradually moved the huge rock in the second cave. Behind it they found another chamber that was made up of a small narrow ledge and a steep slope. Roped together they made the descent down the slope to find their way blocked by rock. Slowly they drilled through the rock until they had a small opening. Below the opening in the gloom of the upper reaches of the bottom cave they found a set of steep steps cut into the wall. They manoeuvered their way down the steps only to run out after about five meters. The rest of the wall was worn smooth probably by the passage of water. They continued to lower themselves to find when they reached the base they were in fact behind the niche in which the symbols were written.

"Obviously" Peter remarked "the niche was once two completely separate walls. Over time or as the result of the most recent earthquakes they have come together. We cannot move them without destroying the symbols, so right now I really need some suggestions as to how we are going to be able to come and go to this cave without having to ride the river."

"Is there no space at the top to come over the walls?" asked Merilyn.

"That is something we would have to look at. Perhaps there is an area there that has nothing on it perhaps we can come through that and over it somehow" Peter pulled at his bottom lip "what we need here is an engineer and we have to get one ASAP. I'll have to go back up and ring Dad and arrange for someone from Perth to come up."

Peter suited up he had already gone back up and come down again, he didn't mind the ride coming down but he found the dragging against the rush of water quite hard to take. The rope was tight pulling his harness tight around his body. He knew he was safe enough but he didn't feel safe.

He slipped into the water and was soon rising up into the pool. Dave was there to drag him out as he surfaced.

"Phew I hate that pull around the rocks just before you actually get into the pool, it is so hard to manoeuver, the opening isn't big and the water is so strong." Peter clambered out of the pool pulling his gear off "all the more reason for us to find another way into the lower cave before something goes wrong and someone gets swept away. Mungaway really likes being down there but he hates the trip back more than I do—can't say's I blame him."

"We are trying boss" one of the drillers told him "but we just haven't found a place to come through the wall. An engineer would know where to go."

Peter nodded "yeah I know it's hard and you are doing a good job I'll get on the phone to Dad and get someone up here ASAP."

He strolled naked out of the cave to his tent he had gone beyond wearing underwear under his wet suit it was always too hard to work the bottom half on comfortably. All of them had taken to doing this because of the long hours they spent in their suits once in the cave. Merilyn made one exception, she wore a bra as once down there they tended to turn down the tops and not suit up properly again until ready to come back.

Peter's call to his father was short and sweet. He knew what he wanted and Cashman senior knew how to get it so there wasn't much else to discuss. The engineer should be there the following morning. Peter didn't want to ride the river down to the cave again, he was tired and wanted only some fresh air a decent meal and a drink. He climbed into shorts and shirt checking some of the drawings they had made while in the cave. Fortunately the gap in the niche was big enough to put the drawings etc. through so there was no necessity to take them when they went back up. Instead they pushed them through the gap into a basket and it in turn was winched up through the hole. He poured himself a good stiff drink added a squirt of soda and sipped while he leafed through the work they had already done. It was going to take too long to catalogue everything they really needed more people but at the same time Peter did not want to break in someone new and hope they would keep their agreement of silence. He already felt there were too many who knew. Then a thought, 'why not John Craznow?' John was experienced, well known and as anxious as the rest of them to find the truth. He would call around and ask him to come and join them, perhaps to, the Italian specialist, Ramono Parvon. At least they were all on the same wave length and all looking for the same answers.

He called Italy's drill site and got Ramono immediately.

". . . so will you come out and give us a hand?" Peter asked him.

"Yes Peter I will drive out tomorrow and fly out the following day, three days at most I should be there. Okay?" he asked.

"That's great Ramono and where in the world is John Craznow do you know?" there was a faint echo on the line and a slight delay as the radio phone relayed the question.

". . . . Bulgaria, I think Peter, I could ring the site in the Urals and see if they have heard from him. It takes a while to get through but I can leave messages around for him. You just want him to fly straight out you don't want to talk to him first?"

"If you can get a message to him just tell him to turn up and bring some equipment as I have requested from you."

"All very mysterious Peter can't you tell me what is going on?"

"No sorry when you get here. Talk to you soon, 'bye." Peter replaced the handset.

He walked back to the cave and radioed the others telling them to call it quits for the day and come up. He then went back to his tent and contacted the pilot in Broome regarding bringing out Ramono and John when he was found.

"I am on my way out now Dr. Cashman I have some mail for you and a new piece of equipment sent up by Dr. Cashman senior, is there anything you want?"

Peter thought for a few seconds,

"Yes how about picking up enough lobster for all of us some fresh salad vegies and a few good bottles of wine I think it's time I gave this mob a little celebration. Oh yes, and several good bottles of Champagne. If you can think of anything else that might make the night pleasant throw that in to. Bill it all to me; have you got the foundations card with you?"

The pilot's voice was loud and clear "I have and I will and I can think of a couple of things that would go down well."

"Fine, we'll see you in a few hours then. Will you stay tonight and go in tomorrow? if so I'll have a bed set up for you."

"I will stay tonight it may be dark or close to it when I get there. I'll see you then."

Peter hung up. This crew had worked so hard and so had the cook under some fairly extreme conditions. The cook did wonders in the big tent, even though the stove was running on gas, fridge freezer lights and cooling ran on solar panels, the constant high summer temperatures of sometimes 53c. made it very difficult for even the most tolerant cook to prepare meals comfortably.

They had never really celebrated finding the lower cave they had just assumed that if there was something there they would find it. But now it was time to put aside work even for a night, put aside the arguments and just celebrate and relax.

Peter walked backed to the cave to watch the other's come up through the pool; they came up together Mungaway and Merilyn. Surfacing simultaneously Merilyn ripped off her mask and with Peter's help hauled herself out of the water.

"Peter I think we have a problem down there, I think the summer rains are affecting the water flow Mungaway almost got washed away." She looked worried.

"No it was alright really" Mungaway told him "she just worries about me."

"Well show him your harness then, I had to help him around the rocks" Merilyn was angry.

Mungaway hauled himself out of the pool and stood up the harness under his right arm had frayed away.

"I think it was just the pull of the water that did that I don't think I was in any real danger" he told them.

Dave stepped forward and checked the harness.

"You could have been killed Mungaway, if this had torn away the force of the water would have pulled that harness off and you wouldn't have had a life line."

"Well" Merilyn said "I think the water has become much stronger I think there is more water coming in down there and it seemed to me the levels are rising."

"I didn't notice it" Peter told them "but that doesn't mean anything. Is it possible those Tsunamis have let more water into the system?"

"If that is so then two things are going to happen. One is the water will continue to rise until it reaches the highest level which is the roof, the second is we will lose the cave" Dave said.

Peter looked horrified "the water wouldn't have to rise far before we lost the cave David. And what about this one if the water down there rises then it will force more water upwards and this cave could be flooded as well."

"I suppose when the engineer gets here we could get him to check it out and maybe blow the area where the water goes down into the artesian basin" offered one of the drillers.

"What would that do?" Peter asked.

"Well . . . . if he could set a charge in just the right place he may be able to blow the rocks below where the water goes in creating a much larger entrance so that the higher volume of water drains more quickly and in turn keeps the river level down" he looked at them all "it's a thought."

"And a pretty damn good one at that." Peter slapped him on the back "tomorrow when the engineer gets here we will put it to him. Meanwhile no-one is to go down until it is safe. If we lose the cave then we lose the cave there is nothing to be done about it, we will just have to finish our work underwater until we have as much information as possible and leave it to the elements. As for this cave we will set up a pump and if the water rises in the pool we will pump it into the desert, night and day if we have to."

The others nodded saying nothing.

The drone of a small plane intruded on Peter's thoughts as he sat sipping a drink, leafing through the day's work and trying to figure out where it was all going.

As the small plane landed the others went out to meet it and help with the unloading. The boxes of food and two cases of wine were unloaded along with some necessary equipment two more carbon lights some more lines a new spectroscope and a new gadget from Alan Cashman, a small computerised hand held sonar which could be used while in the river to determine where the river went. Dave had already volunteered to be the one to use it.

The Pilot had added a few things to the shopping list some avocados, two kgs of cooked prawns and two large fresh made cheese cakes. He grinned at Peter,

"You did say if I could think of anything else".

Peter laughed "I did and I will send you shopping more often."

The dinner that night was the first real celebration they had had since the cave findings. The cook had done wonders and presented huge platters of lobster, prawns and salad both vegetable and fruit. Red wines white wines and champagne flowed. They all sat down together including the cook and no-one left the table until it was all gone including the cheese cakes. Picaninny dawn saw Mungaway, Merilyn, Peter and the pilot all sitting on the nearby sand hill, glasses in hand drinking a toast to yet another new day as the huge orange ball of the sun slowly rose over the edge of the desert.

"I never tire of this sight" sighed Peter "we have a beautiful world I want so much to keep it intact or at least part of it so that humanity can go on. It isn't fair that a world such as ours that just happened to be formed in the right place at the right time should be destroyed by some unknown force about which we can do nothing. Why can't this thing just go and pick on a world where it doesn't matter. I realize we are not alone but the race that we are and the world that we have is unique. We may find other life out there but it won't be like us and their world won't be like ours. Once this is gone it is gone forever. If we can find a way of surviving whatever is going to happen then there is a chance that a fourth race will begin on the earth and the world can renew itself with man. Am I asking too much?"

The others said nothing but all shook their heads, there was nothing anyone could say Peter had said what they all believed.

CHAPTER 28

The night's dining and wining took its toll no-one worked that day, and no-one had a head for riding the river. When they did surface most of what remained of the day was spent going over the previous work. The camp was quiet the workers subdued. The pilot left the site mid afternoon to pick up the engineer in Broome. He would not return that night.

At four o'clock the following morning a loud groaning sound brought people running from their tents. They stood huddled together in the cold early pre dawn light wondering what was happening. They didn't have long to wait. A huge shudder like the land shaking itself was felt followed by wide spreading ground rippling that knocked them all down like nine pins. The ripples rolled away into the hills dislodging rocks and stones and causing sand to run down the hills like water.

"Oh hell" exclaimed Peter "the bloody cave". He started to run toward the hills staggering as another tremor overtook him. Mungaway caught up to him grabbing his arm,

"You can't go in there if it collapses we may never get you out Peter."

Peter tried to shrug off the strong brown hands holding him.

"Let me go Mungaway I have to see what is happening."

Mungaway held him firmly, "there is nothing you can do Peter".

The tremors stopped as quickly as they started a deathly silence spread over the desert.

In the eerie stillness Peter walked slowly toward the cave the others stood watching his retreating back until he was out of sight then slowly one by one trailed after him.

Peter stood at the cave mouth, it was full of sand and small rocks his shoulders sagged but he wasn't truly disappointed it was nothing they couldn't shift it would just put them back a while. Serves them right for becoming too complacent, it had all become too easy. Finding the caves finding the writings finding the key to symbols, nothing had been hard once the caves had been uncovered now they were back to square one. Staring at the cave was not going to get the work done; he turned to the others,

"Well we'll go and get breakfast now that we are all up and then we will start digging it out;everyone okay with that?"

He walked away, back to his tent, not waiting for an answer. He knew as they did that it was all they could do.

Before the sun was too hot the work had started in earnest. They used picks, shovels and anything else including moving the smaller rocks by hand and using the winch to move the bigger rocks away from the opening. Once they were able to get into the mouth of the cave they discovered that much of the roof had also come down landing in the middle of the floor. The entrance down to the second cave was blocked by falling rock but none of it too big to move. This took all day.

The plane landed at 4pm with the geo/engineer from Perth, he didn't get much of chance to sit and talk as soon as he had been assigned a tent and stowed his gear he was taken straight to the caves. Peter introduced him around to the others as TJ full name Thomas John Mason, but never called anything else but TJ.

"At first" Peter told him "you were brought up here to try and find a way through the roof of another cave to a lower cave, however this morning we had two 'quakes which has stuffed it all up and brought half the damn hill down on the first cave. Now we have to find our way back into the second cave and quickly, so that we can find a way down into the third cave. The underground river is rising quite quickly, we have no idea if the rocks in the other caves have been dislodged or what damage there is caused by the 'quakes. We may have already lost the bottom cave to flooding; all our work may already have been for nothing. I know you have just gotten here but we have to really get started because we don't know if we are going to get more tremors and the sooner this big stuff is moved the safer we will be. Okay with you?"

TJ nodded "I understand that's what I'm here for. Do you know whether the caves were fairly stable?"

Peter referred him to Mungaway "he can tell you if they appeared to be he is our resident expert in all things tribal and otherwise."

"The caves appeared to be as stable as any I have seen" Mungaway told him "there had been some shift in the rocks but nothing beyond what would normally be expected with seismic activity and natural ground movement. The large wall rocks had no major cracking certainly the tribes who lived there would not have moved into them if they appeared to be in any way unstable."

The engineer nodded "good that means that except for the falls of rock from the tremors we should not encounter any major shifting in the actual cave walls."

"Is that good for us?" Peter asked.

"Yes it is because it means that if we go in there digging around and disturbing the falls we are not likely to have a large wall slab or similar come down on our heads" TJ told him.

"We did lose some roof though in the upper cave, that could easily come down again couldn't it?" Peter asked

The engineer nodded "I am afraid so that is the risk in any cave, the roof is usually the one part that will collapse. But I would say because the first cave is directly below the hill that is the only one to suffer. The others were probably formed from lava bubbles or water which means the roof will be solid."

Peter breathed an audible sigh of relief and the others looked at each other even managing to smile.

"We cannot do much of this tonight Peter" Merilyn told him "I think we should get an early start, say before sun up, and work all day, what do you think?"

Peter scanned their faces, "Do you all agree on that?"

Everyone nodded in agreement.

"Okay then we start at 4 am. We will take a breakfast break at 8 am that will give us four straight hours before it gets hot. Then we work through all day until it's dark. If we can we will continue under lights; everyone okay with that?"

Again they nodded their agreement.

Turning to the drillers he said "I want you two to set up the new lines and winches for the heavy stuff and for now I want you to go with the engineer around the hills so he can have a look at how the hill came down and where. I also want you to hook up all the lights we have I want as much illumination in that cave as we can possibly get."

Turning to the pilot Peter asked "Do you know if there has been any contact with John Craznow yet?"

The pilot shook his head "not that I know of I have not been told he is coming in. As soon as he is located I will get him here as quickly as possible."

"Thanks" Peter said "I would appreciate that".

While the engineer and drillers walked the hills sites Peter, Merilyn, Mungaway and David had a meeting in Peter's tent.

"Look I have no illusions about what we are doing here, I know it's dangerous work and given the amount of what came down in those last tremors I know that if it happened while we are inside someone could die. I am not going to give you an "it's all for the greater good" speech because you are putting your lives on the line and maybe for nothing. So I am telling you now we will go in there and we will do what we can to retrieve as much information as possible, if things look bad we get out really quick. We all take breathing apparatus and water with us, if something goes wrong we protect ourselves to the best of our ability. If any of us get trapped we wait until whoever is up top can get us out there will be no heroics, okay?" they all nodded in unison "in the event of further tremors I will not ask anyone to go down there you must choose to go as a personal decision. Understood?" again they nodded "I just hope that whatever we are doing here has the answer because we could be putting precious lives on the line for nothing."

The silence grew as no-one spoke there seemed nothing to say. From an animated and often heated group they were now quietly considering their choices.

"Well Peter I for one will go back down because I believe the lower caves are stable. If anything goes wrong it doesn't matter where we are if we are going to die one place is as good as another" Merilyn stared at him "does that make sense?"

Peter smiled at her and nodded "Yes Merilyn it makes sense and thank you."

"Well count me in" grinned Mungaway "I always loved danger".

The others laughed.

"I am here for my services as a scuba specialist Peter, if you need me I am available for whatever you want. Count me in" Dave told him.

"Well I know that John Craznow would not be put off so when he gets here we will have an extra pair of hands and a lot of expertise" Peter told them.

"Craznow is coming back?" Merilyn asked the pleasure in her voice unmistakable.

"Yes I have put a world wide call out for him I need him here he has the experience we are looking for. I see that pleases you Merilyn" Peter teased.

Merilyn Ross's tanned face darkened with the flush that rose in her cheeks. She said nothing.

"It will be good to have him back" Mungaway told them "he is wasted over in Europe there is little he can do there but supervise we need the hands on experience he can bring to drilling and cave work."

All nodded and murmured their agreement Peter adding "I will put out another call and see if he has been located yet. You are right Mungaway I think he is better here than anywhere else."

CHAPTER 29

The meeting broke up as the dinner gong sounded. The drillers and TJ had returned from their walk, TJ having made sketches of the rock structure and land fall.

"I would like to discuss this with you after dinner" he told Peter "I don't think we have too many problems if we don't have any more shakes."

"Good we will have a full meeting in the mess tent when dinner is finished."

Dinner over the Engineer presented his case.

"I know it looks bad" he told them "but it really isn't as bad as it looks. The hill has come down but from what I have seen the hill itself is made from sand stone and limestone. Now this stuff will move and shift quite easily because when unexposed to the outside air it remains soft. However once it has been exposed to water such as most of the hills have been at sometime or another, sandstone and or limestone forms a meld and tends to wear away rather than fall down. The ceiling collapse in the top cave was only the top of the hill shifting with the tremor. There is probably more of it that has been moved and may eventually fall but that is probably only pieces that have cracked through over time and worked their way loose. I don't really think too much more of it will be a problem. The walls of the caves are probably all the same rock because there is nothing much else of note here. There does not appear to be any igneous rock here. The area may well have been under an inland sea at some time and has worn away since surfacing but the hills themselves don't appear to have been created by any form of volcanic eruption the whole area appears to have been cold stable for a very long time."

Peter tilted his head slightly to one side "did my father not tell you what you were coming into?" he asked.

The engineer shook his head "no he just told me to come here look at it tell you about it and help you find a way through some caves."

Peter smiled "ah . . . Typical of the old man, and I suppose he didn't tell you I am a vulcanologist either?"

TJ coloured slightly "er . . . no he didn't tell me that either".

"Well that's okay; he has probably done that so you don't come here with some preconceived ideas of what is expected of you. Did he not tell you either that of all the world sites we are working on at present that is the coldest and most stable we have found?"

Again TJ shook his head "no he told me nothing".

"However you wouldn't think that now given the fact that we have had two tremors since I asked for you. Does that bother you TJ will it worry you to go down into caves that may start to collapse in the event of a tremor?"

TJ stared at him "I don't suppose anyone is willing to risk their lives for a few caves but if it is essential to the human race that I help you find your way through these caves— and I believe from some of the things Dr. Cashman senior has said that it is vital to all humanity—then no it does not worry me. But if this just a matter of searching for lost tribes then I would indeed be wary."

"Tomorrow we will show you what we mean and then you can make up your own mind whether you think it worth it or not" Peter stood up "I think we should get an early night and start this thing fresh, first thing." He turned and left the mess tent.

As he was climbing into bed the phone rang, John Craznow had got his message.

The small plane took off as the sun rose over the desert.

The entire site crew were already hard at clearing the top cave.

Once they had cleared the entry and forced their way into the cave they were able to estimate the damage. As TJ had said there wasn't much really. Some slabs had come down off the roof and a bright carbon light turned upward showed some cracking of the stone which would no doubt would eventually fall. The narrow entrance to the second cave was blocked by a chunk off the ceiling crushing the bones of the two bodies they had left there. With the winches and a lot of hard labour they were able to move away the rubbish and squeeze through to the ledge then down the long sloping ramp that led into the second cave. The lights they had set up were still there, the offset lights came on but of the big lights only two were working the other two had been smashed. They turned them on as they did so Peter heard a gasp from TJ

"My god" he said softly staring at the magnificent wall paintings. "I thought that lot upstairs were beautiful but these . . . ." his words trailed off.

"Now you know why you are sworn to secrecy. These however are nothing compared to what lies below us. Unfortunately you may never see them if the river has its way."

As they neared the bottom of the second cave Merilyn Ross called a halt,

"Peter the water is rising".

They turned the big lights downward and their torches to find the water had risen by at least half a metre.

"This means the river has risen beneath us" Peter said, turning to the engineer he said "is it possible for you to blow the entrance to the artesian basin underwater and give the river more access, and if so will it lower the level?"

The engineer looked at the drawn plans of the cave and river beneath them.

"I don't see why not, I have blown underwater areas before, if I put the charge in just the right place it would widen the access. Once there is more room for the higher volume of water the level should drop quite quickly. Water only goes upwards when it can't go down. If this is pouring into an artesian basin then the opening is probably caused by water wear so it is bound to be narrow. The only problem I see is if I don't get the charge in the right place I could crack the basin and all that stored water will eventually leak out."

"Which brings us to another problem" Peter added "The water goes over a very large drop and is moving at tremendous speed, we have had a net across to stop us from going over with it when we go down there but that may not be in position any more so we are going to have to really harness you up. If you do go over we have to be able to get you back. If you go down into the basin we may never get you back, do you understand that?"

TJ looked thoughtful a frown creasing his forehead.

"I understand Peter and if I go it has to be my decision alone—right?"

Peter nodded "yes I cannot tell you to go nor even ask you to go you have to go and have a look and decide if you will try it or not. If you think it is too dangerous then it can't be done. David is our dive specialist he will go down into the river with you he will tell you how it is running and why and to where and then if you decide to go ahead he will wait for you to come back. Just do me one favour if you do decide to do this no more risks than necessary, no really short charges set the time allowing for all possibilities. Also be aware that we don't know what is below the drop where the water goes over there could be a ledge or another cave none of us has been over to look."

David and TJ suited up. The harness they were fitted with had been doubled and covered the whole body instead of the chest. TJ's harness was reinforced with steel buckles instead of nylon as they had used during the dives. He wore a flat pack for air front and back and a radio helmet. Strapped around him in a waterproof container TJ had arranged two sets of charges each one attached to a thin line which would be anchored once the area was determined. His wetsuit was the type used in the Antarctic dives to protect him from the cold water at a greater depth. All possibilities had been addressed and it was decided to send him down with a dual winch line. He turned and shook hands with everyone,

"I hope this is going to be as we expect I will certainly do my best be assured of that."

He grinned at everyone and with a quick wave slipped into the pool followed by Dave.

The force of the water when they came around the rock into the main river, was unbelievable. If he hadn't been harnessed to a winch which was slowly releasing him he knows he would have been swept away; the pressure on him was enormous. The water was black and impossible to see anything he had no idea where Dave was until he touched something soft and felt a hand grab at him. He hauled himself out onto the water onto a narrow ledge where Dave now stood.

"This ledge was twice as high out of the water so it has risen considerably" Dave told him "we need to cross the net to have a look over the end."

They eased their way across the net feeling the pressure of the water against them knowing they could go to their deaths if they let go.

On the other side the ledge was wide but went nowhere. TJ shone his torch down over the dropped trying to see where the water went to. It was so black and there was no rising mist so the bottom was obviously a long way down. That was not good.

He stared long into the black depths straining his ears for the echo roar of water going through a narrow opening. He stood stock still concentrating all his energy on listening, 'till finally he picked up a slightly different note in the water. A distant swishing sound came to him he concentrated on it trying to locate its origin. He finally decided there must be a gap in the wall below them and the sound was the water slopping into it. This could work in his favour. If he could pick it up albeit not very distinctly, it would not be too far down. He decided to give it a go.

"Dave I am going down there but from the other side this side has an angle and the water is flowing across that angle. The water is higher on the other side and is going over a little slower so let's go back."

They again crossed the net, but before TJ determined where he was going in Dave showed him the opening into the cave. He shone his torch into the opening allowing TJ to catch a glimpse of what lay behind the walls.

"Unfortunately you couldn't fit in with two air packs on but believe me what you are going to do is worth trying. I guarantee you a real look in if this all works."

He grinned at TJ and slapped him on the back "Ready?"

TJ waddled to the edge of the water he called up to the drillers that he was going over the side and to draw up the ropes until he said stop then lower him at a steady pace. He slowly lowered himself over the edge. The water grabbed him and for an instant he was suspended on the crest of the water as the ropes held taut then he went under. At first he was thrown around it was a shocking feeling then as quickly as it started he was against the wall and could only feel a slight push from the water. He slid down the wall unable to see anything but a circle of wall in the light from his helmet. Occasionally he was tossed around and then just as quickly it would all stop. The pressure was tremendous and he was grateful for the two lines that held him. Checking his depth gauge showed he had come down 15 metres, not far but it seemed like he had been there forever. Another two metres and suddenly he was caught in a washing machine he was tossed from side to side the noise was tremendous then he was slammed into a rock. The wind was knocked out of him and he gasped,

"Hey you okay down there?" came faintly through his helmet radio.

He couldn't speak immediately and when he did it came out in a wheeze.

"I'm still here I can't talk right now".

The water boiled around him then he felt as though he was being sucked into a hole but not straight down, sideways. He was close to panic,

"Stop lowering me" he shouted into the microphone.

The harness pulled tight around his body, he could see nothing he felt around looking for the wall it wasn't there, 'it must be another cave' he muttered . . . He switched on the higher powered belt torch and there just in front of him was a swirl of water.

"Oh god" he spoke into his radio his voice strained "the water divides there are two exits and I am right between the two." Then he had a thought.

"Keep a tight hold of me and lower me slowly I am going to look for the dividing ledge when I find it I am going to anchor the charges there and blow the division. That should create one very large exit and if it does then our problems are solved.

The water kept dragging him into the smaller exit he felt panic rising but he knew they had him and if he couldn't fight the panic they would pull him up. As he went further into the small section his knees scraped bottom. He felt around with his hands and found a lip he hung on and yelled triumphantly into the radio,

"I am actually hanging onto the lip now if can just stay here long enough to get these charges anchored we are in with a show. By the way what happens if I blow this cave and it turns out it was all part of it?"

There was silence for a moment then the voice of Peter Cashman came to him,

"We will never know TJ and what we don't know in this case will probably kill us anyway."

There was faint laughter, despite his situation TJ found himself grinning.

"Yeah understood" he said.

Anchoring the charges was just not that easy, he had to bash the line spikes into the rock which in normal circumstances was difficult. He also had to try and stop himself from being sucked into the cave by lying astride the lip and trying to bash the spikes in within the circle of light.

The whole thing seemed to take forever with TJ become irritated at his fumbling. Finally the spikes were in firm enough to wind the lines up so that the charges floated against the lip. If the rock was too solid no amount of charges would shift it. If it didn't collapse the best they could hope for was a large enough crack to create a bigger hole.

"Here goes nothing" he said.

He shone the light onto the clear face of the waterproof container then touched a spot just below it, a set of numbers illuminated in bright red. He continued pressing the button until he had 45 minutes on the clock. 'That should be enough' he told himself.

"Okay haul away" he told them over his radio.

He felt his harness tighten then he began to rise out of the mouth of the cave. Through the washing machine; which was not near as bad going up as it had being lowered into it then slowly hauled up the wall to the ledge in the cave. As he came over the top Dave reached out and grabbed his hands pulling him out of the water.

TJ sank onto the floor he was exhausted his body battered and bruised from the pounding he had taken. He looked at his watch and suddenly jumped up,

"Jesus we have to get out of here, that took longer than I expected."

"What . . . !" yelled Dave "how much time did you set?"

". . er . . . . not as much as I should have we have six minutes to get out."

They both slid into the water yelling into their radios to be pulled up quickly.

They had just come around the rock into the pool when the huge explosion rocked the cave. The water boiled up around them tossing them around like corks. Beside the pool waiting for them to return Peter felt the explosion and the vibration that rattled through the cave, saw the start of a water spout and yelled at everyone to run. The drillers jammed the winches and ran up the ramp to the small ledge above. The water spout boiled up out of the pool going twenty or thirty feet up drenching everyone. One of the winches screamed then unravelled as the electrics blew. Then it was all over, the pool had drained and was now just a long black tunnel. Dangling at the end of the tunnel against the wall was one of the divers. They hauled him up it was Dave and he was unconscious. They dragged his helmet off; Peter felt his pulse and checked his breathing,

"He's okay just knocked out by the concussion, but where is TJ?"

They stared down into the now dry pool. The drillers could not get the winch restarted their only other option was to pull him up by hand. It was slow because they had no idea where the blast had taken him, and if they got caught on rocks they may never get him back. An hour passed before they began to feel a strain on the winch rope,

"I think we have him" one of the drillers said quietly.

"Can you pull him up any faster?" asked Peter.

"I don't think that's wise Doctor we don't know where he went or whether he is caught anywhere. Obviously the river has dropped or the pool would not have drained so I suggest someone else go down and see if they can locate him."

"I'll go"

Peter stared at Mungaway,

"But you hate going down there you know that".

"Yeah true, but I don't have to swim now do I" he grinned at Peter.

They suited him up and hooked him up to the winch used on Dave.

"It won't be easy Mungaway and we don't know what has happened we may have created an even worse situation than before so please no risks."

Mungaway nodded, sliding over the edge of the hole. He kept his feet against the wall to avoid being spun around. When he got to the rocks at the bottom he looked around before stepping forward to where once the river roared. In the light of his torch he could still see the river but in front of him was a narrow slimy ledge. He stepped onto it and asked them to feed out his line slowly in case he fell over the edge. He made his way slowly along the ledge eventually coming to the cave where they had spent so much time. The river still flowed quickly but it was only half of what it was, the blast had obviously opened up a new hole. But where was TJ?

CHAPTER 30

Below the fall of water where once a small cave had worn away to become another opening into a huge artesian basin a huge hole had opened up. The small cave was now dry and on its narrow rocky ledge just above the hole which was once the original floor lay a body in a black wetsuit his belt and helmet lamps were burning, his bright yellow helmet, gloves and fins were illuminated by the brightness in an otherwise coal black environment. There was no movement, no sign of life, the eyes were slightly open and only a small patch of condensation on the face plate in front of his mouth showed that recently the body had been breathing. His radio crackled with static there was no-one to hear it there was only a small cave and a roaring black waterfall.

Mungaway took off his air pack and squeezed into the lower cave. It was very wet inside with water still dripping off the walls but generally there was no damage to the paintings or the symbols. He radioed back.

Peter was pleased at least now they could continue their work, but had he found TJ?

Mungaway told him that the water going over the side was nowhere near what it had been and he wanted to go over and take a look maybe TJ was dangling down there somewhere unconscious.

"No no no! I forbid it Mungaway you will not go down there I can't afford to lose you. Now please return to the surface and we will just keep winching until we get him back." Peter told him.

"But what if he is caught and you can't get him back?" Mungaway asked.

"Well then I am sorry but I forbid you to go after him. He took the risk he set the charges too soon and now he has paid for that mistake. We will eventually get him back but you are not going to do it. Understand!"

"Mungaway shrugged his shoulders 'who's going to stop me' he said to himself.

He pulled on his air pack walked to the end of the ledge where the fall started and lowered himself over the side. Into his radio he said,

"There are some new holes opened up I am going to check them out so just keep feeding me line until I tell you to stop, okay?"

The water pulled at him but instead of struggling against it he allowed it to pull him down quite quickly. The water suddenly bubbled around him and then he was behind it. He switched on his lights and there in front of him was a small rocky outcrop. He crawled onto it slipping and sliding down a small incline. Ahead of him he could see a light in the total blackness. He eased his way over mindful of the huge hole of blackness and roaring water almost beside him. He reached the light and found the body of TJ. He checked him for pulse; it was there but terribly slow and weak.

"I've got him" he said quietly into his radio "I am going to strap us together then you can pull us out of here."

Half an hour later Mungaway and TJ were pulled out of the hole.

CHAPTER 31

Deathly silence reigned over the earth. It had been some time since the last upheavals anywhere. Those who survived in the shattered areas of the world began to breathe easier as they believed the worst was over. Those scientists who had stuck with the Cashman's over the probable cause of unrest on Earth began to have their doubts and were moving more to the other side of the argument; 'it was just one of those things'. Many began to say it was caused by giant sun spots even though the Astronomers could find no evidence of sun spot activity. Whatever they believed they now no longer believed that somewhere out there in the great blackness of space was a wandering star or planet with enough power to create such havoc. If it were really there why did it all stop? And why hadn't they found it by now? All reasonable arguments of course but Alan and Peter Cashman were stubborn in the defence of their belief. The only people who now believed that it was all not over were those who worked feverishly on the drill sites trying to establish the truth of the Earth's history.

The peace continued but the strange quiet was also ever present. No birds were heard and few seen. No animals were seen in the wild—what animals were left. Even the domestic dogs and cats were quiet and tended to sleep away their time in small dark places unwilling to come out unless it was for food. For those who studied the behaviour of their pets and believed in their sixth sense it was unnerving. The long battle for some sort of normalcy began.

In the major cities large buildings were brought down with implosive devices. Badly damaged houses were razed after the last of the owner's contents were salvaged. The splits left in roads paddocks, and highways were simply fenced off there was nothing to be done about them. Damaged bridges were brought down piece by piece. High tension and power lines were brought down and channelled underground. Fire-fighting volunteers were sent into the forests to put out the last of the fires and begin planting new trees. Those areas totally denuded of all life and buildings were left untouched to allow nature to begin regenerating. No-one really knew where to begin. Huge tent cities sprang up furnished by the leftovers, anything that could be scrounged. Government agencies opened food kitchens; those without money ate free those with something donated what they could. Banks and other money agencies unable to access their holdings for their depositors; opened their vaults where possible. Those who lived in the areas where the underground towns had been built in the event of a nuclear war;were offered them in an effort to begin again. Some underground chambers had collapsed during the 'quakes, people sheltering there had been trapped; many died. Before anything else armies of volunteers went in and cleaned them out. All bodies were burnt in an effort to protect their water supply and contain outbreaks of disease. In many parts of the world winter had set in with a vengeance. The sky though clearing on occasions remained a dirty murky grey most of the time caused by the smoke and ash from the volcanoes. Storms of great intensity still raced around the Earth, with a two fold result. Fires were put out and drinking water replaced; landslides and mud slides were still common place in the mountainous areas of the world. Yet the world remained still. Many referred to this period of over twelve months as the great healing period. The Cashman's and those who stood firm in their support of them believed it was simply the calm before the storm. Peter didn't believe they had seen the worst of it he believed that what was coming was going to be far worse than anyone ever imagined. Bad enough he believed, to literally tear Earth apart.

CHAPTER 32

The drill site in Italy was no more; the day John Craznow flew to Australia the entire drill site was crushed under tons of rock as a huge land slide brought down a large part of the mountain on top of them. Ramono Parvon, making final arrangements to leave for Australia was held up when a section of the road collapsed during a rain storm. Rather than find another way through they opted to stay in camp for another night and go out by Helicopter the next day. The next day was too late, at 2am the side of the mountain roared down on their camp; there were no survivors. The drill site on the edge of the Great Sandy Desert would know nothing of this until Peter Cashman sent a message to their contacts at the small town of Chavenna requesting information when Ramono Parvon did not arrive. A fly over by the Helicopter would provide the only answer.

John Craznow arrived at the camp in Western Australia to be greeted by a beaming Peter Cashman, and Merilyn Ross. He shook hands with Peter and kissed Merilyn lightly on the cheek.

"Good to be back" he said smiling at Merilyn.

Peter saw the colour darken Merilyn's face and for an instant this cool clever oh so business like woman, was almost shy. He smiled to he was glad for them if there was a spark there. Given the way the world was they all had to snatch at happiness when it presented itself. Tomorrow none of them might be here. For the return journey to Broome they sent Dave into the hospital for a thorough check up. The evening before the Flying Doctor had picked up TJ for a flight to Perth. He had remained unconscious, sustaining broken ribs, fractured arm and concussion. Dave had opted to go to Broome after the Doctor had checked him over and declared bed rest would get him back on his feet.

The remainder of the day was spent bringing John Craznow up to scratch and getting him down into the lower cave with the view of finding a way through the roof. Outside of their damaged engineer John was the only one with the expertise to do this. He marvelled at the wall paintings and in an hour of examining the paintings and symbols had tied at least two sets together in reference to the same thing; the great Volcano god and his love for a beautiful white star.

Back in Peter's tent they sipped coffee and discussed the probabilities of finding the answers they sought.

"Somewhere John there is a key to these hieroglyphics that we have not found yet. You can see for yourself that some sets of symbols refer to the same thing but we cannot work out what the rest mean. We simply cannot crack the code. It's like nothing I have ever seen before. Yet someone cracked the code or the Book of Vulcan would not exist." Peter told him.

"But how do you know that the Book of Vulcan is right Peter, how do you know the person who transcribed all this didn't just transcribe it as he saw it. Maybe he couldn't crack it either and just wrote it as he thought it should be."

Peter pulled at his bottom lip,

"Something tells me that the author transcribed these hieroglyphics, call it a gut feeling call it what you like, you know yourself, when something feels right you just know it is!

John nodded "what about the others how do they feel about it?"

"Oh they agree, they are finding changes in the symbols sets daily. We have discovered that some sets are exactly the same as others but they have a dot or a curl and we also believe that the colour of the dot or the curl determines who or what it is talking about. Just when we think we have got a handle on where the story is going it all changes colour, sometimes a slight shape change, just like shorthand really."

The two men stared at each other; Peter was the first to speak.

"What did I just say?"

"Just like shorthand" John told him.

Suddenly they were both up and running towards the caves. They didn't speak as the strapped on harness and abseiled down the black hole that was once a pool.

In the cave they found Mungaway sitting cross-legged staring at the wall his eyes were fixed and open, he did not move a muscle even when they spoke to him. Slowly he got to his feet,

"Peter I think I have the answer".

"I think John and I have arrived at the same conclusion Mungaway"

Mungaway continued,

"These people had neither the time nor the space to write everything. They were probably dying from malnutrition and knew that they would not get it all down" he paused.

"Go on" Peter urged him.

"I think what they did do, was write periods of their history in a sort of shortened version, like ah . . ."

"Like shorthand Mungaway"

"Yes, yes that's it like shorthand."

"John and I have just come to the same conclusion. Great minds think alike."

Mungaway continued,

"Each set of symbols represents a major story, we need to dissect the sets piece by piece combine those pieces with the drawings near them and that should give us the answers. I know it sounds simplistic Peter but I believe I am right. These people lived in these caves for a very long time there is no way that these walls cover a very long time unless they were doubled up or like the Egyptians they had a way of putting whole sections of history into just a very small space. There have been other places on Earth found over the years where other tribes did this, but none as complex as these. They must have been very intelligent people, the ancestors of all things and considered the beginnings of man."

"So you consider" John said "these people were an early race, or should I say an earlier race than those which we have in our recorded history. If so it bears out that those who believed we were not the first race of man on Earth were right"

"This is exactly the premise we have been working on the whole time. We were not just looking for cold stable areas John we were looking for the remains of people who lived long before the ice age or ice ages if you like. People who could make the story of the Book of Vulcan either a truth or a lie" said Peter.

"When your father first brought this up to me I believed it was an assumption a maybe a perhaps, not a definite this is what we think scenario. If I had known this when we started looking I could have looked so much further gone that much deeper."

"Yes I suppose you could have John," Peter told him "but what would you have told the others? That you were looking for one of the first races on Earth? It was enough in Italy that they found bones of a long dead race that no-one could tie to any other. I could not tell them that was the only aim we had, we had to protect the secrecy of what we were doing."

"So we were to believe we were working only on finding a cold stable place where people could survive the catastrophic problems being experienced."

"Well yes that is what you were supposed to believe" said Peter "you and of course all the other drill sites we have set up. At the time I did not know you well enough to take you into confidence on the whole project, now perhaps you should read what we have on the Book of Vulcan. It will really make more sense to you to read what is written and then maybe you will understand what we are all up against. It has always been our desire to find a place to try to save humanity but before we could find such places John we had to find out if any of the last race survived a catastrophe, a catastrophe such as we have not seen yet and many of our fellow scientists do not believe in. I am afraid my father and I and our colleagues are losing credibility quite quickly. People need proof to make them understand if you can't show them black and white they just won't believe it."

"Yes I can understand why. Even as I say that I don't really understand any of it. I would appreciate being able to read the book because all I know about it is it supposed to be some sort of future prophecy. Is that right?"

Mungaway and Peter exchanged looks,

"This" Peter waved his hand around the walls "is the Book of Vulcan in its purest form this is what it was based on. If it is prophetic as it is supposed to be then we must find out how to crack the hieroglyphics to fill in the gaps in the book. We have to learn to read those paintings and in the right order so that we know what these people went through. If we do this we may find a way to survive, if it is a prophecy and we don't understand it; we are probably all doomed to die."

John stared at the paintings softly illuminated by a few small lamps. 'What difference would it make?' he asked of himself 'what if we do find the answers does that mean we will survive? Or does it just mean that we know how we are going to die and when'

"Look I know what you're thinking John and I don't have all the answers either, I just know that if we can find out what this all means it could buy the human race some time. Perhaps enough time to create safe havens so that maybe some will survive. That is all we are trying to do."

"But if they didn't survive Peter what is the use of all this?"

"We have more technology; we are better equipped to deal with this sort of thing. We have better food systems, better communications systems, we still have our satellites there is nothing to say some of them won't survive. We have specialist clothing and breathing equipment, drugs and antibiotics and specially engineered seeds for crop restoration, tree regrowth. We have the fertilized eggs of just about every living creature on earth. We have the ability to restore from DNA samples. If we get enough time we can set up workshops in stable safe areas. We may not have all the comforts of home and there maybe too many people to make it very comfortable, but if we can survive John we can start anew. It has to be worth the effort we have to try."

John nodded "You're right of course, these caves obviously were safe and there must be others systems like them, so why didn't they survive down here?"

"They starved to death" Mungaway told him "they didn't die from disease or toxic fumes or anything else they simply could not store enough food to keep them all alive"

"Well I suggest we get to work in one big hurry then, time is wasting and if what you say is right then we may not have very much of that" John walked to the wall and lightly touched one of the symbols "if only you could speak" he told it.

"They do John" Mungaway told him "we just can't understand their language yet."

Two days after John Craznow arrived Peter was still trying to raise the drill site in Italy. He had heard nothing from Ramono Parvon and did not know how to contact him. On the third day he reached the small town of Chavenna where their guide and contact for the project was staying. Within hours of leaving a message for him he had called Peter back from Milan. He had left the area after the problems started and had not returned and would not if all the reports were true.

". . . . say again" Peter frowned and concentrated on the faint voice on the other end of the line "an accident? What kind of an accident?"

The line hummed and went dead,

"We are having major problems getting through to Italy; Gianni tells me there was some sort of accident and cannot go back into the region unless he knows it's safe. The road went out and that held up Ramono, but he has heard nothing from any of them since. I will call the Helicopter base in Bologna and have them send someone up and take a look" he stared at the map "I hope they are alright there hasn't been any seismic activity in the area in fact the whole world has been quiet."

Merilyn Ross touched his arm lightly "I am sure it will be alright Peter it's probably just heavy rain. Truth is Ramono is probably on his way to Australia as we speak."

That night as they sat around the now cleared dining table talking of the days' events and the work they would do the next day, Peter received a call on the satellite 'phone.

"Yes, yes," he frowned deeply then his face seemed to pale beneath his tan, "oh . . . , thank you for calling".

Peter replaced the receiver slowly.

"They're all dead" he said slowly "Ramono and the entire crew, gone. It appears there was a rock slide and it brought down a huge portion of the side of the mountain and it all landed on the drill site. It was early hours of the morning they think because nearby villages heard a roaring sound. The only one to survive is our guide from Chavenna he couldn't go back to the site because the road collapsed. It was thought that was why Ramono didn't make it out; poor devil must have waited for a chopper."

No-one spoke it was a blow to lose such valuable and experienced people. John Craznow looked stunned; he had worked beside Ramono since day one and would still have been there with him if the site in Bulgaria had not found some bone fragments in the core drills. He was excited and had flown out immediately by Helicopter. He would have returned to the site had he not received the message from Peter Cashman to come back to Australia.

The next morning as the sun rose over the desert and the early light turned to glorious gold, seven people stood in a group their hands clasped as Peter Cashman recited a small prayer for the dead in Italy. They bowed their heads and remained silent for one minute.

In front of them a soft slab of sandstone was etched with the date of the disaster in Italy and on the rock was taped a single silk rose supplied by Merilyn.

As their minute of silence ended, Peter spoke, his voice sounded older weary,

"God I hope this was all worth it."

Slowly they walked back to the dining tent for breakfast. Each busy with his or her own thoughts.

Little was said over breakfast and as each finished they headed for the caves to start the days work. So many people were dying they had to hurry now it seemed like time was running out for all of them.

CHAPTER 33

'The Lord of the Air and Wind made clouds and caused rain to fall washing clean the earth. The Lord of the Earth then made all manner of things grow.'

A year of peace and quiet followed. No major eruptions, even some of the smaller volcanoes went quiet altogether. No 'quakes, but a lot of rain and still the huge storms played around the Earth in the form of Tornadoes and Hurricanes in the northern hemisphere and Cyclones in the southern hemisphere. The only advantage of these killer storms was that they cleared the skies of the greyness that had hung over many parts of the world. They also washed the buildings—what was left after they passed through—clean, and the decimated forests again looked green instead of black.

Many areas that had been denuded by Tsunamis or earthquakes began to show a flush of green. Mother Nature was the most amazing creature, her ability to continue life in all manner of things was nothing short of miraculous. Even the birds began re-appearing. Domestic animals left their hiding places and some sort of normalcy began to return to the survivors.

Although this year would be known as the healing year for many it was a year of fear.

Peter Cashman and his crew, his father Dr. Alan Cashman and his colleagues now based in Perth, were worried. Why had it all stopped? This did not bear out their theory of a wandering star or planet wreaking havoc across the universe! If it were so then everything would have continued and gotten progressively worse. If they had looked silly for espousing their views before they were now beginning to look down right ridiculous. Those who had gone along with their ideas, some only half heartedly, were beginning to laugh and call them names; charlatans, fear mongers, crazy! There was even talk of the scientific community asking the government to rescind the funding going to the Cashman's, for research. Alan Cashman was furious; he was highly respected in the scientific community around the world. He was one of the most sought after seismologists and was renowned for knowing what would happen next. His appointment book was booked all the way for several years.

Alan Cashman strode up and down the laboratory he was so angry he couldn't speak.

After some time he stopped pacing and stared at those gathered around him watching in silence. They were not used to their leader who was normally reserved and self assured, losing his cool. They were amazed when he had exploded after opening a letter from the funding committee.

". . . . therefore Dr. Cashman" it read "we believe that unless you can substantiate the use of research funding presently granted to you while the Earth has been experiencing seismic and volcanic disruption, then we will have no option but to withdraw the remaining three years funding or make it available for other research if you submit information for same."

When he found the words Dr. Alan Cashman drew a deep breath,

"I am sorry people, I am really sorry, but if they take away our funding then I will fund it personally. I will write and tell them that if I have to do that and if the outcome proves what we have been working on is correct then they will have to look after themselves. As a private fund investor I will place all these people and their respective families first on the list of those to be saved. The government can go hang. The rest of the people will be told via our own web site and other forms of communication including a privately funded radio network which several colleagues and I have had use of for some time. I know this is hard on you and I know you are finding it all difficult to believe but believe you must. I would not be doing this if I did not believe myself that we are right. My son and his crew plus several other sites around the world are working very hard to prove that we are facing an Armageddon. I need you to have faith and trust in what we are doing. I realize you are not seeing much for your hard work but you will. I must also tell you this I believe this lull is just that; a lull. Don't allow yourselves to become complacent and think it's over because it isn't; not by a long shot. Truth to tell it is just beginning; if I and others like me are right, it will get much worse and we will be facing a universal final solution. If any of you want to believe I am crazy and there is nothing to be concerned about, that what we have been experiencing was just 'one of those things'! then you have my blessing to go. I will pay you what you are owed and you will be given the best references to find further work."

He stared at his crew, they were tired none of them were getting more than four or five hours sleep a day. Meals were haphazard and often skipped in favour of sleep. Families were rarely seen. He knew they were giving their all to his project but so was everyone else, they were not doing an 'everyday job' here they were trying to save the world.

"Well?" he lifted an eyebrow and stared at all of them "anyone?"

The head of his anthropology team stepped forward,

"Dr. Cashman you have my loyalty, I would just like to see a bit more of my family".

"Then bring them into the complex and install them in the apartments we have enough of them not in use. We can bring in teachers for the kids or your wives can take them to school each day it's up to you. If this is the only stumbling block that any of you have then don't hesitate, whatever you need to remain here; you can have; just name it."

One by one they stepped forward and shook his hand their loyalty was unanimous.

On the edge of the Great Sandy Desert Peter Cashman was also tired. They had been working night and day to try and establish a common link in the hieroglyphics. Just as they managed to work out a whole section and began to weave the threads of the story together they would a find a new symbol introduced into a particular phrase which meant that the entire phrase meant something entirely different. No-one had taken a break since long before John Craznow had arrived and tempers were beginning to fray. Merilyn Ross had been on site for over two years and had not had a break at all. She was becoming irritable and unsociable; the long hours in darkness had taken their toll on her. Many days she was in the caves before sunrise and did not emerge until after sunset. For an entire month she did not see the sun. After one evening of arguments and constant bickering the normally quiet peacemaker of the group, blew up!

"That's it" she screamed at them all "I have had it, you keep going over the same ground, when is someone going to come up with something new that we can discuss. It's not as if we all agree. Isn't it time that someone else stood up and told Peter and Mungaway they are not always bloody well right!"

With that she stormed out of the tent grabbing a bottle of red wine as she went.

John Craznow stood up excused himself and went after her; he found her sitting on the small hill overlooking the desert. He quietly sat down beside her saying nothing. She was sobbing and her shoulders shook under the thin cloth of her shirt. As the sobs subsided she poured wine into a foam cup and gulped it down offering him the bottle. He took it and without a word took a swig.

After she had calmed down he put his arm around her shoulders,

"Come to Broome with me Merry, let's just dump the work for a week or so and go and have some fun while we have the chance."

Merilyn didn't speak she didn't trust herself to, she nodded pouring more wine.

John approached Peter the next morning about going to Broome for a while.

"By all means go" Peter told him enthusiastically "you have earned it particularly Merilyn she has worked so hard. In fact I think everyone should take a break, I am going to send Mungaway back to his family for a fortnight, the cook needs some time off and the drillers can go and whoop it up somewhere. I myself am going down to Perth to see my father and try and persuade him to meet my mother in Sydney for a family gathering with my sister and brother. We haven't been together for too long" he smiled and patted John on the arm "enjoy your time together".

That afternoon John and Merilyn flew to Broome. By 4pm they were installed in a beautiful suite overlooking the Indian Ocean in the 'Blue Indian Resort'. Broome had remained untouched by the tsunamis, they had come over the coast further south. The cyclones had also pretty much left the town alone with only an occasional blow and a lot of rain. The town was jumping with people especially those who believed that the cities would go therefore the further up they were the less likely they were to be hurt. True, Broome was not shaky, but it was in the cyclone path and it did have an enormous tidal change from zero to 10 meters of water in minutes. That could be devastating in the event of a tsunami. John went out shopping while Merilyn showered and changed for dinner. He booked them into a small seafood restaurant for dinner and managed to pick her a single rosebud from a garden he passed. At the Ocean Pearl he bought her a stunning necklace with a gold clasp holding two diamonds. 'Too much'? He thought 'nah she deserves it!'

Merilyn had also done a spot of shopping while he was gone and had bought herself a black dress short and strapless with a tiny lace jacket. She had lost so much weight since being on the desert and though she had spent much time in the caves her skin was a deep gold. When dressed she stood in front of the long mirror, 'hmm not bad' she told herself. Merilyn was turning thirty three and despaired of ever getting married, her job was not the type of job where it was easy to meet eligible single men; John Craznow was the first such male she had met in years. Presuming of course he was eligible she had no idea, he may have had a wife tucked away somewhere she had not asked and he had not volunteered, what's more she didn't care. She heard him come through the door letting it slam as he walked in. He didn't go to the bedroom but went straight through to the ensuite from the other door. She was glad she didn't want him to see her yet. As soon as the water was turned on she finished her makeup and headed out to the lounge. She poured herself a cold glass of champagne turned off the overhead lights and turned on all the lamps. Even though she knew she was attractive Merilyn wanted as much help as she could get. Apart from her black frock and lace jacket she wore only tiny diamond earrings. Her red gold hair was swept up off her face and neck and held with a diamante clasp. She had poured on the skin lotion to add shine and softness to her arms, legs and shoulders. Then glass in hand she waited. About twenty minutes later John Craznow emerged from the bedroom he was classically dressed in grey pants soft cream silk shirt (just bought) and a navy Reefer jacket. As he came through the door he saw her and his eyes widened.

"Merilyn is that you?" he smiled

She casually handed him a glass of champagne,

"Yes John is that really you?"

They burst out laughing.

"You are stunning" he told her "I never imagined you out of your shorts or jeans and shirts and in a little black dress my god girl you are beautiful".

He reached into his pocket withdrawing a beautiful blue box; he placed the rosebud on it and handed it to her.

"For you" he said.

She smelled the sweet perfume of the rose it was the first time she had smelled anything so sweet in such a very long time. She brushed the soft velvet petals over her lips a gesture that did not get missed by John.

She opened the box and was stunned by the glorious string of pearls with their gold clasp and tiny diamonds flashing in the light.

He took them from the box and put them around her throat clasping them in the front.

"They look wonderful with your earrings" he told her.

She walked to the wall mirror, they were beautiful and yes they did match her earrings.

He took the now empty glass from her hand,

"This is going to a wonderful evening, come let's go to dinner, I want to show you off."

He opened the door for her and laughed at the appreciative whistle he heard as they crossed the outside paving to the car he had ordered.

CHAPTER 34

Peter Cashman flew to Sydney with his father three days after the camp had been temporarily closed. They were meeting his mother, sister and brother at the apartment before going on to a family dinner with other relatives. It was time they had a family reunion. Life had been so hard for all of them since the Earth's problems began. Fortunately all had survived so far without so much as a scratch.

During the flight they discussed the reasons behind the sudden quiet around the Earth.

"I suppose" said Peter "that the object has moved into another stage of its wanderings and gone behind a large cluster or similar and that in turn is shielding this part of the universe from the effects!"

"Or perhaps there is no object Peter, perhaps it is just the time for the Earth to begin to disintegrate. Or maybe we have just outlived our time on Earth; we have been top dogs for a long time you know. We cannot remain so forever it just doesn't happen."

"Disintegrate? Earth? No way that won't happen, the Earth is relatively stable the centre is cooling there is no reason for any of this to be happening as a normal process. I thought you of all people would come up with something better than that Dad! What has happened have you lost your dedication are you beyond doing this job?"

Alan Cashman could hear the pain and anger in his son's voice; he knew he didn't really believe what he was saying yet what else was there to believe. All their work for the past three years had come to nothing! They had been ridiculed, their funding withdrawn, some of their supporters had moved on because they no longer believed. It pained him to think that his son was disappointed in him, but right now with the most recent astronomers report in his brief case and the latest seismic activity figures; it really looked like there was nothing!

He patted Peter's arm,

"No Peter I have not lost my dedication but I think you should read these reports then make a decision for yourself based on the facts that we have."

He handed his son the reports.

Peters faced was flushed with anger, it was he who had not believed The book of Vulcan to be any more than a story, it was his father who had given him reason to believe it could be a chronicle. Even if it didn't happen in their life time did that mean it wasn't so?

He took the reports, without a word he read them all thoroughly before throwing them back into his father's lap.

"So? What does that all mean. The astronomers are only saying they can't find a large object capable of having this effect upon the Earth. Note father they said a large object. Does that mean that any object they have found is not capable of having this effect upon the Earth? Does it also mean that there never was an object capable of the same? Do they say anything about any object out there? No! And do you know why?Because they don't know what they are looking at!"

Alan sighed,

"That could be so we don't even know ourselves Peter."

"Look Dad in those paintings the object in the sky was white, huge. As the tribe moved further down into the caves the object became larger and more dominant, doesn't that tell you something?"

Alan nodded, "Yes it means that it was coming closer."

"Right! Now we have to figure out how long they recorded the journey before dying. Did they actually only record the last bit before the object left that orbit or was it as it came into the Earth's orbit. If it was moving at a rapid pace it could have had an horrendous effect on the Earth anywhere between a few years and a million years depending on its speed. If they did not record anything prior to seeing the object other than the every day things and then suddenly they started recording it's arrival, couldn't that mean that it came swiftly did much damage then left as swiftly?"

Alan pulled at his lip a gesture shared by both father and son when in deep thought.

"So you are saying that any object in the Universe within a reasonable neighbourhood could cause this damage, if it were big enough, without being seen until it actually comes zooming into our path or behind us. Then assuming it is moving at great speed, and your argument is based on the size of it in the drawings, it does the damage and moves on. The damage is the changes of the continental structures, the oceans, and the various life on Earth. If this were so Peter then you have your reason for evolution. It would kill off what could not survive and force evolution of those that did, whether it be man or beast."

Alan's voice became animated Peter detected the excitement and smiled.

"Yes Dad, which means we don't have to die, not all of us anyway but we do have to continue to find a way to survive. There is something out there whether it can be seen or not and it will suddenly appear one day and it will all be too late. Assuming that the speed is great the time of its arrival and departure should be no more than a few weeks perhaps months at the most. Then we will have to put up with the after effects as it moves away. They will diminish quickly though as they will probably be shielded by other celestial bodies."

"Peter what if it is in front of us and not behind us?"

"Then we stand to lose our satellites at least, especially if it has gotten any bigger than it was; which by the way, is quite on the cards. We may collide or worse, go out of orbit. We are only ninety three million miles from the sun if that happened we would fall into the sun and that would be that. But we would be all dead long before that happened. Either way it would be quick."

Alan stared at his son, "so matter-of-fact about it all Peter aren't you afraid?"

Peter nodded, "Yes I am afraid, but not of dying Dad I am afraid of living I am afraid of being a survivor. What if I survived in a place on my own, how could I live knowing everyone else had died, yet I would have to just in case there is someone else out there who also survived. Don't you think that is frightening?"

His father nodded, "yes Peter it's the old saying 'there are far worse things than dying'.

They fell silent each closeted within his own thoughts.

The 'plane landed at Sydney amidst a rain storm that appeared to be a curtain. There was no wind or storm just solid steady drumming rain.

Barbara Cashman, wife of Alan mother of three met them at the airport and guided them out through to the car-park where she had Alan's car and driver take them to their apartment.

"Peter it has been so long" she slipped her arm through his and squeezed it "I have been so looking forward to this reunion I was hoping we wouldn't have any . . . you know . . . . problems?"

Peter laughed, "No just for you I asked Vulcan for some peace and he granted it."

They arrived at the apartment as the rain stopped. Instantly the sky became that glorious blue that Australia knows so well. The clouds drifted off and the sun poured down onto the streets turning the water to steam. Eddies of almost ethereal mist flowed around the cooler spots on the footpaths and roads. The air smelled clean and fresh and the buildings took on an air of being freshly painted.

"How long are you with us?" Barbara asked of her son.

"About a week, then back to Perth to catch up with some old friends and enjoy some R&R with them, then back to the desert unless the people in Perth can come up with anything that will keep me there" he smiled at her.

"Are you going to tell me about Vulcan?"

Peter glanced at his father,

"Has Dad not mentioned this to you?"

She shook her head, "not often and as usual he tells me nothing, he just says 'nothing to worry about my love when I know you will know' of course he lies though Peter."

They all laughed. Peter patted her hand,

"When I know you will know mother."

She sighed, "Like father like son."

His week in Sydney was great. He spent a lot of time with his Geologist brother but discussing work was banned by the wives and the husband of his sister.

His sister Emma, a scientific Photographer, had brought her husband and daughter Carli. His brother Damien had brought his wife and their three children, India, Cassidie and son Daniel.

Peter marvelled at how the children had grown, not surprising though, since he hadn't seen any of them for three years. He had photos of course but it didn't really do them justice.

"And when are you going to settle down?" his brother asked him.

"Who would want me" Peter pulled a face "I am always stuck in a lab or remote places, I am never happy unless everything is blowing up in my face, what sort of a husband would I make? Besides I don't know any lovely women and the only one I have met recently just went off to Broome with my cave specialist."

"Hmm slow as usual" his sister chimed in with a laugh.

"I saw Jenna the other day Peter, she was just strolling along the Mall in Adelaide" his brother told him.

"Adelaide? I wonder what she is doing there she was supposed to be based in Perth now."

"Well she told me that Adelaide was getting quite a few shakes and she had been transferred there from Perth because someone had gotten hurt and they were short one."

"Yes well Adelaide did cop it for quite a while but it has always been a bit that way."

"Anyway she also got a promotion so she is now heading the graphs section of the S.A. Seismology unit. It's quite a step up for a woman but then again she is very smart. She is not doing field work anymore she now sits in her office and tells everybody else what to do."

"I can't quite see her doing that" Peter said "she always loved the field work, too much really. We broke up because we just never saw each other. Three weeks a year and an occasional weekend is no way to conduct a love affair. I am constantly surprised we lasted four years."

They discussed everything that week, from the sunrises on the desert to the price of food 'these days' they laughed a lot, ate a lot drank much good wine and told some awful jokes but the time went by so quickly. Soon Peter was back at the airport en route to Perth to catch up with his friends before returning to the Great Sandy. He kissed his mother goodbye holding her tightly; he hugged his father brother sister, nieces and nephew, and shook hands with his brother-in-law.

"I'll call you all soon, and don't worry about anything we will get through this and more" he waved to them before disappearing into the 'plane.

Back in Perth he was met at the airport by Mungaway.

"Good to see you looking so well Peter" he told him.

"Yes it was a wonderful week catching up with everyone."

"We have some news Peter" Mungaway told him "but I don't know whether it is good news or bad news."

"Tell me Mungaway what is it?"

"Can you wait 'till we get home? My wife picked up the news from University and I'd rather her tell you in her own words it will sound better than second hand."

They arrived at the beautiful Colonial home just a stone's throw from the beach at Point Filer just below Mandurah. Mungaway and his wife had bought the property as a holiday destination when the children were very small and the land very cheap. As the children had grown Mungaway had begun building the house. Slowly the old shed was converted to a flat for visitors and the Colonial home with its four side wrap verandah was built. Mungaway and three brothers with the help of a builder friend slowly over three years block by sandstone block, had laboured until it was complete. Only the roof was done by a full tradesman. The house was fitted painted and serviced by Mungaway subcontracting the work and acting as labourer. The whole time, he worked and studied for his degree. The house was a wonderfully warm and friendly environment that his whole family adored. Besides the separate flat, it boasted five bedrooms, three bathrooms with a separate shower outside for the pool and sea swimmers. His wife commuted daily to the University unless kept late at night then she would stay overnight in their small unit in Perth city. Peter loved the house, he loved it's size the way it was furnished with casual comfort, and a wonderful housekeeper who had been with them since the children started going to school; a cousin of Mungaway's.

He settled into his bedroom then strolled out in shorts and T-shirt to be greeted by Linda, Mungaway's wife and a long cold Vodka and Cranberry juice, a household favourite.

"Now Linda" Peter said as he settled into a large cushioned wicker chair overlooking the sea "what news have you that my friend refuses to divulge."

She glanced almost nervously at Mungaway before speaking.

"I . . . er overheard something that I suppose I should not have. I was going past the outer chamber of the observatory when I heard a colleague mention that they had been picking up an object in the night sky. They were excited because it didn't seem to be on any of the comet lists and they, this person, were going to request that it be named after him and the person who was with him. I went to another colleague and casually asked if he had seen the object in the sky and what did he think of it. He positively froze Peter, his face went white, and then he asked me how I knew. I told him a lie; I told him I had also seen it during a routine check. That I had become interested in Astronomy since everything started happening and had noticed it two night's previously. He believed me and said that it was assumed to be an unnamed comet but to keep it to myself because people were worried about everything that had been happening. The following night I went to the observatory after hours and the caretaker and I had a bit of a chat, he even let me use the telescope. There it was just where it had been the night before but a degree further south. I watched it for ages it wasn't white but it has a hazy look about it." Linda sipped her drink and stared out across the Indian Ocean, no-one spoke.

Peter sat quite still digesting Linda's news. At last he and his father were vindicated. However, if the University Observatory could pick up this object, why didn't the big observatories pick it up? Answer—they had, the Astronomers were lying!

'Guaranteed' thought Peter 'that they had been told not to divulge the information to the Cashman's because it just might prove they had been right for a long time.'

"Linda may I use your 'phone please" Peter asked.

She indicated the study to him, "go ahead".

Peter rang his father in Sydney, it was 9pm there and his parents were readying for bed as he called.

He told his father about the object and heard just what he expected—nothing!

He knew his father would be fuming silently so as not to worry his mother.

Then he spoke,

"I'll go to Canberra tomorrow Peter someone owes me some answers and they had better have them ready. Did they really think I would not find out? I will call you tomorrow night will you be at Mungaway's house?"

Peter answered in the affirmative and after a further short conversation replaced the receiver.

He returned to the sitting room overlooking the Indian Ocean,

"My father is livid, not that I can blame him. He goes to Canberra tomorrow. But please don't let this spoil our week together because when we get back up north we are going to be flat out. There are so many things new to tell you all and much to do."

He lifted his glass in a silent toast the others did likewise then they polished off their drinks.

CHAPTER 35

One week later Peter and Mungaway flew back to Broome. There they met up with a radiant Merilyn Ross and her soon to be husband according to the rather large rock she was sporting on her left hand. Peter and Mungaway congratulated them, and made sure they took a case of Champagne with them when they flew out. There were no discussions on the 'plane there would be enough of that when they got back to the campsite.

The small plane landed and Peter noted with satisfaction the drillers had returned and were setting up equipment. The cook had also returned the dining tent was open for business. Another arrival was Dave their scuba instructor, looking a little worse for wear.

Peter hailed him,

"What brings you back here?"

"I wanted to see you before I went back to Perth" he answered.

Peter and Dave shook hands.

"How are you?" Peter asked.

"Yeah pretty good, a bit tired but nothing that a holiday won't fix. I only got out of hospital this morning. I had concussion as you know, and a couple of fractures that we didn't know about, one across the top of my shoulder blade and one through the wrist. Anyway everything's okay now and I am looking forward to catching up with my family. TJ's been in a pretty bad state he was in a coma up until a week ago."

"Yes we have been keeping tabs on him. My father arranged for a very good neurosurgeon for him so we can only hope for a full recovery. I think it will be a long time though before he works again. My father has arranged for the Department to pay his salary as per usual plus all his medical bills and a one off payment to his wife for expenses. It's is the least we can do under the circumstances. As for you Dave you will also be paid in full and your position at the centre in Perth is quite safe until you are back on your feet and able to go back to work."

"Thanks Peter I appreciate it. I guess now that the pool is dry you won't be needing me here anymore will you?"

"No Dave I think if there is any further swimming to be done we can manage it by ourselves. Mungaway has been able to tell us exactly what happened down there. The explosives worked very well creating a huge hole and sending the water down in one direction. Of course that caused the river to drop and we are now able to come and go to the cave as and when we like. Of course we still have to abseil down the hole but it is a whole lot easier than going down in scuba gear. Eventually we hope to be able to find another way down but when that will be is anyone's guess."

"So what happens now? The way things are I mean it's all quiet isn't it does that mean it's all over?" Dave asked

Peter shook his head,

"I don't know what to tell you Dave I know you are married to a promise of silence but we have things happening now that I don't think I can go into, suffice to say, no I don't think it's over I think it's just beginning. Whatever we have experienced up until now is just a taste of what I believe is coming. I wish I could tell you something different but I can't. I'd rather you be prepared. Take your family somewhere safe Dave set up something for yourselves food and equipment wise that will keep you going for years. Don't take no for an answer and don't listen to anyone else I guarantee you I am right. Even if doesn't happen in our life time it will happen so if not yourself think of your family and their families. If you don't do it now you may as well not do it at all because when the next wave of unrest starts and that shouldn't be too far away, it will be very bad."

"I am listening to you Peter and I will do it. I have great faith in both you and your father. I just don't know how I am going to convince my family."

"Find a way Dave, just find a way or no-one will survive" Peter shook his hand "thanks for everything you did here I hope it goes well for you."

Dave waved at the others as he climbed back onto the plane. It took off climbing steadily into the wide blue. He looked at the coloured land flowing beneath, catching the occasional sparkle as sun caught water, the magnificent blue dome above them, it was wrong so very wrong that this magnificent planet could die so easily. He was sure there would never be another one like it. For all the years scientists sent unmanned space craft to the nearby planetary systems they had never found another one like Earth. He felt like crying it was so unfair. He would do everything he could to survive what was coming and he believed it was coming, he saw enough in the caves and heard enough from those around him to make him believe it was just a matter of time. His family would just have to humour him.

CHAPTER 36

Back at the campsite congratulations were being heaped on Merilyn and John. Peter had never seen her look so happy.

"See" he told her "what a holiday in Broome can do for you!"

Everyone laughed.

They spent the rest of the day unpacking sorting paper work and helping the cook get his kitchen organised again. Once done cook made one of his roast dinners they all loved.

They had wine and champagne for the toast to the happy couple. Cook made a magnificent Pavlova in celebration then joined them all in eating it and toasting.

They chatted and told jokes until quite late. A new moon rose over the desert, Peter glass in hand walked over to the hill to watch it, surely outside of sunrise it must be the most magnificent sight in the world. He could hear the laughter floating across the cool night air. He was so pleased for Merilyn and John he was glad that they could share a happiness that may well be all too brief. He cleared his mind and just gazed at the spectacle of the rising moon, the ever quiet Mungaway slid onto the sand beside him with a bottle. He replenished their glasses then lifted them high in a silent toast to the new moon.

"May it not be the last time we see you" intoned Mungaway.

"Why do you say that Mungaway?" Peter asked.

"I feel something coming Peter I feel it inside me way down deep where my grandfather told me to look for things that would go wrong. It's like a vibration that works its way up my spine. I simply can't explain it in any other way you would have to be aboriginal to understand."

"Sometimes I wish I were aboriginal, Mungaway so that I could believe in the continuation of all living things. Yet right now I don't believe in anything anymore. People have betrayed us Mungaway they have listened to our hypotheses then shredded them one by one. Then when they had all the information they needed to look for that which could be our undoing they got rid of us, gave us the 'old heave ho' then continued to do what we had expected they would in the beginning; scan the heavens for our Idoli. Even when they maybe found it they didn't tell us. Do you realize that for that object to now be visible in our telescopes, that it was visible to Hubble and maybe the longer range telescopes much sooner! Why didn't they tell us? Was it because they couldn't stand to believe that humanity was facing the end, the final solution to being too smart for its own good."

"Maybe Peter they didn't tell us because they were facing their own mortality and didn't want to believe it."

"Yes I suppose you're right, you should have been a scientist you know".

Mungaway laughed, "no way I couldn't stand being tied to one ideal for the rest of my life. I have so many irons in the fire, every time I go to another job I have to remember which one I am doing."

They both laughed then.

"I guess it's time I went and told them isn't it" Peter said quietly.

Mungaway patted him on the shoulder,

"Yes Peter it's time, we'll go together."

Peter and Mungaway went back to the dining tent where all were still sitting.

They refilled their glasses and stood at the top of the table.

Mungaway tapped his glass,

"Peter has something to tell you so please fill your glasses and listen."

He sat down then and folded his hands in his lap, a glint of light sparkled off his wedding ring; he twisted it and continued to do so as Peter began talking.

When he had finished there was dead silence.

"I wish I could tell you that it is not the Idoli sphere and although it cannot be positively identified at this distance I believe as I am sure you all do, that it is what we think it is."

John lifted a finger,

"Go ahead John" Peter told him

"Assuming that it is the sphere, with an assumed distance how long will it take to get here?"

"Until I hear back from my father in Canberra I can't say. He will be able to ascertain the distance and I should think by now he has accessed Hubble so he should be able to tell us within the next couple of days what we are looking at. One of the big problems is this, there is going to be panic because I will guarantee you this will get out. Someone at the observatories will not be able to keep their mouth shut especially once the next lot of problems begin and that will be very soon.

For the moment I believe this past year has been quiet because the sphere has been behind other large clusters of stars and planets thus we have been shielded. Now that it has become clearly visible, we are going to start having problems. I believe it has been visible for a very long time but as I told my father they simply did not know what they were looking at and discounted it as an asteroid or distant comet that just suddenly disappeared. That disappearance will be their argument for not telling us. I cannot ask you to stay here as much as I want you to. You have a right to go back to your families and try and take them somewhere safe. Stockpile food blankets water and equipment, if they are near the sea move them inland but not near the mountains. You all know this state is not dry there is water underneath, it is safe and we do not have volcanoes here so your only real worry is earthquake. Take as many precautions as you can and try to survive. I will call back the plane when you are ready to leave so please let me know quite soon. Okay? Any questions?"

No-one spoke nor moved they all seemed to be frozen in position. Peter let his gaze drift around the group trying to determine their thoughts. Then one of the drillers spoke.

"er . . . . Dr. Cashman, sir, I have a wife and daughter in Perth can I bring them here please I don't know of a safer place."

"Peter smiled at the young man with the worried frown,

"Of course you can, you can go and get them whenever you like and I want you to bring as much as possible with you because you will be living in tents and you will need to be comfortable. You also need to stockpile food which I suggest you get while you are down there I don't think we are going to have a water problem. Anyone else?

"Well I can't do anything about my father" John Craznow told him "he lives in England with my sister and I have already asked her to try to find a safe place until I tell her otherwise. She is smart and understanding and to my knowledge she is either doing that or has done it already; I haven't yet heard."

"I don't have any family" said the quiet voice of Merilyn Ross.

"You have me sweetheart" answered John.

"Cook? You want to go?" Peter asked.

"Go where? Why do you think I work here? My wife died five years ago and I don't know where my son is, no sir I'll stay thank you. Besides who will look after you all if I don't?"

The second driller stood up,

"If you don't mind I would like a week to arrange for my parents to find a safe place and to help them out, then I would rather come back here if that's okay with you."

"Do you want to bring them here?" Peter asked him "you can, they will have to live in tents but there is no reason why they cannot come here."

"It's too hot for them Dr. Cashman they live in the south I will just take them to my little farm they will be safe there."

"Okay take your week or as long as you need to get it all fixed up then we will see you back here. Mungaway? What are you going to do?"

"Linda won't leave the University until the going gets really rough. We do have a unit in Perth but I think that's a bit risky. I have an uncle who lives on a small farm in the south west quite a way from the sea, I will ask Linda to take the kids and go there but I need more than a possibility for a reason."

Peter smiled, "tell her I said so!"

Mungaway nodded "I will do that. I will leave sometime in the next two days if that's okay with you."

"Of course, go take care of your family and I hope we meet again one day when it's all over."

"Okay that's settled then, any other questions."

"Yes Peter what are you going to do?" Merilyn asked him.

"My father has a property in N.S.W. out near Orange. We used to spend time there with my Great Aunt. When she died she left it to my father. They will be safe there. It's a big place big enough for all of them and then some. I am not worried about them. Well I guess that's settled then we all know what we are doing and tomorrow we will begin doing it."

As he walked out of the tent to again stare at the moon now well risen, John Craznow approached him.

"Peter a word."

They strolled toward the small hill. Peter waited while John found the words.

"I am going to ask Merilyn to come to Broome with me and get married now or at least as soon as I can arrange it. I want you to come with me, be my best man, will you do that?"

Peter smiled "it would be an honour."

The two men shook hands.

The following morning as the sun rose over the Great Sandy Desert a small band of people busied themselves for what they believed was to come. More tents were erected; the drillers ran more power lines setting up a power board in each tent. The two largest solar generators were brought into domestic use. The smaller generator that had powered most of the camp was now the sole use of the kitchen and dining tent. Fuel was stockpiled in the hills under covers and closer to the camp in pits. By midday both drillers had left the site and most of the work was complete. Peter's satellite phone started burping; he knew it would be his father. Everyone in camp stopped and listened while he took the call.

CHAPTER 37

"Hello?"

From then he said nothing for about fifteen minutes. Everyone sat in the dining tent waiting for the call to finish; there was no point continuing work if they didn't know why they were doing it. Finally the call finished with Peter's last words "I'll tell them, thanks Dad, bye".

He came into the dining tent four pairs of eyes glued to him.

"It's the sphere and it has just come out of a giant gas cloud which could account for our last year of peace. We have had our funding restored and upgraded and even an offer of more staff but he told them we don't need it, and we don't. My father is heading to our farm in N.S.W. and has advised us to be ready for anything and everything. The Government is going underground with its military advisers and other select people. We have to spend the next week or so collecting as much seed and grain as we can get, anything that will grow should we survive. We don't know how long we will have the sphere in our immediate range but if what we have so far worked out from the paintings and symbols is anything like correct it should come into range quickly and out of range just as quickly but being what it is the damage will be total. I cannot guarantee any of us will live through this. There are other possibilities. It may be out of our orbit or it may not even come into our range it may have shifted since last time it visited. It may be in front of us which means we could collide, that is total destruction of the Earth and death will be quick. It may just be too close to us and pull us out of orbit drawing us in and destroying us, again death will be quick. It may be on a path to the our sun and if it falls in it will cause huge sun spot activity, or worse depending on it's size, then we may have a lot of destruction on Earth but with a good chance of survival. There is another thing, it is unstable and its course is erratic, it is not following any specific orbit through the Universe. Last time it may have even come from a different direction. Its movement seems to be decided by what appears in front of it. A highly magnetic field will push it away, in a field of stars and planets with high iron content it will draw in the garbage the litter around them. This in turn will increase its overall size. Earth has a high iron content core that is why we believe we are having so many problems with volcanoes and earthquakes. It is, at the moment, far enough away not to do anything more than just cause the unrest that has already occurred; and I don't mean that lightly. As it comes closer everything around us will begin exploding. Western Australia has one big advantage it was one of the first pieces of land to rise from the sea during the formation of the Earth and has a deep stable crust except for the fault line that runs through the southern areas into the Indian Ocean. Our biggest problems are going to be earthquakes, landslips and last but by far not the least; Tsunamis. The Indian is deep and already decidedly unpredictable with high tides and a huge mountain ridge that runs from Malaysia down to just about level with Perth. This is where some of the cones popped up last time. To the north of us we have the Java trench. This is not big but it could be nasty, Krakatoa came from it and so did the Son of; these are the things that could bring us undone. If the ridge rises or falls, as it is closest to us it will directly affect us. Our coast could rise by many metres which we could cope with, or if the mountains blow up it could drag our coast down. This ridge is called the Ninety Ridge and is the closest to W.A. there are others behind it all the way to Africa. The one that caused the most damage last time in Africa was the Atlantic Indian ridge which exploded into life inundating South Africa. If it happens again and I can't see that it won't, the whole Indian basin could go. As I said we could either rise or fall, regardless the tsunamis will keep coming because there is nowhere else for them to go. Sometime in the next few days the Government will be making an announcement requesting people to leave the coast, we could well see an influx of people here, those caves must be protected at all cost, they may still be our only answer."

Peter had just finished speaking when an ominous groan echoed through the hills, everyone dived to the floor and waited. They did not have long to wait.

Suddenly the ground heaved beneath them and then rolled away. The noise was like a huge moan, the earth creaked and groaned. The hills shook and rattled as stones and sand poured down their sides. Every piece of equipment was shaking the cook lay there listening to his pots and pans hitting the floor. This time he had set his breakables down low in specially created cupboards to protect them. Now though they were rattling like mad, he didn't think they would be breaking. It seemed to go on forever but in fact it only lasted about 30 seconds, then it was gone. They got to their feet stepping cautiously outside the tent not knowing what to expect. The first hill before the turn into the gully that led to the caves, had a great slice sheered off the face of it and there for all to see was another cave.

Peter literally ran to the cave which was filled with dust still settling. There on the walls were the now familiar paintings, yet they were different, they showed everyday life. They showed babies being born, food being grown and stone houses being built.

All around them was forest, trees and plants that had never been seen before; flowers as big as dinner plates, and beautifully coloured. This cave was definitely the home of the tribal scribe or scholar. He was their historian. On the floor of the cave toward the back where a long deep hole would indicate a well Peter found a tablet, an inscribed tablet, and there at the very back wall was a small gap that he just knew would take him into another cave, possibly the scribes own home. Merilyn Ross arrived beside him, seeing the gap she walked to it and squeezed through. She switched on a torch and there was an almost unbelievable sight,

"Bring torches!" she yelled to the others "you have to see this".

Peter squeezed in beside her and shone a torch around.

"My god Merry we've found it".

The others came with more torches and all squeezed into the cave. Piled up on the floor, on shelves of stone and stacked against walls were tablets of varying sizes. Some were painted with colours some were simply written in white with small black symbols included in them.

"We have their library" Merilyn said so quietly she was barely heard.

Some of the larger tablets had been broken by the tremors but not shattered and they were easily placed together. All the tablets were of soft sandstone the same stone was still available in the area; they had used the same to mark the shrine for the Italian crew.

John quickly brought up a carbon light and switched it on. The bright light flooded the cave showing it to be much bigger than first thought. Way at the back it narrowed into a small tunnel which again Merilyn was given the job of crawling through.

"Just be careful Merilyn we don't want you falling into something like the water fall. Just put some light in there and let us know what is there okay?" Peter said.

Merilyn put on a line harness and attached a light to her arm and around her forehead. She crawled down the tunnel into absolute blackness. She felt fear yet exhilaration at the unknown ahead of her. She could hear water running and stopped she had no intention of going over the falls. The tunnel had been sloping downwards gently until the last few metres when the slope became much steeper. She stopped easing herself forward bit by bit. Then she unclipped her big torch and shone it forward, there in front of her the tunnel widened and she was able to stand though still stooped. She stepped forward and found herself looking down a set of stone steps cut into the rock. They were damp and quite slippery so she sat down and eased herself toward the first step. When she reached it she shone her torch straight down and there below her was an almost replica of the second cave on the other side but bigger by far. The walls were painted and there were many symbols. The tablets were stacked everywhere. A stream poured into the cave from the right down into a large pool which must also have been able to drain slowly. The edge of the pool was built up with rocks as though there may be occasions when the water was higher. Over on the back wall were what appeared to be cooking implements and something that may have been matting or similar. There were also bones, quite intact skeletons. Merilyn couldn't see enough to count them but there were a few people here.

There was nothing she could do they needed to get equipment in here it seems they had found the last home of the Tribal scribe, this must be where they sheltered from the terror of the outside world. She shone the torch around the cave there didn't appear to be any cracking or individual rocks therefore the cave was either created by a lava bubble or worn through by water; either was a plausible reckoning. Slowly she retreated, only turning around when the tunnel became to low to walk and she resorted to crawling again. She came out into the library where anxious faces greeted her.

"Well? Well?" Peter couldn't contain the excitement in his voice.

"It is, I think, the last home of our tribal scribe. I'd say this is where he and his family sheltered during those last terrible days. The cave is intact has no splits or cracks so it either was formed by lava or water, either way it makes it very safe and unlikely to move in an earthquake. I believe we could survive in that cave and because it is very large, much larger than the second cave on the other side, it could hold a lot more people. There are bones cooking pots and what appears to be matting of some sort. Oh yes it has its own pool with a stream coming in so I think it is a small branch from the river that has found its way through the walls. You are going to love it!"

Mungaway smiled "it's what we have searched for, for so long, now we have it all, the only thing we don't have is who wrote the Book of Vulcan?"

"That may well be answered in that cave. If someone went there even a thousand years ago and translated those tablets and wrote the book then his foot prints may still be there in the dust. Or he may have left something else there a food wrapper or something that says he was not one of them" Peter told them.

"I would like to see the Book of Vulcan Peter I think at this late stage there is nothing more to hide and the sooner we all know about it the better. Don't you think so?" John asked him.

Peter nodded "yes I think we all need to read it and see how someone else translated those tablets and drawings. I suppose once we establish those particular writings with what is on the tablets then we have the answer to it all don't we. Of course I never did consider that before because I wasn't even sure that the book was an accurate translation, and even now I am still not sure but anything is worth a try."

"Peter I would like to go back to Perth as quickly as possible if you don't mind" Mungaway told him "I would like to get my wife and children organised and then I want to come back here but I want to bring my wife with me. She is wonderful with languages especially the ancient ones she would be a great benefit here I am sure of it. I don't necessarily mean in translation I mean in being able to tell who where and when the Book of Vulcan was written."

"Go Mungaway" Peter told him "go quickly and do what you have to do then we will see you as soon as you can get back. Time is short for all of us, we must get done all that must be done then we will start to work out how we are going to make these caves liveable before the worst arrives."

Mungaway left the following morning just before sunrise; his truck seemed twice as loud in the still morning air. The cook quickly assembled everything in one place so that when the time came he could pick up quickly and move everything that was needed. The only real problem they faced moving into the caves was the generator they would have to keep one running at all times as there was a decided lack of cooking fuel. In the days when the old ones had lived there was probably coal, peat or wood or a bit of everything. These days there was only bare desert, shale and sand. The generators would have to be placed in the library and shielded against noise. They would have to set up some sort of a system to keep it powered if they lost the sun. There was also the problem of having to hide the opening of the cave. John suggested they stack rocks inside and out leaving only a small gap at the top for the last person to come through then complete the stack from the inside. It sounded reasonable but Peter said no, the cave would have to look after itself. What they could do was fill the gap between the outer cave and the library which was simpler and more effective. If anyone then came this far looking for safety and found the cave they would probably not give a thought to what may lay beyond it. He doubted though that anyone would come this far it was very remote and to most people considered waterless.

CHAPTER 38

That evening after a long and hot days work Merilyn, John, Peter and the cook sat down to a light meal in the dining tent. The radio was blaring the latest news of upheavals beginning around the Earth. Nothing too dramatic, an earthquake in South America, China and Alaska, Mt. Kilauea which had never really stopped erupting, exploded with a vengeance. The news went on; many of the areas being devastated were already uninhabited anyway. Then an interruption,

'We interrupt this broadcast to bring you the news that Sydney has been hit by a large earthquake measuring 7.6 on the Richter scale. The bridge which is already damaged and buckled has been twisted, with one pylon crashing into the harbour. Water front properties have been reported as sliding into the water. Several large apartment blocks on the north shore have been destroyed as have many homes in the west and north of the city. Some city buildings left intact after the last earthquake are now beginning to collapse and in several instances late office workers have been trapped as lifts and stairwells became unsafe for use. Fires have broken out across the city as gas pipes rupture. A huge fire has begun at an oil refinery in Wollongong, ten teams are at present working to contain the blaze.'

Peter sighed noisily "well here it is it's begun, that tremor we got was only small by comparison to what is coming. To have a 7.6 in Sydney is devastating for a city that size and there will be aftershocks. I . . ." he was interrupted as the satellite phone burped.

He went to his tent to answer it. No-one could hear what was being said but when Peter returned to the dining tent his face had paled considerably under his tan.

"My father just called . . . I . . . ah . . . my mother has been killed. It seems our apartment block on the North Shore has collapsed. Mother went back to get some things before leaving for the farm and she was caught in the 'quake. I have to go out first thing in the morning I will probably only be gone for a few days, you all know what we must do" as he walked out of the tent he turned back to them "these are dreadful times for everyone but we must survive all of us, somehow. We may all lose loved ones but there is nothing we can do we cannot bring them back we can only hope to perpetuate them by surviving ourselves and telling our children about them. Be safe people."

CHAPTER 39

Peter flew to Sydney the following day.

His father met him at the airport, Peter could not believe how haggard he looked he seemed to have aged ten years since his last visit

They stood hugging each other not speaking.

Peter stood back wiping his eyes,

"Oh Dad why did she go back there why weren't you at the farm?"

"We were on our way Peter; we had gone down to see my brother to see if he would come with us. As we started out for Orange she asked if she could go back and get her rocker, it's not that big and would have easily fitted on the trailer. I couldn't deny her Peter it was the only thing she really wanted. So we went back. I told her I would go and get it but she insisted on getting it herself, she said she just wanted to check the apartment one more time. So I let her go, oh god I let her go!"

He sobbed; Peter put his arm around him.

"The quake hit as she was coming back down. She had waved to me from the balcony to let me know she was on her way. Then we got the first movement, the driveway heaved and the old house behind the apartments started to fall apart. I ran the car out of the driveway and out onto the main parking area. Then the shuddering started and the building started swaying like mad then it just started falling down. I tried to get out of the car I wanted to go and get her, but I couldn't stand up. I sat there and watched it collapsing piece by piece and inside was my beautiful wife of thirty six years, and I couldn't do a damn thing about it. Bricks were falling like rain, bouncing off the car and the trailer but I wouldn't move I wanted to be there when she came running out looking for me. I wanted to go to the building but I couldn't even get out of the car. The 'quake only lasted about 30 seconds but it seemed like a lifetime and in that 30 seconds the building and the one next to it and another one further along just collapsed like so many packs of cards.

Oh Peter she's gone my beautiful wife is gone what am I going to do without her" Alan Cashman sobbed like a child while his youngest son held him.

"Did SES or anyone get into the building Dad were there any survivors?" Peter asked.

His father nodded, "Yes I went in with them yesterday, they found Barbara's body in the lift, it had crashed to the bottom of the lift well. Our next door neighbour there, George? you remember? he was with her. He must have seen her carrying the rocker and helped her down with it. They only pulled two survivors out of the bottom apartment."

"Please Dad you can't blame yourself we can't change what is happening."

His father pulled away from him and wiped his eyes.

"It is my fault Peter because I should never have let her go back for the rocker I should have told her there was no time, or I should have gone in and got it myself, it was probably too much for her to carry. Yes it's my fault I killed her, I let her die."

Peter shook his head, "She would never forgive you for talking like this, she was an independent woman who didn't ask anyone to do anything she could do herself. That includes fetching a rocker from the apartment down to the car. All the years you were married and moved around did you do the packing? no! mother did. All the times we went on holidays did you load the car and trailer? no! mother did, so why are you so convinced that by allowing her to do what she has always done was your fault. Dad she would always do what she wanted to do and no-one could stop her. You did not cause her death you couldn't know that there was going to be an earthquake. Please Dad we have to get on with trying to save ourselves now and perpetuate mother's memory by surviving."

He led his father out into the car park where his car and driver were waiting.

"Where is the car and trailer Dad?"

"I think they are still in the main car park. I don't think they would have been moved."

Peter spoke to the driver.

"Can you take us to a Motel or Hotel away from the main city please preferably on the south side and then can you get a cab back to the apartment block and see if you can retrieve my fathers' car and trailer."

The driver nodded, "yes sir. I believe Dr. Cashman Senior was driving the four wheel drive sir."

"Good. Well when you get it, if it's drivable, bring it to where we are because after my mothers funeral I want you to take my father out to Orange, I will drive the Nissan, then you can bring me back to Sydney. Okay?"

The Driver touched his hat "Yes sir."

Two days later Barbara, wife of Alan for thirty six years, mother of Damien thirty five, Emma, thirty three and Peter thirty one, grandmother of Carli, India, Cassidie and Daniel, was cremated. Her ashes were taken to Orange to be scattered over the Rose garden that she loved so much.

The following day an exhausted Peter Cashman came back to Sydney, wishing their driver well and telling him to find a safe place or go back to Orange. His flight left for Perth at 9pm there was only one seat left, in first class; he took it.

CHAPTER 40

Back up on the campsite Peter was pleased with the results. Much of what they would need had been taken into the library cave and stowed against the wall.

Both drillers had arrived back and had laid a non-skid rubberized matting on the steps. Peter could only assume that the earlier people were not only small of stature but incredibly nimble to be able to traverse the steps.

Their camp had now swelled with the arrival of Mark's, the youngest driller's, wife and child. Peter was introduced to her; she was a teacher and an artist in her spare time.

"I want you to meet Dr. Peter Cashman" Mark told her "he is my boss here".

Peter smiled "Peter please" he extended his hand "no time for formalities now.

She smiled back at him "Denise" she said "and this is our little girl Belinda whom we call Bindi."

"Nice to have you here I hope you don't find it too uncomfortable."

Peter walked toward the other driller who was talking to two older people.

"Ah Dr. Cashman I would like you to meet my parents" Joe Mackie told him "this is my father John and mother Isabelle Mackie—mum dad this is Dr. Peter Cashman our site boss."

Peter shook hands with them both, he looked puzzled.

"I thought you wouldn't bring them here because it was too hot!"

"Yes that's what I said and that's what I thought but when it came time to move them they didn't want to be on their own away from their friends and I couldn't leave them where they were so they asked could they come here to be with me. I am all they have Doctor I hope it's alright."

"Of course it's alright . . . er what can you do—anything?"

"I was a nursery man for years" the older man told him "I have been dabbling in hydroponics for the last ten years and doing quite well at it, I brought a lot of seedlings and seeds with me to see what I can set up. My wife was nurse. Gave it up about five years ago but is very good and knows what she is talking about. We thought we could be of more assistance here than stuck on a remote farm by ourselves."

"Well you certainly have a lot to offer between us we are developing quite a community here. Welcome aboard." Peter continued his tour of the site.

The only one missing was Mungaway and Peter was becoming worried that all had not gone to plan with him. Perhaps Linda had chosen not to come back with him and insisted that he stay there with them. His children would be left with their uncle maybe that caused friction. Peter hoped that he would return he was a great inspiration to all of them and managed to think of things that no one else did. He also had an uncanny knack of knowing when things would happen. His concentration on a particular thing was amazing and often brought results. He was a talent that Peter knew they would need if and when things got bad.

His first week back on site, was a week that was long and difficult in many parts of the world as that great erratic sphere began exerting a lot of pressure on the Earth. The tides became very high and there were fears that the moon may be pulled out of orbit. Peter had been rising early each day to hear the radio broadcasts and to fine tune the base radio which in the very near future may be their only form of communication with the outside world. He had joined the cook for early coffee most days as they discussed how they were going to accommodate everyone in the caves if necessary. The cook had some good ideas and Peter asked him to write them all down for their discussion meeting. They were still deep in conversation when a faint engine sound echoed across the early stillness of the desert.

"Mungaway!" Peter said "he's back."

They walked outside and there on the horizon a dust cloud rose hanging steadily in the windless air.

"He must have come up through the centre maybe the roads are blocked or something."

"I'll go and make fresh coffee" the cook told him.

Peter nodded but didn't take his eyes off that dust cloud.

Half an hour later Mungaway drove into camp with his truck loaded to the hilt and towing a very large trailer also full.

"Good grief" Peter muttered "he's brought the house with him."

Mungaway jumped out of the truck grinning broadly,

"We have had a terrible time getting here Peter, the highways are full of people getting out of the city, I had to use all my bush nous and take the back tracks to get us here it's taken nearly a week."

Peter and Mungaway shook hands warmly,

"Good to see you my friend what have you brought?"

"Besides Linda you mean."

Linda jumped out of the truck and kissed Peter warmly,

"Hi Dr. Cashman how goes it."

"Linda! I am so pleased you came" Peter looked back to the truck "and the kids?"

"With my uncle, Peter, and they have some friends with them so uncle won't get lonely and neither will the kids" Mungaway told him

"Well I hope they are safe that's all"

"Oh yes" Linda added "they are safe they wouldn't want to be anywhere else they think it's all a big holiday."

"I hope they realize it's serious Linda and not to take risks or go back to the City."

"Yes they do know Peter we sat them down and told them the truth and what to expect I couldn't see the point in not being honest with them."

"Well we have developed quite a large community here and everyone can do something and now we have you two which will just cap it all off. Tonight I am having a discussion meeting you will be introduced to everyone and I am going to tell you all exactly what I know and how. It's not going to go down really well because we are all facing death but it is something we have to talk about."

Mungaway nodded, "understood Peter, but I really think we have a pretty good survival chance. We can only try."

"Now!" Peter eyed the truck and trailer "what have you brought for us."

It took the rest of the day to unload and stow everything Mungaway had brought with him. He had forgotten nothing from cases and cases of food, wines and dried vegetables to medicines, radios and parts, cables, extensions, lamps, carbon lights, two more generators, canvas and tents, blankets pillows, linen, toiletries, books by the dozens, painting apparatus and sketch books.

Mungaway grinned when he unpacked these,

"These are our walls Peter our place for painting and drawing history."

The list of the goods he had brought was endless and many things that others hadn't even considered. By the time they had finished the previously three quarters bare library cave was full.

"I think we could sit this out for many years to come Mungaway" Peter told him "short of all being killed in some sort of cataclysm we now have enough goods for twice as many people. We won't starve, we won't be cold or hot and we will never need for water or any of the other necessities of life. We have a fully qualified nurse amongst us who also brought her own case. She has done everything from nurse the terminally ill to delivering babies so we are right there. We have a resident artist and teacher, a nursery man who dabbles in hydroponics, two drillers who are also a dab hand at electrics and mechanical maintenance, we have a linguist, two seismologists one who is also a vulcanologist, a specialist in drilling and caves who also can turn his hand to just about anything else, a superb cook and caterer and little girl who could grow up to be brilliant at any or all of the above."

They both laughed.

That evening, now that everyone was on site, Peter called a meeting.

CHAPTER 41

"I have called you all together for several reasons. I want first to introduce you to Mungaway and his wife Linda" they stood and acknowledged the "hello's" "I also want to introduce you to Vulcan" Peter picked the old book up off the table and held it up "this is the Book of Vulcan this is what we based our search on when we first came here."

He went on to tell them the story of how he was sent the book thought it a good story showed it to his father and they moved on from there when it was determined to probably be a chronicle.

He spared nothing, he told them everything, even invited any or all of them to read it in turn and to offer something that may give them a clue as to what to expect.

Peter knew that some would find it difficult to believe so he did not dwell on the book instead he moved onto the last printouts he had on the position of the sphere and the pull it was beginning to exert on the Earth.

"We may all die but I will say this, if we die, that is us particularly, then you can rest assured that there is probably no-one else alive, because this is one of the safest places in the world. We are far enough from the sea to not be affected by the tsunamis that will come. We are far enough inland not to be directly affected by cyclones that will come. We may get a lot of rain but the caves are above the desert and away from it so even if water pools, which I doubt, we are safe from it. We will get earthquakes but because of our position they will be the type that simply roll away from us similar to what happens when you drop a pebble in a pond. Underground these may be frightening because the earth is old and will creak and groan a lot but try not to be afraid it will pass quickly. The caves are safe and have been in their present state since long before what we consider the dawn of time. These caves were once lived in by the ancients. This was an original race on Earth, it may have even been the second race on Earth but certainly it was long before so called modern man. They were small built people who wrote, painted, grew food and built their homes in this place which was once a forest, a virtual jungle. We have found their bones and their libraries and you will all get to see them so that you know how it was. They went through what we are experiencing now and they survived. Why didn't they continue, I hear you asking, well for one very good reason, food, or should I say the lack of it. They were smart capable people but they could not store enough food, so they all died of starvation. We on the other hand, have the technology to store food for many years, to grow fruit and vegetables without sunlight and without soil. We have food that can be reconstituted simply by adding hot water. Much of it may not look inspiring but we have an excellent cook who can make it taste great you have already experienced his cooking and some of the food he has been preparing for you is reconstituted. We have heating and cooling apparatus and apparatus that can pump oxygen into the caves to keep the air reasonably fresh. We have in our midst people who can all do something from just about most walks of life, we do not have high flying businessmen in our midst" everyone laughed or smiled "but these people can keep us alive and keep our stomach full and this is more important than anyone who can make lots of money. I am grateful that you all decided to come here I am glad to be able to offer you this safe haven which, though it may also become our prison, hopefully we can remain alive. Living is our prime importance because if we can get through this like others in other safe places, the human race can continue. We have a little girl with us and we all want to see her grow up just as any other children who may be born here. I have much faith in you people. I don't know you all but if the people who brought you here are any example then we are going to be good friends and close allies. If you have any questions about anything no matter how small or even if you think it insignificant, please ask there is always someone who can answer your questions. For now are there any questions?"

John Mackie raised his hand,

"Yes John" Peter nodded to him.

"What is the most likely reason we would die."

Peter pulled at his lip,

"If the sphere is in front of us when it passes we could collide. We wouldn't know anything and death would be instantaneous assuming it is as large as we think it is. Or it could pull us out of orbit, again death would be quick. It could block the sun for long periods of time depending on how big it is and how fast it is travelling that would have a terrible effect on earth, it may not affect us directly, but could mess up survival for others. It could pull our moon out of orbit which in turn could do one of two things. It could crash into Earth which of course would be the death knell for the human race or the moon may be pulled out of orbit and taken away with it and leave us without the natural rise and fall of tides that the moon creates. That probably would not affect us greatly but it would be strange without it. That's getting away from it a bit. Or one scenario which my father and I have thrown around which indeed has me worried. There is a possibility that this sphere has being picking up rubbish from around the universe accumulated space junk, bits of asteroids left over comets, dust and gas, chunks or rocks etc. from old novas, then when it shoots past us some of these pieces could break away if they are too near us and crash into Earth. We would not survive a big strike. Several small strikes we could survive living underground as long as the oxygen nitrogen content of the outside air does not become compromised. In the event of major strikes the dust clouds or water clouds and whatever else that got thrown up could cause a winter for a millennia. There is also a possibility that some of those strikes could be here in Australia it seems to be a magnet for space junk to fall on to."

Peter stared at the faces in front of him there was no easy way to tell people to prepare for death because the human race always believed it could never be wiped out. Of course it was pure arrogance on their part to believe they were invincible.

Denise raised her hand.

"Peter if we got a strike and it hit say Europe what would happen to us and how long would it take. Assuming it was big."

"Well if it hit the sea the tsunamis would be of such horrendous size that the oceans would just pour over all the land the exceptions being the very highest peaks but even they may not be immune. We would not be safe. If it hit land the result would be catastrophic. A huge cloud of dust would be thrown up that would cover the entire world for maybe many hundreds maybe thousands of years. The fracture zones would react causing tremendous earthquakes and quite probably some very big volcanoes. The chance of survival would be remote, the outside air would be compromised we would probably suffocate."

"If that were to happen would we die slowly or would we be able to take the easy way out?"

Peter stared at her it was something he had never addressed yet it was a question that must be debated.

"Under the circumstances if we survived the initial strike then the decision to end it before anything else happened would have to be personal choice. Anyone who wished to, of course would not be stopped, if, if the rest of us believed there was no hope. I would welcome anyone's thoughts on this matter."

The night wore on, little Bindi fell asleep on the floor on her favourite blanket. The debate on self administered Euthanasia was a main topic and not readily decided upon.

CHAPTER 42

Peter continued to talk to his father; he noted though that many of the calls were riddled with static and often so faint that he could not hear. Small tremors located in the Northern Territory were being felt fairly often and the group had become quite blasé about them barely stopping work unless things got a bit rough. Everyone did something throughout the day. Those who weren't involved in setting up the caves were taken on tours of the other caves, the galleries as they were now referred to. The library tablets were moved to the lower cave once entry and exit had been established. The areas at the very back of the lower cave were very cool and very dark and it was decided because of the size of the cave that this area would be used as a food storage area. Nearby closer to the water source there were two flat rocks raised above floor level as air movement was most pronounced in this area Cook set up his second kitchen. The drillers and John Craznow had designed an intake system based on the old evaporative air conditioning system. They brought fresh air into the caves and sent stale out via a small duct system. It worked very well. Below the steps leading down to the lower cave and to the left looking at the steps there were several dark recesses, these were nominated as sleeping areas. The recesses were cold but dry there were old mats there which they carefully removed and placed wrapped up with the old bones they had found. These had obviously been used for sleeping areas because of their depth. The cook decided that behind his working kitchen area would also be his home and set about making it warm and comfortable. They had noticed that no matter how hot it became outside nor how cold the desert could get at night the caves barely changed. The monitored temperature stayed at a general 23 degrees Celsius sometimes up a little sometimes down a little but a very liveable temperature. Peter also insisted that when there was daylight outside then the lights must be on in the caves. They had positioned the big white carbon lights to give as much light as possible. When it was dark outside then smaller lights would be on throughout the cave and in and around the sleeping areas. This was to get people used to the changes while underground. Only sleeping areas would remain totally black throughout the night. The library cave became not only a storage area but a work area.

The generators would all run from this cave and would be powered by a system of reflectors. The remainder of the cave would be storage for everything they could not take below. The idea of closing off the small opening had blossomed into a reality with John Mackie using his skills to make fake rocks out of cement and sand and colouring them to match the surrounding area. These were then pushed into place when needed to be. The exhaust pipes from the cooking area below were brought across the roof and out into the roof of the outside cave. They then followed that line to outside the cave where they curved over the hill, carefully camouflaged. In the event of the cave becoming covered again by another slide the pipes would still be safely doing their job. When they had set the caves up as far as they could Peter again called a meeting.

"People" he began "you have done a tremendous job we have completed project cave, and now we can only take a 'wait and see'. The tremors or small temblors we have been experiencing are nothing to worry about. The Territory has been experiencing them for some time and we have been getting them here fairly frequently. They are not big enough to send us underground so I want you to get used to living on the desert. Now I know we live in tents which is a very light bright existence because the tents are all white, so if you find that the early sun is getting you up too early Mungaway has a store of water proof canvas tarps which you can have to create a fly cover. This will keep your tent much darker. It also stops rain leaks but as we don't seem to be having any of those you wouldn't have to worry too much about them. If you are finding it too hot, I mean uncomfortably so, don't rush off to the caves because you will never become acclimatized. See John Craznow or either Joe or Mark our drillers and ask them to set up an aircon pipe for your tent. The dining tent has one and it can be extended or we do have evaporative coolers which work well and fans if you want them. Though the desert is very hot in summer it is very dry therefore a much easier heat to put up with. This area has actually recorded in excess of 50 degrees Celsius now that is too hot to be out in but if you have shade and drink plenty of water you can get used to it. At night the temperature can drop below zero particularly in the spring and winter months. Autumn and summer tend to stay fine and mild. We do get rain here especially during the cyclone season depending of course which way it is coming. If it is coming in from the Torres Strait we will get it and if Broome or Derby have cyclones we will get it. When it rains the desert turns green and the wildflowers come out and it is beautiful. I can understand how once this was a beautiful jungle. I believe we have what it takes to maintain a complete community here we could possibly take in one or two more people but if you ever see strangers in the area or are approached by any you must not mention the caves they must be protected at all costs. Your story here is that we are working on a drill site that is government funded. Nothing else! I don't think anyone will come this far but you just don't know. Any questions?"

The next hour was spent in general discussion and people raised their hands and gave their names as the next day's jobs were allocated.

Three months after they had set up their community Peter received a message via the base radio that Adelaide had had a devastating earthquake, 7.9 on the Richter. There wasn't a lot left of it. He thought of all the people he had met whilst spending time there during his early study years. Some who had remained good friends. Then he recalled that his brother had told him Jenna was there. Ah Jenna!, he had loved her since he was a young student but too afraid to make his feelings known. They were both 23 years old when she asked him out for dinner. They spent the next two years together both working in the field of Seismology. Then he changed studies to Vulcanology and they worked separately for much of the year seeing each other only on weekend breaks and annual leave. He had asked her to marry him she had said yes but it never went anywhere from there. Their respective jobs took up all of their time. Then one weekend she told him it was over. They drifted apart and had never seen each other again. Now she was head of seismic graphics or graph section as it was fondly called in Adelaide, or at least was until the 'quake; where was she now?

Other reports came in; tremors here and there nothing major outside of Adelaide. It was a forgone conclusion that Perth would experience a 'big one' sooner or later. New Zealand was taking a bit of a hiding with the remains of the Taupo Volcanoes continuing to rumble and spew ash and lava at odd intervals. The Southern Alps had settled down but the whole of the South Island was very shaky.

Palmerston North in the North Island the great University and college town; suffered a lot of damage after two 'quakes made themselves felt up to 6.5 on the Richter. Tasmania the one state that had not suffered at all in recent times was making it known that one of the old cones of the Lake St. Claire national park had started smoking and there had been mild tremors around the lakes area. Still the poles had not quivered and for that Peter was grateful, if anything happened to them and they melted they would all drown. Alaska had had its earthquakes and big ones which had broken up huge sections of the ice shelf but the 'year of healing' had seen these chunks refreeze giving everyone in the far north of the planet a bit more breathing space. He knew that the Earth was to suffer much more than this and it would be far worse than it had been before the sphere disappeared from view. If only he knew when it would get here and what its course was maybe they could work out the possible survival rate. But it was so erratic no-one could work out its course. His father had said anything from six months to ten years. Peter thought that sounded ridiculous, even with something erratic surely the Astronomers had worked out its approximate speed that was all they needed to determine how long it would take. Making allowances for it's erratic behaviour they could still give everyone some idea of what to expect and when. As he sat thinking over how he was going to keep these people alive, he heard his old call sign being broadcast. It was faint but it was definitely his.

". . . . say again . . . . calling PJC do you copy?"

He listened intently twiddling the knobs and dials to get a clearer sound but it was still too faint as if it were thousands of kilometres away.

"Peter are you out there . . . . calling PJC . . . . anyone? Do you copy over?"

He picked up the handset and started broadcasting on a higher strength signal. When he got nothing back he switched to satellite tracking.

He strode to the tent doorway and yelled for John Craznow,

When John arrived Peter was sitting listening to the faint call.

"John I need to track this call I switched over to satellite tracking can you try and get something clearer for me, you know more about it than I do."

John worked on the tracker for sometime then suddenly

"PJC are you listening can you read me over?"

It wasn't loud but it was clear.

"Where is it John" Peter asked him.

"From this I would say about here" he pointed to a track somewhere above the South Australian border into Northern Territory. She has left the main road and is trying to head west on a track called the Bilton track it leads nowhere. She has to come further north if she is trying to get here if she continues that way she will run into the Gibson Desert and may never get out. Who is she do you know?"

"I'm not sure it sounds like an old girlfriend of mine Jenna, but she sounds tired and a bit panicky so it's not easily identifiable. She does know my old call sign though so I guess it could be her. Let's try using her name and we can find out where she is trying to get to."

John picked up the handset,

"To PJC caller is your name Jenna? Is that your name please? Over"

Nothing!

"If you can hear me stop where you are turn back until you get to the track marked Angus Downs turn left and follow through till you reach the station then wait and call again over"

The line buzzed faintly then and faint voice came back on the line.

"I hear . . . . back to . . . . Downs . . . . thanks will . . . . over"

"No name Peter but at least now she is not heading into the middle of no-where. If it is Jenna where has she come from?"

Peter smiled, "the Seismology centre in Adelaide. The 'quake must have been a big one if it made her get out she would have stayed regardless. She has been head of Seismic Graphics there I don't know where she was going but she probably heard from my brother that I was on the desert in Western Australia and she is trying to find me. There is an awful lot of desert in Western Australia though."

"Well if she makes it to Angus Downs we can call her and we should get a good reception. At least there she will be safe for a while until we work out how to get her here if she wants to be here. John saw the interest on Peter's face.

"Fancy after all this time she wants to find me, I wonder why?" Peter stared at the radio he had spoken so quietly John felt he was talking to himself.

Peter left the tent and went looking for Mungaway.

Finding him in the outer cave folding tarps, Peter told him what had happened.

"How can we get her here if that is what she wants? She is obviously looking for me for a reason she was either very brave or very frightened to take off on her own into the desert."

"If she goes to Angus Downs and we can call her there we can get her onto the Tanami. Once on that she can come straight through to the Bells Well turn off then I can go and meet her and bring her on to the site."

"What about the winds Mungaway, you know yourself at this time of the year unless you know the Tanami track the winds can cover it and a person could finish up driving into no-where and they may never be found. That has happened too many times."

"Yes" he nodded in agreement "that can happen but if it does I think she would have enough brains to stop and wait before trying to work out where she is. And if she is very smart she wouldn't go on anyway if she couldn't see the track."

"She is scared Mungaway she must be to come looking for me."

Mungaway put his hand on his friend's shoulder,

"It's okay Peter I will find her; can I take someone with me?"

The next morning before sunrise Peter sat at the radio a freshly brewed pot of coffee beside him and started calling.

"Caller to PJC where are you over?"

For two hours he called constantly switching channels and boosting the radio as far as he could. Satellite tracking could not find her the area was just too big.

At 6.30am cook started serving the first breakfasts bringing Peter's to the radio desk.

"Eat" he commanded "you will feel better with a full stomach."

Peter ate sausages, bacon, scrambled eggs and toast followed by fruit juice and more coffee. He was finishing as the faint call came over the radio,

". . . . PJC? . . . . read? over"

Peter yelled to John,

"We have her John she's calling now."

John hurried to the radio and started typing in a program for the satellite tracker to find her; suddenly a small ping heralded a sighting. A tiny green spot appeared on a broad brown expanse.

"Gotcha" he said quietly.

Mungaway joined them,

"I can get there she is okay for now. Go back and tell her to drive north until she finds a wide track that is fairly well graded that is the Tanami. Turn left onto the Tanami and continue straight ahead until she reaches Bells Well it is signposted and there is water there. We will meet her there. I will take Linda you can do without her until this is all fixed. I will also take the drillers four wheeled drive because it has a winch, we may need it."

He and Linda hurried to their tent packing food and clothing for themselves and extra food for the person they were going for.

"Take plenty of water in case you get into trouble" Peter told him "and if you do get into trouble let us know immediately okay?"

"Linda you stay on the radio and I will be on this end" John told her "your voice is a bit clearer than Mungaway's, no offence," John said turning to him "your voice is a bit too soft."

Linda nodded "no problem I will call every hour on the hour."

Linda and Mungaway left the site. The morning was clear and warm without any wind and Mungaway hoped it would stay that way. They drove across the desert heading south east before finding a small track that would take them to the Tanami. It was a long time since he had gone this way but some things just never changed and the Tanami was one of them.

CHAPTER 43

The day progressed smoothly enough John getting hourly reports from Linda. By evening they were stranded in a huge dust storm and couldn't move. Mungaway had been trying calling to Bells Well but got no response, John also had no response.

"It will be the dust storm I suppose" he told Peter "I think it is probably dispersing some of the radio waves particularly if there is a lot of silica flying around."

The night wore on John only breaking from the radio for meals. He was often joined by Merilyn or Peter or anyone else who happened along just to keep him going.

By 4am the following morning John heard a call. He had been dozing head on arms refusing to leave the radio until the girl was found and he was sure Mungaway and Linda were safe.

The caller was distant but clear, it was Linda.

"I hear you" John told her "are you alright? Over"

"We are well John the storm has gone but the road has gone with it we are going to be a bit late finding Bells Well can you give us a position on the GPI? Over"

John tapped in the information and started scanning on the Satellite tracker. He picked up three green spots on the Tanami before finding the right one. Mungaway's vehicle was fitted with a tracking device which made it easy to pick up. The cross hairs blipped then started zooming in on the sighting.

"I have you Linda. You are still going the right way if you continue straight ahead for approximately 5 klicks then a slight veer to the left you should see the track clearly it is showing up well I am surprised you can't find it on the tracker over"

"We can't find it John because this tracker has not been fed in the information for this area. It sort of makes it a bit hard it doesn't know where to look. But I have that information can you see the girl's vehicle? Over"

John zipped over the landscape finding nothing. As he reversed toward Mungaway's vehicle a faint blip showed directly in front of Mungaway about 10 kilometres away.

"Yep, I have that vehicle Linda it's directly in front of you about 10 klicks away and is very faint I would suggest it is probably covered in a lot of sand. Over"

Four hours later a call came through loud and clear.

"Base this is Linda over"

"Go ahead Linda" John told her.

"Base we have the vehicle. Both people are safe though dehydrated they had run out of water and had not eaten. We will make camp here at Bells Well then when they are feeling better we will make the return journey. I repeat both people have been found. They are alive but dehydrated I will call when we are leaving the area. Over"

John called Peter in and told him.

"Did she say both people John?"

John nodded, "yes but did not elaborate so I guess she has brought her husband with her".

"Uhuh, oh well they are both welcome" Peter walked out of the tent.

John heard the utter rejection in Peter's voice, after all this time it sounded like he still cared.

Two days later both vehicles rolled into camp.

Mungaway jumped out first shaking hands with Peter,

"Even the Tanami has people on it, a lot of people actually. They all seem to be heading anywhere that isn't near big cities or towns. Families with trailers carrying everything they own looking for somewhere to set up camp. I told a couple of them they are in the wrong place it is too dry there they need to head to where the underground springs are. I gave two families a map of the areas in Northern Territory and South Australia. They are simply wasting their time out here."

Linda walked towards them helping a young woman with a child.

"Someone to see you Peter" she told him.

Peter looked hard at the woman, she looked like Jenna but much thinner and her once long black hair was cut in a short curly style. He still wasn't sure though until she got close then she said,

"Hello Peter long time no see" reaching out her hand toward him.

Peter clasped her hand,

"Jenna it is you! I almost didn't recognise you, you are so much thinner and your hair . . ." he trailed off "take them to the mess tent and tell cook to give them some food and water or whatever and I will arrange with John to erect another tent."

He strode away without even speaking to the little boy who stood beside her.

She took the boys' hand and walked with Linda to the tent. Cook laid out breakfast in front of them within minutes they were both very hungry even though they had meals with Linda and Mungaway.

"Did I do something wrong?" she asked Linda between mouthfuls of food.

Linda shook her head,

"No I don't think so, Peter has a lot of responsibility and you haven't been in his life for a very long time. I think he probably feels as though you are using him."

Jenna turned quite red, and continued to eat.

"I'll say this for you Linda you are blunt."

Linda laughed,

"Being married to an aboriginal helps, he always says exactly what he thinks no feelings spared; it rubs off."

Jenna continued to eat in silence; Linda realized she had not heard the little boy speak at all. She wondered why.

"I'll leave you to eat in peace, help yourself to whatever. Cook will help you if you need it. I will go and see about your quarters and I'll be back here in about fifteen minutes. There is an ablutions block and toilets behind and to the left there are clean towels etc. if you want to take a shower and change your clothes and perhaps the little bloke's. I'll see you soon." Linda stood up and left.

John and Mark erected a new tent, adding a canvas tarp as a fly to darken it. It was one of the larger tents divided into two rooms. It was decided Jenna and the boy should sleep separate as all the families that were there. It was reasonably close to the ablutions block for convenience with the boy.

Peter joined them,

"Give Jenna one of the bigger beds and the boy can sleep on the smaller cot type he isn't very big. You can give them an evaporative cooler as well. Make sure they have enough furniture. She doesn't seem to have brought that much with her, but she will need a couple of clothes racks and portable robes."

He watched the proceedings for a while before wandering off to talk to John Mackie about setting up another hydroponics section.

By the time the evening dinner gong sounded Peter had not spoken again to Jenna. He wandered towards the mess tent thinking about how they were going to allow for washing and toileting underground when he almost walked into her.

"Whoops! Sorry I just didn't see you, miles away I suppose."

Jenna smiled,

"It's okay Peter. Look could we talk after dinner I really need to tell you why I am here and the reasons behind it all. Please Peter" she smiled briefly.

He looked at her for a long time then at the solemn little boy tightly clutching her hand.

"Okay" he said "my tent about 8.30pm".

On the dot of 8.30pm Jenna came into Peter's tent.

She looked younger in the soft light of the tent just as she had all those years ago when they first began to go steady. Peter was surprised though how slim she was. Jenna always had a soft round feminine figure; he had loved her shape.

"Peter" she began "I have to be able to speak without interruption if I am to say anything at all. If you ask me questions I will stop talking and I don't think I will have the courage to start again."

Peter frowned but nodded his assent.

He poured them both a glass of wine, propping his feet up on his desk he waited.

"When we broke up Peter it wasn't just because I wasn't seeing you very much or that our jobs took us away in different directions, I had also met someone else. You may remember him from uni, Dr. Philip Mores? Well he was very good to me I was the only woman in my field working in the field and he sort of looked after me. I guess because you and I were so far apart in time I began to see more of him. Yes I know he is a lot older than me, twenty years older actually. I was flattered by his attention. Then we had that last weekend together you and me, and I told you I wouldn't see you ever again. I loved you but I wanted more than that I wanted attention and romance and fun, and I was not getting it. Even when we were together we only ever went to dinner or stayed home. All our friends were the same friends and all we ever talked about was work, I was sick to death of it all. Anyway I went to South America with him on his next trip but I took sick and they flew me home six weeks later. The doctor said I had some kind of virus. I was in a Sydney hospital for a week and I had a lot of tests done before they found that I not only had a virus I was also pregnant. Because they didn't know what kind of virus I had, they asked me to have the pregnancy aborted. I wanted to but I believed I was in love with Philip so I decided against it. I had Steven 7 ½ months later. He struggled for the first three months of his life because I had developed blood poisoning during my pregnancy. Finally he started to grow and eat and then crawl and walk. He was always a little slow in talking but when he talks his speech is clear and he is very smart. He is a very quiet little boy though. By the time he was twelve months old, Philip was dead; he died of a stroke. I never married him because he had never divorced from his wife. But I had Steven and I was happy with that. Steven developed a kidney problem when he was only two, the Doctors thought it was genetic and wanted to know if anyone else in the family had a problem such as this. I went to Philip's wife and told her and asked if the other children had suffered any similar problems. She was infuriated, screaming at me that Steven wasn't Philip's child and I was just after Philip's money. I was so distraught I went back to Steven's Doctor and asked him to do a DNA test for me so I could show her. The test results came back about a week later and they showed that Steven wasn't Philip's child; they were so different it was unbelievable. I went to the Lab. and asked if your blood sample was still available for DNA testing. I suppose you remember when we all gave them in case anything happened in the field and we needed to be identified." Peter nodded, he remembered. "Well it came back an almost precise match, a 99.9% sure. I didn't know what to do I knew you would never just accept me landing on you with a child purported to be yours so I decided to say nothing. Then I was transferred to Adelaide and ran into you brother in the Mall. He told me you were living and working out on the desert not far from the Territory. I wanted to contact you but it just didn't seem right. Then that last big 'quake Adelaide had, I lost my home and some of my friends; it left Adelaide in a state of chaos. I wanted to protect Steven at all costs so I resigned my position. I took all the money we had and packed up the car and went looking for you. So you see Steven is your son Peter not Philip's, I am sorry I didn't tell you sooner but I really considered that you wouldn't want to know after all this time. Steven is four and the only father he ever knew was Philip. He doesn't remember him now but they were very good friends. Philip adored him and spoilt him rotten. After Steven was born we would take him on my back or Philip's back every where we went we were never apart from him. I knew that the 'quakes etc. we have been experiencing must be more than just that otherwise you would not be living and working on the desert. I decided that I too should get out and find safety and I had hoped that you would be in a place of safety where I could bring Steven and let you get to know him, before something worse happens. I didn't even know if you were married or not I never asked your brother and he never volunteered" she gave a small laugh "that would have been a very bad joke wouldn't it?"

Peter stared at her for a long time only looking away when she became noticeably uncomfortable under his gaze.

"You have the DNA result with you?" he asked her.

Jenna nodded, producing a slip of paper from her jeans pocket.

Peter took it and read it there was no doubting the likelihood of his paternity, the two tests, both his and Jenna's showed the child to be 99.9% their child.

"Well, I have gone from being a lonely bachelor with little chance of offering anything to future generations to a father in one fell swoop. I can't say I am unhappy about it but I would like to take the time to get to know the boy. Also Jenna that doesn't mean that you and I are anything more than colleagues. I know you are his mother but I was not his father for a very long time and if Philip had not died I would never have been his father so I really need time to get used to the idea. Okay?"

She smiled and nodded,

"I understand. Does that mean we can stay here?"

"Yes you can stay, you will work like the rest of us and Steven will have classes with Bindi's mother, she is a teacher. When we have our next meeting I will inform you of what we are up against meanwhile I suggest you get settled in and find your way around the camp. When you get some time take in the galleries and I will show you our underground quarters for when the time comes."

"For when the time comes Peter?" she stared at him "it's going to be that bad?"

Peter nodded,

"Yes and quite possibly worse."

"Worse? You mean total annihilation?"

Again he nodded,

"Maybe. No-one really knows Jenna we are just taking every day as it comes."

As she walked out of the tent Peter called to her,

"By the way, that kidney problem Steven had? My sister had it too."

"Thanks for telling me now I feel happier that not only was the test right but his ailments also place him in your family." She smiled at him and left the tent.

On the following Saturday Peter, Linda, Mungaway, John Craznow and Merilyn Ross, flew to Broome. John had chartered the flight to pick them up at 6 am. In Broome a taxi deposited them all at the Blue Indian Resort. Three hours later on the lawns of the resort John Craznow and Merilyn Ross became husband and wife.

At 6pm. in the main restaurant, the five of them joined by the celebrant and the Manager of the Resort sat down to a wonderful seafood dinner, with wines and champagne. The Resort Chef had created a beautiful wedding cake as a gift for them. The following morning feeling a little the worse for wear, Peter, Linda and Mungaway flew back to the site. John and Merilyn Craznow stayed on at the resort for a week before returning.

CHAPTER 44

In Europe all hell was breaking loose as Idoli charged toward this tiny section of the universe, hell bent on destruction. She was coming back to reclaim her love with Lord Vulcan.

The rain started on the desert just three months after the arrival of Jenna and Steven.

It was so heavy it that it was almost impossible to hear yourself think. The entire camp was on call to help out anyone with problems. The biggest problem by far being the rain coming into the tents. The tents they used were specifically designed for hotter climates and were of a lighter fabric to allow good air circulation. The tarps supplied by Mungaway to increase darkness were the only thing that kept out the rain, unfortunately not everyone had them nor did they cover the side walls. They had to break out the big igloo tents that Mungaway had brought with him meanwhile those who were dispossessed slept in the caves. The rain lasted for a week, steady solid drumming rain. The lower level of the desert to the east of them filled with water and spread out. When the rain stopped the animals and bird life came to the desert, it was the most amazing sight in the world. Huge Pelicans and Jabiru, some Ibis and myriad of green bush budgerigars and yellow finches. Some of the small birds Peter had never seen before glorious little black birds with an oily green breast and tail feathers.

Mungaway was also impressed with them,

"I think they come from New Guinea, I have seen them before but only once or twice and that was years ago" he told them

The desert turned green overnight, and from somewhere came the tiny fish the birds were so intent on eating. Within days flowers burst into bloom, the gums dotted around the Edgar Range flowered and the scent of honey hung heavy in the air particularly at night or in the early morning. The hard dry edge left the desert and though it was summer and tremendously hot there was magic all around them.

"Where did the birds come from?" a small voice asked Peter as he sat on a small outcrop of rocks above the water filled desert.

Peter turned around and sitting beside him was Steven.

"How long have you been here?" he asked him.

"Mummy brought me" Steven said pointing to his mother who was closer to the water taking photos.

"Did you walk all this way?" Peter looked around for a vehicle.

Steven shook his head,

"No Mr. Craznow brought us."

Peter looked for John and Merilyn but couldn't see them,

"He's gone now; he's gone to look for stones."

John loved to collect Australian Gem stones and many times found some lovely pieces around the hills of the Edgar Range.

"I see" Peter told the boy "well then what do you think of this?"

Steven smiled briefly a beautiful smile that lit up his little face and for an instant he looked just like his grandmother, Peter's now dead mother. Peter's heart gave a little lurch, she would have loved this serious little boy she would have coaxed him into smiling more and talking more she had that way with children. The grandchildren had adored her they would tell her anything and she would keep their confidence. He felt his throat tighten, how he missed her. Each time he spoke to his father he would almost forget and it would be on the tip of his tongue to ask to speak to his mother. How hard it must be for his father now, he would never love again like that if ever at all.

Peter again considered the little boy's question.

"So you want to know where the birds came from? Well Steven it is all a bit of a mystery really. They just know when these inland lakes fill up and the flowers are going to bloom and that the fish are going to be in the water. They are very clever creatures far cleverer than we are. But where did they come from? Well I don't really know, from all over the place I suppose from the Territory and the Coast and South Australia."

Steven crouched down beside Peter on the rocks,

"It is really beautiful isn't it!"

Peter was amused and amazed at the boy's ability to grasp things, his mother was right he is as smart as a whip.

"Yes it is" Peter answered him "more beautiful than anyone imagined I certainly never thought I would see this."

They sat together this father and son, the father dreaming of a safe world to raise his son, hoping that it was all a nightmare that would just go away, the son happy to be sharing this magic with the man he had learned to call his father.

The days reverted to long and hot and slowly the desert lake receded until one morning all the birds were gone and the only evidence of anything unusual happening were the flowers and a few little fish that still flopped around in the remnants of the lake.

If anything the temperature rose to a point where Peter considered moving into the caves for the duration of the summer months. Even the air conditioners could not keep up with the constant heat. Work outside was impossible with most people opting to sleep away the afternoons and start work when the late afternoon coolness approached. Finally when April had ended and still no sign of relief Peter had everyone go to the caves for the hottest parts of the day. It was easier to sleep with the cool air constantly being pumped in. Gradually they began sleeping there at night and within a month most of them had moved into the caves for sleeping and recreation purposes. The cook also brought his new kitchen into play creating the lunches and dinners there. He was more than happy with the way it all worked out. Sometimes the cooking smells hung around but the exhaust system worked very well and no-one really minded.

They saw no-one even though often in the distance a motor could be heard more often than not moving away from them. They all took turns in the radio room which was now located in the library cave and a bulletin was posted everyday on the world news. The TV was on every night for anyone who chose to watch it and those who did also posted bulletins for those who had not. The world was still, but winter did not come to any of it.

Australia of course was used to Indian summers where the heat went on interminably often right up until June. But Europe had had a warm and dry winter and now they were going into a sizzling early summer. The death toll rose, with heat exhaustion amongst the very old and the very young being the biggest killer. Those areas that relied so heavily on snow melt for their constant water supply found themselves short of good drinking water. Crops failed, animals died and plagues of mice, and locusts invaded the store sheds and dying crop fields. It was worse than the upheavals.

China, Russia, and South America suffered famine, Africa literally died.

First came famine then plague and pestilence then starvation. Peter and his group watched in horror as cameras went to Africa to record the death throes of nations just recently inundated by huge rain storms. It was the tsunamis said the scientists. They had killed the land by forcing so much sea water down into the artesian basins. Then a bad season and the water they brought up was no good it was tainted. Peter was concerned about their own water but tests showed it to be pure and clean they would never have a problem.

Reports from Dr. Alan Cashman became more frequent as he tracked the Idoli sphere across the Universe. She was huge now and clearly visible to the naked eye in the night sky.

Peter often sat out on the little hill with his glass of wine and watched for it tracking its movements across the sky when he found it. Merilyn occasionally joined him but more often than not it was Steven who sat with him and learned about the sphere.

"Will we all die father?" he asked one night as they sat quietly watching it zooming across the horizon.

Peter shook his head,

"I hope not Steven I hope not but I cannot promise you it won't happen I can only promise you I will protect you as much as I can."

Peter had grown to love this quiet little boy who absorbed information like a sponge. He had problems with Jenna though. As much as he still admired her even loved her a little bit he could not bring himself to go any further with it He had tried, they had shared a laugh and joke had played partners in the quiz games that they often played at night had discussed Steven's upbringing and education at great length; but he could go no further. Something just wasn't there the spark had died.

John and Mungaway had both urged him to examine his feelings for her to see if he could compromise. But try as he might he just did not yearn for her. If he didn't see her he didn't miss her even though he enjoyed her company. They were his good friends and he knew they were trying to help him but there was nothing he could do about it. Jenna tried hard to please him and he knew in his heart she would have loved to have renewed their relationship but somehow he felt betrayed. Steven would never have been his, he would never have known about this lovely little boy, his son, if Philip had not died. How could he forgive her for never trying to find out who Steven's father really was. Surely she had known it was possible from the very beginning that it was his child and not Philip's? He supposed she wanted to be with Philip so it was easy to accept this child was probably his rather than find out the truth. That made him feel unimportant in her life. When she did find, out which was now three years ago as Steven had since had his fifth birthday, even then she didn't look for him, she didn't call him and tell him, she chose not to. Now he had nothing to offer her it was all too late.

CHAPTER 45

As they sat staring at the magnificent dome of the night sky Peter heard his name being called.

"Here!" he yelled in return.

John Craznow came into view,

"Phone Peter it sounds like your father he is a bit distressed".

Peter jumped to his feet and ran to the tent.

He picked up the handset he was breathless from his run,

"Dad! What's the matter" he asked.

There was silence at first but Peter could hear the soft hum of the line

"Dad!"

"Peter I have just gotten back from Canberra" his father's voice sounded old, tired "I think we are all in trouble somehow" he paused Peter said nothing waiting for him to resume "It's Idoli . . . . she has picked up speed and is heading straight toward us I don't think we have more than a month or so before she gets here. I suggest you make your arrangements quickly to get your people to safety. We must survive Peter we really have to try. When this is all over there may only be a few of us left if we don't get a direct hit or similar, we have to make the effort to survive."

"Dad you said a direct hit or similar what do mean by similar?" Peter asked him.

Again the line hum was the only thing that told him his father was still on line.

"Peter we think she has picked up a lot of rubbish on her way here so it's possible as she nears us the heat of the sun or just friction could knock a lot of that rubbish off into our atmosphere. Even if she doesn't strike us or pull us out of orbit we are still facing a death threat. She is so big the pieces she has picked up are huge just a few of those pieces in the right spot and we are all dead."

"Hang on Dad" Peter told the older man "if Idoli is moving that fast the possibility becomes less. She may well zoom past us so quickly she will remain cold and stable after all we aren't a very big planet. If she is picking up speed then we have a better chance of survival. My only worry is if she hits anything between there and here that could slow her down or force her to change track."

"Oh yes that's another thing Peter" his father told him "she was so erratic in her course on her way toward us but now she has straightened up and is coming straight in the only thing we don't know is just where she will arrive. There are a lot of things out there that could well change her direction let us hope that there is something big enough to do it without affecting us."

"Could the sun do that?" Peter asked him.

Again the silence then his father's voice became hoarse and quiet,

"Oh god pray that does not happen with the size of Idoli if she hits the sun we will be cooked. After all we are the third out not far enough away, it would be awful."

"I doubt prayer is going to help us now Dad, now we just need an awful lot of luck"

"Take care my son" his father told him "and protect that little grandson of mine I want to meet him one day."

Peter smiled to himself,

"I will Dad and you take care we will meet again somewhere I promise."

Peter replaced the phone on its cradle. He stood for a moment considering his father's words. Surely if Idoli was moving that fast it was to their advantage, he hoped he was right. Now to tell the others there was no easy way to do this it just had to be as his father told him.

Everyone with the exception of Bindi assembled in the dining tent.

Peter stared around at the faces of these people faces now browned by the sun. They were good people, they had created a great place for everyone here, they had everything they wanted or needed considering their circumstances this was not going to be easy.

"People I have news of the Idoli Sphere I just wish it was good news but we have to accept the fact that what I am about to tell you is the worst case scenario."

They listened in silence as Peter told them what his father had found out. Even when he finished speaking no-one spoke, no-one moved. Then John Mackie stood up.

"Well if we are ever going to survive this thing then we had better get a move on. I suggest we set up the solar collectors tomorrow for the other generators and get to work moving into the caves and making them as comfortable as possible. A month isn't very long and we have ice to make vegetables to freeze and dry and more seeds to plant so I say let's get going."

Everyone murmured their agreement. Although they all looked somewhat shaken and a few were considerably paler than when they had first walked in, they were all calm; for this Peter was grateful.

"Okay people I go along with Mac I think at dawn we start the move into the caves we have to work on one month at the most. Now in that month we are going to start feeling some magnified effects of the sphere. I would say we are going to have some rather strange weather patterns and more tremors. We may experience rock and shale slides which underground will sound unnerving. So I suggest we make up work parties to move some of the bigger loose rocks from around the cave in case something bigger comes down and blocks it off. I also want someone to formulate an exercise plan I want us all to be fit, if we are going to move into the caves we can't sit around. We have been working hard for months and we need to retain that fitness if we are going to get through this. Everything that is now above ground including all tents are to be taken into the caves. Mac I want those make up rocks finished so we can block it off once we are in" Mac nodded "I want absolutely no trace that we ever existed above ground can I rely on you?" he looked at John Craznow, Mungaway and the drillers, they all nodded. "Ladies I think you should see to the bedding and helping the cook get organized, generally outfit the cave and use who-ever you need for help we are all available. Our priority is to keep those children safe make sure the nursery section is away from the main areas where it is coolest and darkest and hopefully safest" all agreed. Peter watched them as they compared notes drinking coffee and deciding who would do what. They were well organized and it showed he was proud of them all if anyone would or could survive it was these people.

By noon the next day it was hard to believe that anyone had ever had a camp there. The only sign that someone may once have been there was a small pile of corrugated iron left over from the old sample shed they had built when it first become a drill site. Peter decided to leave it there in hopes that if anyone did come their way they would see it and be deterred.

CHAPTER 46

They moved into the caves by evening then the real work began as they marked out their sleeping and living areas and general recreation areas. The long trestle tables were now set up beside the kitchen area fold up chairs stacked neatly along the wall. Cook and the drillers had devised a hood system which was larger and worked better than the exhaust system they had been using. The hood was large and sat directly over the stove drawing up the fumes and smells more easily. The sleeping areas were tucked directly under and away from the steps giving privacy and complete darkness. The nursery was in the largest section at the very back of the cave in the sleeping area. Washing and toileting had always been a problem. Getting hot water to showers and children's baths was not the problem creating an area of total privacy was. The closest point to the water which would have been ideal was too close to the kitchen area. Toilets also had to be place as far away as possible. Finally Peter decided that his sleeping area would be given over to showers and toilets and he would take a smaller area off the recreation section. Others offered to give up their space for him he chose not accept the offers. He needed to keep his desk and radios close to the general area anyway, so it suited him to have his sleeping area close by where he could keep an eye on everything. The toilet problem had been solved for some time with a composting toilet. No smell no waste that could not be used. Mac was in charge of that area as the compost created then went to feed his plants, those that weren't grown hydroponically. The artificial light for the plants was softened by a filter he discovered the plants responded better than to plain white light. He also discovered if he added vitamins C and D to his plant food they thrived. There was nothing he could not grow, his only concern was, if there was a strike and they lost their solar power. He had discussed this with Peter at length.

"The only thing I could suggest if that happens that we use our diesel supply for the generators. This of course will mean noise which we will have to get used to and some fumes even though they are in the library cave. But they will keep us and the plants alive. Let's hope it won't come to that."

The news from around the world was monitored constantly by who-ever was rostered to the radio that day. The radio shift lasted six hours per person and as something new came to hand bulletins were posted in the dining area. Within days of moving into the caves permanently the reports started filtering in of more upheavals. At night the creaking rumble of tremors some minor some much larger, was unnerving and no matter how hard they tried they could not get used to the sound. During the day was little different except everyone was up and about and all the lights were on it was easier to accept. The radio broadcasts were becoming weak with a lot of static. Even though Peter was able to still get calls on his phone he knew from a government broadcast that several of the Communications satellites were no longer working.

Life in the caves for the first week was difficult for everyone. They all felt the urge to go outside, and whenever something had to be done in the library cave there was never any shortage of volunteers. The small mock up rocks created by Mac had the desired effect of cutting off the outside world but one was moved daily to check on the outside world. It was during these times that everyone wanted to be there.

It was at the beginning of the second week that Peter almost lost his son.

The children had accepted the cave life quite happily. It was cool, they could play to their hearts content and they had many teachers. Cook made sure there were plenty of snacks on hand for them and the drillers with the help of Jenna had set up a kiddie gym to keep them fit. When they weren't sleeping or playing or learning they could wander around the different areas of their home with few limitations. At the very far reaches of the sleeping area the roof of the cave sloped quite suddenly down to a small opening. Merilyn was the only one who had explored this section hoping it had led to another large cave. It didn't it was just a series of rock shelves that went downward to nothingness. Her torches had not penetrated the depths of the ledges.

"I don't think it worth roping up and checking it out it is probably a lava tunnel or an old water course that is no longer active. It probably goes on ad infinitum, not worth worrying about." she had told Peter. He had agreed with her.

Bindi had been restless and been put down for an afternoon sleep Steven found himself at loose end and decided to play a game of pretend. He had crawled to the back of the sleeping area with his toy soldiers and played quite happily for some time. Then he noticed the opening and decided to go exploring. When it had first been found Peter had placed some smaller rocks in front of it to deter anyone from going into the area. Steven simply crawled around the rocks and with his torch wriggled through on his belly until he reached the ledge. He looked down.

"Wow it's so deep." He wriggled forward trying to see how far his torch light would shine, and then he was falling.

"Daddyyyy"! He screamed.

Peter was getting coffee when the panicked cry of 'Daddy' tore at him.

"Steven!" he yelled standing listening "Steven!" he shouted again not knowing which way to run.

Merilyn grabbed him

"The back of the cave Peter" she ran towards the sleeping area dropping onto her belly she wriggled around the rocks and leaned out over the edge "I can't see oh god I can't see, get me some light" she screamed.

Mark pushed a portable white light toward her,

"Just hang it over the edge it will work better" he told her.

She slid the light over the edge lowering it slowly. Way down below her on the second ledge she could just make out a small glimmer. She moved the light backwards and forwards to see if it would shine on something, 'Yes! there it was again.'

She eased backward out of the small opening.

"I am going down there Peter I want harness, ropes and as much light as I can carry I think he has fallen onto the second ledge. If I am right then he is safe as long as he doesn't move. He may be unconscious if he comes around he could fall even further."

Jenna stood quietly beside Peter silent tears flowed down her cheeks. Peter turned back to help with the harness when he saw her. He put his arm around her shoulders,

"We will get him Jenna, Merilyn is very experienced."

Why can't it be someone else? One of the men perhaps?"

"No-one else can fit in there she is the smallest built expert we have. You would be surprised if you knew the places she has gotten into. Most of these caves were found by her because of her ability to go into small places. I have complete trust and faith in her."

He turned away then and began helping Merilyn to harness up.

As she slipped over the side Merilyn felt no fear only that Steven would wake before she could get to him.

Slowly she lowered herself down the rock face to the first ledge. She felt the urge to hurry but knew it would be of no benefit to either of them if she did and something went wrong. No she had to take it slowly watch where she put her feet; she couldn't take the risk of knocking down rocks and maybe sending them down onto the boy.

As she approached the second ledge she heard a small sound. She stopped looked down and saw Steven beginning to move.

"Steven!" she said firmly "don't move stay exactly where you are I am coming to get you now but if you move you may roll off then I can never get you. Okay!"

He whimpered then she heard a small voice say,

"Okay."

Merilyn continued her descent to the second ledge realizing just how far down it was. This little boy was very lucky the ledge was narrower than the one above it if he had been a bigger child he may have missed it altogether and continued his plunge down the tunnel. The third ledge was far below them barely discernible in the blackness. The lights Merilyn had strapped on only showed her what was immediately in front and below her nothing else it was just too deep and too wide for light reflection. She reached the second ledge hanging there searching for a foothold. She realized she could not reach it comfortably it was too much of a stretch how on earth Steven had landed on it she didn't know. She would have to swing and hope the momentum would carry her onto the ledge.

She moved her body backwards and forwards to get the rope to swing, as she came inwards she pushed forward her feet just touching the ledge. For an instant she hung there teetering expecting to fall backwards at any moment, and for that instant she felt a stab of fear, it was the first time she had ever felt fear in all the caves they had been in. Then she regained her balance and tipped forward. Though the ledge did not jut out far it did go back a long way and opened into a cavernous great hole. She did not have enough light or time to inspect it but she was certain it was yet another very large cave.

Steven lay on the rock his eyes huge in the unaccustomed darkness. Dirt and tears streaked his cheeks; he didn't speak. Merilyn knelt beside him feeling for broken bones.

"Does anything hurt Steven?" she asked him.

"My arm hurts" he told her with a hitch in his voice.

She felt his arm it didn't feel quite right, she had to assume it was broken.

"If I help you will you stand up for me so I can put a harness on you."

"I'm scared Merry" he started to cry.

Merilyn gathered him into her arms and rocked him soothing him,

"It's okay there is nothing to be scared of now I'm here. You have been very brave so far we will back up top in no time."

Merilyn spoke into her radio,

"I think he has a broken arm which I am strapping to his chest he will probably have a lot of bumps and bruises but otherwise seems okay. I am going to harness him up and when I say go, I mean go. I had to swing to get onto the ledge so when you take up the slack do it slowly at first then when I say okay get us up quickly."

She harnessed Steven clipping his harness to her own she then clipped a second line to the back of his harness. If anything went wrong with one line they could both be pulled up by the other. Holding Steven in her arms facing her his legs wrapped around her, she walked to the edge of the ledge.

"Go now" she told them. The lines pulled tight and slowly they were drawn away from the ledge.

"Okay! we are clear".

They were drawn up quickly to the small space at the top. Merilyn unclipped Steven from her harness so they could drag him through the hole. She soon followed.

Cheers rang out through the cave as she emerged. Jenna threw her arms around her.

"Thank you, thank you."

Steven was whisked off to the medical area where Isabelle Mackie had been preparing to check him out thoroughly.

"I am so grateful to you Merilyn I owe you for my son's life" Peter told her "if I can ever do anything for you, you only have to say, I have no other way to thank you."

Merilyn stripped off her harness,

"Peter look we are all here for each other you would have done the same thing: while we are on the subject though. That ledge is actually quite big it doesn't show much but it goes back a long way. Behind it is a huge hole that appears to be yet another cave. It is so big my torches didn't even show into it. I didn't dare walk in because it could be just a hole with a bloody great drop on the other side but it is something I would like to have a closer look at. I know I said before that it didn't seem to be worth worrying about but I think it is worth a look."

"Then if you go I go" John told her, "I thought I was supposed to be the cave expert in residence".

She laughed, "You are, I just like going into them, I don't know anything about them."

Steven's arm was fractured, without the use of an X-ray Isabelle wasn't able to determine how far the fracture went. She aligned the bones to their correct position, and once satisfied that there were no other breaks, she set the arm in a light plaster and sling.

"This will take about six weeks to heal" she told Jenna and Peter "he has a lot of bruises from the fall but apart from quite a nasty bump on the head, this is his only real problem. I would suggest he be kept quiet for the first week, lots of rest and small light meals and plenty of sleep and he'll be up and around again in no time. I'll check him daily to make sure he doesn't show any signs of concussion, but in one so young I think you will find he will bounce back quite quickly."

The sedative she had given Steven had begun to wear off and when he saw his father he began to cry.

"I'm sorry daddy I won't go near it again I promise."

Peter held his son saying nothing. In all the time they had been with him, Jenna and Steven, Steven had only ever called him 'father' now he was calling him Daddy and Peter loved the sound of it. This was something so unexpected even Jenna looked puzzled.

CHAPTER 47

As time wore on there didn't seem to be any real evidence of unusual upheavals. Certainly they were hearing problems from around the world but none of them seemed to be as bad as the original, some smaller 'quakes and the volcanoes though still erupting in parts had more or less stayed reasonably quiet.

Peter could not understand this; the end of the month had come and gone yet still nothing major. Perhaps the huge sphere had changed its course over time and now, though still affecting Earth, was far enough away not to do the worst damage as originally thought. He was pleased in many respects because now there was a good chance that the human race would go on, the damages repaired in time. They could all pull together it could be done there was enough of civilization to prevent anarchy.

After some deliberation Peter called a meeting and asked if anyone wished to go outside. He told them that as they had now been in the caves for some time and there didn't seem to be any great cause for alarm perhaps they could go back to the galleries and continue to pursue their studies of the old race and maybe finish deciphering the language.

All agreed so they set a roster. There always had to be a male and female in the caves with the children and the radio. Both of them would, in turn, would help the cook as and when necessary.

That night for the first time in weeks Peter stepped outside. The night sky was clear and billions of huge stars gleamed and glittered and there in their midst was the biggest luminescent body he had ever seen. He froze, the thrill of seeing it so close and the fear it engendered made him shiver momentarily then he was shouting for everyone to come and see it.

They all rushed out and stared open mouthed at the monstrous sphere that seemed to be within reaching distance. Not as big as the moon when full but very big.

Then suddenly a huge flare danced across the sky, there were oohs and aahs from everyone.

There was no wind; the desert was still and very warm; there were no animals.

Linda reached over and touched his arm, Peter jumped.

"Sorry" she told him "Peter I really want to go into the galleries I have an idea".

"Tomorrow then? at dawn?"

She shook her head,

"No Peter, now! There is something I really need to look at."

"But Linda they may not be that safe if we get a shake, the front entrance collapses frequently and we have had quite a few rock falls."

"I will be on my guard and I need not go alone Mungaway can come with me he understands the caves and I might need him anyway."

Peter sighed returning his gaze to the huge sphere which seemed suspended above them,

"Okay Linda go get your equipment."

"Thanks" she told him.

Linda and Mungaway made their way through the galleries and down the long well to the lower cave.

"What are we looking for?" Mungaway asked her.

"Anything that pertains to the actual sphere anything at all, drawings letters phrases, anything."

Mungaway carefully copied anything he found and made good copies of the relating drawings. They worked solidly for four hours before Linda called a halt.

"I think we have what we need; I just hope we haven't missed anything."

Mungaway was puzzled,

"Why so secretive Linda? What's going on?"

"I can't tell you yet until I am sure of myself if I tell anyone and I am wrong it will seem stupid, so you will just have to wait."

He smiled to himself he never considered his wife stupid, she was brilliant. It was not her teaching, ancient languages and hieroglyphics, but she had a natural talent for them and often broke the codes where others could not. Now he really believed that she had some knowledge that no-one else had seen or understood. No doubt he would find out the same as everyone else did.

They stepped back out into the brilliant night. Peter sat on the small hill that had so often been their night time seat for star gazing. Above him the sky flared a multitude of colours; sometimes it would be clear almost ghostly at other times almost like a broad rainbow.

Linda touched him on the arm,

"Can we join you Peter?"

He nodded.

"What have you got for us Linda, a way to save the world perhaps?"

Linda smiled,

"That would be good, but no not quite. I have been doing a lot of thinking since we have moved into the caves and I have also being doing a lot of reading of the library tablets and I think I have found a correlation between what is happening and what was written."

Peter stared at her, her face clearly discernible in the reflected starlight. She was looking straight ahead and he knew if he could see her clearly she would not have her eyes focused instead she would be reading from an invisible paper in front of her.

"We have always thought the volcanoes the earthquakes and the general disruption of the Earth caused by the sphere would wipe us or most of us out, it may still, but it isn't the sphere Peter, Mungaway" she patted her husband's arm letting him know this was for him too "it is the sun, our sun. The sphere is probably a natural phenomenon in the universe something though large probably doesn't amount to much. It probably traverses our universe every few hundred thousand to several million years or so. It probably was a goddess to the old ones, hence the creation of Lord Vulcan's story. He was the master of the volcanoes and the fire on Earth and she became his goddess. They wove a story to account for the return of the sphere and the result of that return, fires, volcanoes meteorite showers, huge solar flares . . . ." she waited for the penny to drop.

Peter started, solar flares? Of course!

He jumped up dragging Linda onto her feet,

"You are a genius you are an absolute genius you've cracked the code Linda."

"But it is all coincidence Peter. The sphere does not cause it and it probably doesn't happen every time it arrives but **sometimes** when it has returned there have been huge solar flares which **do** cause major problems on Earth. That is why no matter how much nearer the sphere got the problems didn't increase in fact they diminished somewhat. Yet the temperature climbed, the rains didn't come, we had famine, drought, plague and pestilence, all caused by the big dry, which in turn was caused by the huge solar flares. It doesn't mean that we are not at risk any more on the contrary we are even more so because we have to worry about fires and lack of water, loss of fertile soils and a massive encroachment of deserts on good land. We will continue to experience periods of severe magnetic storms which will cause volcanoes and 'quakes. None of the satellites will ever be any good to us they would have all been burnt out by now. The sphere because of its sheer size is in some respects shielding the Earth. I would say when it begins to leave our region the huge disruptions will return. At the moment it is probably reflecting a lot of what is coming off the sun, hence the beautiful rainbow colours; solar flares refracting through the moisture of the sphere. This was how the story formed;people probably thought that the coming of Idoli calmed Lord Vulcan, and when she left he rages at his loss. That's it Peter we are in for more of what we went through before and we don't even know how long it will last and if the Earth will even survive it. The worst of it all there is nothing to be done we have to go underground and we have to stay there until the flares stop. Whatever and whoever is left on Earth, assuming it won't be cooked completely, will have to start again."

Peter stared at the sky knowing now Lord Vulcan's secret knowing that for all their preparation they still may not survive. Still if any one is going to it will be them he thought.

"Okay Linda now let's go and tell everyone else."

They walked back to the cave together.

There in the huge cavern that had become their home with full coffee cups and a little fearful of what was to be told to them they assembled.

Fourteen people, a small community and maybe a lifeline for humanity.

"I wish to draw your attention to the changes we have witnessed" Peter told them "the volcanoes have diminished and earthquakes have lessened though we don't really know about tsunamis. We can only assume from the broadcasts we have been monitoring that they too have virtually ceased. This may seem like we have come through the worst however I have to tell you this is not the case. Linda has just completed a study of the galleries and the library tablets and would now like to share with all of us her findings. Please listen to what she has to say then we will answer your questions."

Linda now brought out her drawings and pinned them to the board,

"I want you first to understand this is a lot of supposition on my part but because of what I have found, it leads me to believe it is right . . . ."

She then proceeded to tell them the history of the people who lived in the caves and the way in which the Book of Vulcan came to be written,

". . . . in conclusion I can only say that if anyone can survive this it is our group. We have the necessary provisions and technology. If the heat continues to intensify to a point of heating these caves I think we could probably move down even lower. Merilyn has not yet investigated the lower reaches of the tunnel where Steven fell but I believe it has some rather large caves which John and Merilyn will be looking at in the next few days. If necessary our cooking arrangements could become as we need it. We would do a certain amount of cooking then to conserve our fuel, not cook again until that is gone. This is how the old tribes survived and we too can do this. We have a lot of dried food that can be reconstituted with the use of hot water; if necessary we can live on that. There are many ways that we can survive the food problems and anything else; our biggest problem will be what will happen to the Earth."

For the next two hours they threw questions at Peter and Linda and argued about the right way to do things but in the end they all agreed that no matter what happened they would do whatever it took to survive.

Peter was proud of them all, he knew they were afraid.

Then a small voice asked,

"If the end comes will we know?"

Denise was very pale and had said very little about anything in the time she had been with them.

"I don't know if I can answer that" Peter told her "I don't know what the overall effect will be. The Earth will burn up, and I am assuming that the intense heat will penetrate through the layers of the surface finally everything will just die. Similar I suppose to heat exhaustion, you will collapse and go into unconsciousness and die."

"Then by the time the Earth is in its last moments we won't know anyway?"

Peter shook his head,

"No you will be long dead."

"That's okay then" she said quietly.

The questions came thick and fast then it was over. They all stopped talking and drifted off to their respective sleeping areas. Peter, Linda, Mungaway, Merilyn and John Craznow remained at the table each immersed in his or her own thoughts.

"Is there a chance that when the sphere goes the solar flares will stop"? John asked.

Linda shook her head,

"I can't see that. If you study the drawings and the tablets you will see the drawings were made up until the sphere arrived and while it was in the sky, most of the tablets written about it, were written at the time it began to leave the region, and what happened afterwards. When you put it altogether you will see the complete story. It spends a long time getting here, it stays for a long time, and then it moves away. Once it moves away the upheavals begin in earnest and there are drawings to support this. We thought the drawings were all of the sphere arriving but in fact many of them relate to it leaving. The worst of what happened to these tribes was written after that time. That was when Lord Vulcan literally stamped his feet and tried to blow the world to bits."

"But surely someone survived? How did humanity survive?" John asked.

Linda sighed she knew it was not easy for some people to grasp that they may have only months, weeks or even days to live.

"Humanity didn't survive John," she said quietly "it started again. Nature took over, the world regenerated and everything started again. That is why the pictures on the walls the animals flowers fruits everything is what it was like then and they have never been seen in our time on Earth. I am sorry I know it is hard to accept because we believe that we will prevail but humanity didn't once before and it might not again."

They separated then each going to their own place, there was no late chatter no laughter nothing, silence reigned.

Days turned into weeks and then months. The hottest of days were spent in the caves and in the first found galleries. Each person had returned to his or her own work; the community thrived. The only contact they now had with the outside world was a small radio which was solar powered. It had a huge range and usually clear. At the time when the solar flares were at their greatest the radio simply gave up. Then it was a matter of waiting until the flares had eased before being able to listen to the world again. Peter had heard nothing from his father for a long time and was beginning to wonder if any of his family had survived.

One evening after dinner with everyone outside enjoying the spectacle, the radio crackled into life. John Mackie was on duty in the caves when he heard their camp call sign.

". . . . I say again . . . . calling Peter Cashman at Oasis do you read me over . . . ."

John hurried up top calling for Peter.

"I can't be sure of the voice but it is male it may be your father"

Peter sat at the radio filtering out the static and the whine that often accompanied the solar flares.

"This is Oasis, Peter Cashman, over"

Then in a lull in the flares the voice came over loud and clear,

"Peter? Hello this is Jim Milburn, do you remember me?"

Peter grinned,

"Of course Jim how goes it with you? where are you calling from?"

"I am calling from your father's house in N.S.W. he contacted me quite some time ago and said if I wanted to come and work for him I could. I gave up the rangers' job and came here. He needed help and didn't want to bother you because of your work out there."

Peter felt a twinge of guilt,

"If he needed help I could have gone and got him and brought him here."

"It's okay Peter, but I do have to tell you what has happened. This area received a bombardment of meteorites about six months ago, just after I got here. With the big dry it started fires which burnt out a lot of N.S.W. country areas. I'm sorry Peter but your brother his wife and one of their children were killed when they were caught in a big bushfire. Their car ran off the road. I'm sorry we couldn't tell you sooner we couldn't get the radio to work."

Peter stared at the wall in front of him,

". . . dead?" he whispered,

John Mackie touched his shoulder then went to get him a cup of coffee.

Peter flicked the handset,

"Where are the others Jim?"

"There is just your father and I here your sister and family have taken the others with them and gone to some place in Northern N.S.W. your father won't leave the homestead. The house is still standing but everything around us is burnt out. We have water and food so we are right but he wanted me to let you know. He won't leave Peter but I will stay with him and make sure he has everything he needs."

"Why didn't he tell me?" Peter asked

"He can't come to the radio he is laid up. During the bushfire he broke his collarbone and sustained burns to his feet, but he is on the mend and we have a Doctor come by each week and check him out. Probably another month or so before he is back on his feet again but he is getting there. Don't worry about him Peter I'll look after him."

Peter pulled at his bottom lip,

"Can we keep in touch Jim and I can let you know what to expect?"

"We have one of your father's friends coming to stay with us I think his name is Rob Newcraft he worked with your father over there for a while they are going to set up the big telescope. His wife died and he lost his house so he will be here in about a week. We are hoping to build a small community here."

"Well let's talk at least once a week if the flares let us and tell my father as soon as he is well enough to sit up in a chair I will give him the run down on the Book of Vulcan. By the way Jim you might tell him we cracked the code or a least Linda did we know what is going to happen and how! I will talk again soon and . . . ."

The radio suddenly crackled and squealed then went dead.

Peter flicked off the switch and returned the radio to monitoring,

"Well at least some of my family is still alive" he said quietly.

He walked back out to the sand hill joining Jenna, John and Merilyn, Mungaway and Linda. Two bottles from their precious hoard of wine had been opened,

"Here's to your father's good health" Merilyn toasted

They raised their glasses to the now fiery flashes in the sky, and drank in silence.

EPILOGUE

In the first three years of cave dwelling the group swelled by two.

Denise had a little boy named David and Merilyn gave birth to a girl they called Caroline. John doted on his daughter and was often seen doing his work around the community with the sleeping baby strapped to his back. Both women had their babies easily with little cause for alarm. Merilyn had despaired of having children and though she adored her baby daughter often mentioned she was not in a hurry to have another. The community was growing, all the more reason for them to survive to bring their children to adulthood and teach them to survive and help others to do the same.

Peter's son Steven was often seen playing with the babies after his lessons, teaching them colours and sounds. He adored them both as he adored Bindi. The children were everyone's responsibility and each adult would impart their knowledge to the babies as they were doing with Steven and Bindi, now aged nearly nine and six.

POST EPILOGUE

Twenty years after the beginning of the upheavals Earth had completely changed its face. If there were now Space Stations and satellites in orbit still you would see the beautiful blue of the oceans the drift of white clouds the verdant green of some of the forests. But the forests were diminished by two thirds across the world; the oceans were no longer dotted with huge trading ships and beautiful sailing yachts. Great tracts of land lay bare of all life reminiscent of parts of the Australian outback or a Mars landscape. The deserts encroached on much of the fertile land in the northern hemisphere. People who would have been farmers had become nomads living in small oases. The trading ships that plied the oceans on closer inspection would have shown smaller craft that did not require running on computers but could still carry some livestock and goods as in the old method of transportation.

With the solar flares at times violent and frequent, the temperature rising constantly, the possibility of volcanic cones suddenly erupting and monstrous storms which could spring up quickly, it was a hazardous job being the skipper of a ship.

Yet for all the problems plaguing the Earth many scientists still felt that the solar storms were diminishing.

Idoli had not stayed so long and after ten years she had begun to move away from Earth heading outward to the farther reaches of space whence she came her soothing influence on Lord Vulcan diminishing with each passing year. Lord Vulcan stamped his feet and often, screaming his defiance at the Lords who had again taken his Idoli away. The eruptions continued as he roared his protests. The 'quakes signalled his temperamental stamping, but all who knew him knew that he would eventually lie down and go to sleep.

Would he take humanity with him this time?

Or would humanity have learned how to survive the foulest tempered of the Lords and Earth?